Undead All Over

A Brooke Roberts Mystery

Undead All Over

A Brooke Roberts Mystery

Nancy Labs

PARAMETER PUBLISHING

Doylestown, PA

Library of Congress Control Number: 2023914823

ISBN: 978-1-944280-00-0
ISBN (ebook): 978-1-944280-01-7

Printed in the United States of America

 Doylestown, PA   2023

Undead All Over

One

"Wait 'til you see Nina's set designs," Amy said, her eyes bright beneath a mane of pink and purple hair. "Black and white except for a touch of red in each scene—for blood. Like they did it on Broadway way a long time ago. And like that poster over there."

A massive image of Dracula stared at Brooke from the rear wall of the Sussex Academy art studio. The only hint of color was a drop of red at the tip of a sharply pointed fang. Beneath it were the words: *Black and White: Undead All Over.*

"Nina's design. Clever, isn't it? And by the way," Amy said, suddenly serious, "in case you're wondering, my name might be Amy March, but I'm nothing like the character in *Little Women.* Nothing at all, so don't let the name fool you."

It was true. While this version of Amy March had an oval face, blue eyes, a delicate chin and full lips, that's where the resemblance to Louisa May Alcott's character ended. Amy March 2.0 sported thigh-high leather boots, a short black dress that clung to her curves like a wet tee-shirt, and long blond hair accented with streaks of pink and purple. Thick eyeliner, pale makeup and nearly white lipstick made her otherwise lovely features appear cadaverous, and her accessories—serpent rings, skull earrings and an eye of Horus necklace—could have been stolen from a necromancer's jewelry box.

Adolescent rebellion. Two decades ago, Brooke could have written the definitive book on the subject. Like Amy she'd gone through a *noir* phase. Black tee-shirts. Black leggings. Black boots. An attempt, she supposed, at looking bored, anti-social and scary. Sadly, she was the only one who'd been scared.

"Funny," Amy said, her eyes sweeping the vast studio with its easels, computers and pottery wheels. "It's not like Nina to leave the lights on and the door unlocked. And it's not like her to skip out on an important meeting. I guess my dad got to her when he came in after school today—you could hear him yelling at her all the way down the hall. But just wait—before long, he'll have you running out of here in tears, just like Nina."

Brooke didn't like the sound of that. She'd taught theater at the school nearly fifteen years ago and was filling in for the current teacher who'd been sidelined in an accident. *Dracula* was a drama on the stage, not in real life. The brief, seven-week rehearsal schedule was stressful enough without the stage manager's father showing up to cause trouble.

"Let's call it a night," Brooke said with a glance around the studio. "I'll catch up with Nina later."

"Okay, but before we leave, I promised I'd set up a still life for tomorrow's drawing class." Amy crossed the room, to a pair of double doors. "It won't take long to get the stuff out of the storage closet—just a few minutes and we'll be..."

She opened the doors and the words died on her lips.

Two

"No!" Brooke shouted into her cell. "I'm not a student, and this isn't a prank." She glanced back at the body on the storage closet floor. Caramel brown skin. A shimmery white pantsuit. Silver jewelry. Eyes bulging red in their sockets. "Sussex Academy. Send someone—please."

A door opened behind her and Headmaster Dr. Alan Pierce rushed in. "I was on my way out of the building. I heard screams. Is everything…" He looked into the closet and fell silent.

Another man was right behind him, a youngish guy who appeared to be in his mid-thirties. In seconds he was on his knees, his fingers probing Nina's wrist for a pulse. Finding none, he sank back against a shelf of art supplies, a tortured expression on his face as he stared at the body. Several seconds passed before he looked up, and when he saw Amy, he got to his feet and opened his arms. She rushed toward him and fell into his embrace, her slender body wracked with sobs.

"I called the police," Brooke told Dr. Pierce. "They should be here soon."

The headmaster nodded, his face ashen. He shifted his gaze from the victim to Amy and the man who comforted her. "Perhaps you should sit with Amy in Nina's office until the police arrive."

It took some coaxing to pry her from the man's arms, but Amy finally allowed Brooke to guide her away from the crime scene and into a tiny space with bookshelves, a couple of chairs and a desk. A phone sat on the desk, a red light at the base blinking hypnotically into the darkness.

Amy collapsed in a chair and slumped forward. "Who did this?" she wailed through strands of pink and purple hair. "Was it my father? He hated Nina. They argued today, but I never thought…"

Brooke didn't know how to respond. Did Amy actually think her father would do such thing? No—she was hysterical. Traumatized. But more than that, she was a seventeen-year-old kid, and Brooke was the adult in the room. It was her job to say something—but what? Education courses years ago hadn't prepared her for a moment like this. But she had to do something, so she placed her cell on the desk, knelt beside Amy and took her hand.

"I'm sure your father had nothing to do with this," she said softly.

Amy jerked her hand away. "How would you know? You never met my father—did you? And you didn't know Nina." Sobbing, she wrapped her arms around herself, her hands clenching her shoulders as though building a fortress to keep Brooke away.

Feeling helpless, Brooke rose to her feet and leaned against the wall. She stayed that way as minutes ticked by, and then, with a bang, the studio door opened and footsteps thudded on the linoleum floor, keeping rhythm with the metallic clattering of a gurney. Other footsteps followed. Voices as well, muffled except for an occasional word that rose to the surface.

The murmuring continued and then a familiar face appeared in the doorway. Barely a year ago, Detective Jason Radley had played a major role in Brooke's life. It felt strange to see him again in a different setting and a different context.

He acknowledged her with a nod. "Brooke Roberts," he said, tall and lean in his black suit, gray shirt and narrow black tie. Surprised to see you here." His eyes shifted to Amy. "Is she alright?"

Brooke shrugged off the question. Of course, Amy wasn't alright. She was seventeen, she'd stumbled on a dead body and she thought her father was the murderer. How could she be alright?

"You ladies have had a rough time of it," Radley continued. "Let's get you out of here and find a quiet place to talk."

He hurried them out of the studio and down a long corridor toward the offices at the front of the building. Brooke had been there earlier that day, filling out forms, picking up her ID badge and paging through brochures that showcased the private academy's landscaped campus, multiple gyms, a state-of-the-art media center, and brand-new fine arts wing. Notably absent were images of a stunning African American woman lying dead on a closet floor.

"You okay?" the long-faced detective asked as they entered the office and took seats around a coffee table. "Not going to faint or puke?"

Brooke shook her head—she wouldn't do either. Amy said nothing. Instead, she sat in silence, her face streaked with black eye makeup and her eyes fixed on a spot on the carpet.

Once Radley'd made sure they were more or less okay, he went to the door and looked back down the hall toward the fine arts wing. He seemed antsy, like he'd he rather be at the scene of the crime than in this quiet space with two shell-shocked females. "Nina Powell, of all people," he said to no one in particular. "Just wait until this story hits the news."

At the sound of approaching footsteps, he stepped aside, and his boss, Detective James Burleigh, entered the room. The senior detective hadn't changed much since last fall when he'd arrived at Brooke's door to investigate a break-in and a murder. A year later, his suit jacket seemed a bit snugger across the middle, but everything else was the same. Unruly gray eyebrows. Narrow, piercing eyes. A bulbous nose. A gruff slant to his lips and an overall rumpled appearance.

"Ms. Roberts," he began. "It's been almost a year since we last spoke. You're still at the same address?"

She wasn't. She provided the new information along with a brief history of her relationship to the school. "Tonight was the first rehearsal," she said.

Burleigh glanced at Amy who sat catatonically still, her skull-shaped earrings peering through strands of tangled hair.

"The headmaster asked me to tell you he called your mom," the detective said gently. "She'll be here soon to pick you up."

Amy didn't look at him. "I drove to school," she responded, her voice flat. "I can drive myself home."

"You've had a shock. We want you to get back safely."

"Then you shouldn't have called my mother."

Burleigh let the remark slide and instead, directed his questions to Brooke. She told him that she'd met with the cast of *Dracula* at 6:15 that evening. After reading through Act I, she gave the kids a ten-minute break while she toured the tech booth at the rear of the auditorium. And no—she couldn't account for the students' whereabouts at that time. She'd just met them and hadn't yet matched names with faces.

"And the victim?" Burleigh continued. "Do either of you know of anyone who had issues with Ms. Powell?"

The question seemed to shake Amy out of her stupor. "Other than my father?" she asked, her eyes meeting the detective's for the first time. "He had a ton of issues with Nina. He hated her and she hated him. He was here this afternoon screaming at her."

"I see. Any idea what triggered that outburst?"

"Wait a sec and I'll show you." Amy reached for her phone and after scrolling around, found a picture and handed it to the detective. Burleigh took a look and passed it to his sidekick who glanced at it and passed it to Brooke.

The image on the screen showed a dozen pink and white baby dresses mounted on a sheet of plywood. Amy's school photos—twelve years' worth—were arranged at the necklines while vertical lines suggesting prison bars stood in the foreground. The entire panel was splattered with red paint—or at least Brooke hoped it was paint and not blood. *I've been damaged!* the piece seemed to shout. *I'm wounded and broken and trapped.*

"I named it *Little Women*," Amy said proudly. "The pink and white dresses represent the struggles of girls growing up in our patriarchal society. And in case you're wondering, I'm nothing like the Amy March character in *Little Women*. My parents have tried to force me into that mold all my life, but I don't fit."

The announcement drew a look of confusion from the detectives who appeared to know nothing about the novel or the characters in it. But rather than admitting ignorance, Burleigh shrugged off the matter and continued the interview. "Okay, so you've showed us an interesting piece of art, but what's it got to do with Nina Powell and your dad?"

It didn't take much prodding to get at the details. Amy created *Little Women* in a workshop at Nina's church. Late in the summer, Nina selected it for an exhibit of feminist art at a local gallery. When Amy's parents arrived at the opening, her dad took one look, flew into a rage and ended up in a heated confrontation with Nina.

"There he was, losing his mind in front of everyone," Amy said. "But instead of backing down, Nina laughed in his face. That's how she was—gutsy and tough. Nobody could push her around."

But somebody had pushed her around, and now she was dead. Brooke kept the thought to herself. There was no need to state the obvious.

"Your father's name?" Burleigh continued.

"Rupert March. I already know he's a jerk, so don't be afraid to say it."

The detectives exchanged glances. Real estate developer Rupert March was a well-known entity in Pennsylvania's Lehigh Valley. He'd recently launched a radio show and podcast to spotlight his political opinions. People either loved him or hated him. There wasn't much in between.

The interview moved on to questions about Nina's relationships with her colleagues. Brooke, of course, had no way of answering those questions, and Amy, having voiced her thoughts about her father, retreated into silence.

As things were winding up, there was a knock at the door and a female cop poked her head into the room. "Fern March just arrived. She's anxious to see her daughter."

When Burleigh gave the okay, the officer stepped aside to admit a petite woman in a lavender jogging suit. Short, frosted hair surrounded a florid face, tear-streaked cheeks and a pair of frantic blue eyes. A whiff of perfume followed Mrs. March into the room, barely masking the scent of alcohol that entered with her. Her gaze shifted from the detectives to Brooke and then to her daughter who'd resumed her catatonic pose, her eyes once again fixed on the floor.

"Oh, Amy," Mrs. March squawked. "This is terrible. Ghastly. A nightmare. Nina—dead? It doesn't seem possible. And there you were—just a few doors away. If anything ever happened to you I'd…"

She careened toward her daughter, arms outstretched, but Amy jerked away and held up her hands to block the embrace. "I get it, Mom. You're upset. So am I."

Mrs. March drew back like she'd been slapped. "Of course, I'm upset. Everyone at the school is upset—or they will be when they hear the news. When Dr. Pierce said you needed a ride—that it wasn't safe for you to drive—naturally I came running. What was I to do? Your father's away on business, I was all alone, and..."

"I'm not getting in the car with you. Not when you're..." Amy left the words hanging, but her meaning was clear.

By now Brooke had sized up the situation and was pretty sure the detectives had as well. "I'd be happy to drive them home," she offered.

"No need for that," Burleigh said. "Our people will see that they get back safely."

"Seriously, it's no problem at all."

Fern March waved a hand in Brooke's direction, setting gold bangles clattering and clanging on her wrist. "That would be fine. Anything's fine."

"That settles it then. But before we leave," Burleigh said, rising to his feet. "I have a question for you, Mrs. March. You said your husband's away on business, but your daughter said he was in the building after school today, arguing with the deceased."

Amy's mom seemed confused by the statement. "Rupert was here after school? That's odd. He was on his way to the airport. A business trip to..." She frowned, a look of bewilderment on her face. "My husband's always on the road. I can't keep one trip separated from another."

"No problem. We'll check into it later."

Burleigh nodded toward the door to indicate that the interview was over, and as they left the office, Brooke pointed toward the fine arts wing. "This way," she told Mrs. March. "My car's in the faculty lot behind the school."

The woman let out a gasp. "We can't go back there. Not when the parking lot's crowded with news vans. Amy's a minor.

I have to protect her privacy."

The detectives appeared to agree. After a brief consultation they decided that the Marches should wait in the office while Brooke circled around to pick them up. That settled, they escorted Brooke down the long corridor and past the police tape that cordoned off the studio.

At the exit Brooke reached in her pocket. Her keys were there but not her phone. That's right—she'd laid in on the desk when she knelt to comfort Amy. In the chaos she'd neglected to pick it up.

When she explained, Burleigh dispatched his younger sidekick to lift the tape and escort her into the studio. Once through the door, Radley wandered over to the storage closet to check out the proceedings while Brooke slipped into Nina's office to retrieve her phone.

It was right where she'd left it, next to the office phone that blinked one-two-three in the darkness. Seized by a sudden impulse, she pushed the button. The first message confirmed an appointment earlier that afternoon at Zack's Auto Body Shop. The second was a male voice reminding Nina to meet him for an early dinner at a restaurant called Don Giovanni's. The final message clicked on, and for a few seconds there was silence. *"This is Jay,"* began a breathy male voice. There was another pause and then he spoke again. *"This is my last offer, Nina. I mean it this time."*

Three

"All set?" Jason Radley asked from the doorway.

Brooke turned around. Did he notice what she'd done? Would it matter? She put it out of her mind, and together they joined Burleigh and left the building.

A heaviness in the air heralded an approaching storm while in the distance, lights flickered, fairylike, in the woods bordering the school. Fireflies? Heat lightning on this warm September evening? No. Flashlights searching for evidence before the rain could wash it away.

The distant glow was dwarfed by brighter lights in the parking lot. Flashes of blue, white and red exploded from the roofs of a dozen cop cars, the colors bouncing off storm clouds and casting an eerie glow over an ambulance idling nearby. Meanwhile, cops huddled together, speaking among themselves or talking into their phones while trying to ignore the reporters buzzing around them.

Seeing Brooke and her escorts, the reporters gave up on

the cops and swarmed in her direction.

"Say no comment and keep walking," Detective Burleigh muttered between his teeth. "You'll be seeing a lot of these so-called journalists in the coming days, Maintain your distance, and if anything new springs to mind, don't tell them about it—tell us."

They stood guard at the car, keeping the reporters at bay while Brooke slid behind the wheel. At the front of the building, she waited while an officer escorted Amy and her mom to the car. When Mrs. March indicated a preference for the back, Amy slid into the passenger seat next to Brooke.

No sooner had they left the campus than a long, mournful sob erupted from the backseat. "This never would have happened at that other school," Mrs. March wailed. "You were safe there, and your father and I never had a moment's worry—not until…" She paused for another sob and kept going. "You were only fourteen when they found liquor and marijuana in your locker. I'm still mortified when I think of those horrible, humiliating meetings with the head master and the schoolboard."

"So, duh," Amy shot back. "Don't think about the horrible, humiliating meetings, and then you won't be mortified. Is that so hard to figure out?"

The question elicited another round of sobs. Frowning, Amy turned her face away and stared silently out the window. By now a faint drizzle dotted the windshield, and the slow, steady rhythm of the wipers kept time with the noise from the backseat. Swwwissh, sob. Swwwissh, sob. Swwwissh, sob.

Further down the road, a deer darted out of the woods and came to a halt in the middle of the lane, its eyes fixed on the approaching headlights. Brooke slammed on the brakes, her tires squealing on the wet pavement as she swerved to avoid a collision. The close encounter sent her heart racing. Was that how Drama Teacher Rachel Leventhal lost control of her car just a week earlier?

The trees soon yielded to rolling fields dotted with farmhouses, barns and silos. Tract houses appeared, clustered together in identical rows, their lights blurred by the rain. After five more miles Amy directed Brooke down a gravel lane that twisted and turned for half-a-mile and ended at a ten-foot wrought-iron gate hemmed in on either side by stone walls. Amy pulled a device from her backpack, and when she pushed a button, the gate creaked open to allow them to enter. As it closed behind them, flood lights sprang to life on either side of the driveway while others shone on a large, Tudor-style dwelling and the manicured gardens surrounding it.

Amy turned to her mom in the backseat. "You can quit crying now. We're home."

Brooke brought the car to a stop and got out to assist Mrs. March who clung to her arm, sniffling as they made their way toward the house. Amy walked ahead to open the door, and Brooke was just about to guide Mrs. March into the foyer, when the woman held out a hand to stop her.

"This is far enough. Thank you for your help, Ms..." Amy's mom hesitated, a look of bewilderment on her tear-streaked face. "I'm sorry. In all the confusion, I didn't get your name."

"Brooke Roberts. I'm filling in for Rachel Leventhal."

"Brooke Roberts. Rachel Leventhal. Of course. Well, Ms. Roberts, thank you for the ride home." With that, she ushered her daughter inside.

Brooke caught a glimpse of Amy's face as her mother closed the door. She wanted to reach out to this traumatized kid with a touch, a hug—something to say she cared. But the door closed in her face and she was left staring at a plaque that said: *Ring twice and speak slowly into the intercom.*

She returned to her car and watched the house recede in the rearview mirror. Ahead of her, the wrought-iron gate creaked open to allow her to leave and clanged shut to make sure she didn't return.

▾ ▾ ▾

Ted Roslyn unlocked the door to his row house in Allentown, exhausted but still pumped from the prophecy conference in Houston. *Deception 101* had played to a massive audience, and for reasons that were fairly obvious. The atmosphere these days was thick with lies—on the news, online, everywhere. People were hungry for the truth, and hopefully the conference had helped assuage that hunger.

He tossed his duffle bag on the floor, went to the kitchen and stuck a frozen lasagna in the microwave. While waiting, he leaned against the counter to review his messages. After scrolling through half-a-dozen, he stopped at a text from his ex-wife. Well, look at that. A photo of Becca's brand-new baby girl—a pretty little thing with chubby cheeks and rosebud lips. Ted was glad Becca was remarried and starting a family, and he was glad that she and her second husband were happy. Ted hadn't made her very happy, and that's why things ended the way they did.

He clicked out of his messages without looking at any more—the news of Becca and her baby had thrown him for a loop. Not that he still carried a torch for his ex—he'd long ago closed the book on that chapter of his life. Even so, the message was a painful reminder of the fact that, unlike his colleagues from the conference, Ted had no one to come home to. At age 39 with the big four-o looming on the horizon, he was all alone in a cheesy, rented row house that offered little in the way of creature comforts.

The microwave beeped and shook him out of his thoughts. Food, after all, was his most immediate concern. He took the steaming lasagna to the living room, flopped down on the sofa and clicked the TV remote.

"BREAKING NEWS!" shouted a bright red banner. The

breaking news turned out to be a murder—not exactly a novelty these days when homicides were at an all-time high. Except, as it turned out, this wasn't the usual drive-by shooting or gang-related crime. Someone had sneaked into a pricey private school and offed Nina Powell. She was an art teacher, but more significantly, she was supposed to testify in an upcoming police corruption trial. It looked like that wouldn't be happening.

An image of the crime scene appeared on the screen—well, not the actual crime scene, but a photo of the building where the victim was found. The two-century-old prep school looked bright and cheerful in the sunlight of an autumn afternoon. Steps led to a portico supported by graceful columns. Wide windows looked out over the world. The place reeked of knowledge, history and tradition.

From there, the camera cut away to a scene completely unlike the one on the website. Police. Flashing lights. Reporters. Back in the day, Ted would have been one of those reporters, and even now, he felt himself salivating at the thought of covering this juicy story. It had it all. Dirty cops. Human traffickers. Hush money. And an elite prep school where rich snobs sent their kids to protect them from all the above. Oh—and a dead witness who just happened to be African American. Things didn't get much better than this.

The camera shifted and came to rest on two men and a woman hurrying through the crowd. Wait a minute! Ted knew those people. The short, stocky guy was Detective James Burleigh and the tall lanky individual next to him was Jason Radley. And the third person? Ted blinked and looked again. Yes, the third person was Brooke Roberts. What was she doing at a swank private school in the middle of a murder investigation?

Memories flooded back as he stared at the screen. Her chestnut hair. Her blue-green eyes. Her lipstick that left a trace of coral on a coffee mug.

He glanced at his phone. He wanted to call her, but it was

way too late. Even if it weren't, he doubted she'd be interested in hearing from him. She'd been grateful that he'd helped her through a rough spot last year, but she'd made it clear that she wanted to be left alone to grieve her husband's passing. Ted had respected her wishes—he'd had no choice—and he didn't think she'd appreciate him barging back into her life.

He closed his eyes and greeted the images that arose from the past. Towering trees, an isolated cabin, rain, guns and in the distance, lights bursting through an angry sky.

And just like that, it was over. Or was it?

He chased the thought away. Of course, it was over. There'd been nothing there to begin with.

▾ ▾ ▾

Rain streamed down the windows, sparkling and glistening in the glow of the streetlight in the alley. The effect was hypnotic, but even so, Brooke couldn't sleep. The sofa bed with its wafer-thin mattress wasn't meant for every-night use, and after tossing and turning, she still hadn't found a comfortable position.

Three weeks ago she'd sold the house she and her late husband shared, and she still hadn't adjusted to life at the Beacon Arms Apartments—a temporary residence while she shopped for a new place to call home. But that wasn't what was keeping her awake. Every time she closed her eyes, an endless loop began playing in her brain. Amy March, her youthful chatter giving way to shrieks of terror. Nina Powell, her eyes bulging red in their sockets. Amy's gruesome artwork and her mother bursting into the office, too caught up in her own personal melodrama to support her daughter in a time of need.

Role reversal—Brooke was familiar with the syndrome. Her own mother had acted out a similar script. Needy. Dependent. Afraid. Her descent into suicide when Brooke was in her early twenties had come as no surprise, and yet suicide is always a surprise, horrific in its cruel and desperate hopelessness.

Her phone squealed and the images fled. She didn't want to talk to anyone. Not now. But since it might be important, she forced herself to take a look. The caller was Jocelyn Fisher, the receptionist at Sussex Academy.

"Can you believe it?" Jocelyn shrieked into her ear. "Nina Powell—murdered on school property? It's a nightmare—an absolute nightmare. Poor Amy. How's she supposed to cope with this tragedy? And you—your first night on the job. I can't imagine what you're going through."

Once the hysterics subsided, Jocelyn got around to the reason for the call. No school tomorrow—police orders while they scour the campus for evidence. School would reopen on Wednesday with a memorial service followed by grief support workshops instead of classes. After-school activities would go on as usual, except for play practice. At 6:15, Dr. Pierce would meet with the theater students and their parents to discuss safety procedures being implemented for the rehearsal season. It shouldn't take longer than an hour.

Brooke was stunned by the news. She'd assumed the play would be canceled out of respect for Nina. It seemed appropriate to do so, but when she said as much, Jocelyn fell silent.

"To put this in perspective," Jocelyn said, "*Dracula* is the kick-off event of the school's three-week bicentennial celebration. Two-hundred years is a big deal—a really big deal. For the students, their families, the alumni—everybody."

It was easy to read between the lines. *Dracula* marked the beginning of a three-week love fest designed to get fat-cat alumni to open their wallets. With big bucks at stake, the show must go on.

Four

Morning light flooded the gallery, illuminating the works in mixed media, each piece a testimony to women's creativity and resilience. The show on Sunday had brought out a huge crowd to see the work of young, feminist artists, and other than an awkward moment when Rupert March made a scene over his daughter's contribution, the event had been a resounding success.

Entering her office, Madeleine Hewitt settled down with a cup of decaf and her latest self-help book. So far, the author's advice had proven surprisingly helpful. Cutting back on caffeine and turning off the news had done wonders for her state of mind, and while she missed the morning jolt of java, she didn't miss the media's daily onslaught of fear, rage and despair. Life provided plenty of all three.

Celebrate success! the current chapter instructed. Well, that was easy enough. All she had to do was look back at Sunday's spectacular opening. And yet, a note of sadness had hung over the event. Until recently, Sid would have been at her side, pouring champagne and charming artists and patrons alike. A tough decision loomed on the horizon: begin divorce proceedings and move out of the house that had been in Sid's family for generations, or continue to live separate lives beneath a shared roof.

The buzzer sounded from the front of the building. At first Madeleine ignored it, but when the noise persisted, she looked up at the monitor and saw a young woman with dark, shoulder-length hair peering through the window. What was wrong with people? The sign on the door said the gallery opened at ten, and here it was—only nine-thirty. Sighing, she tossed her book aside and got to her feet. She'd come to value this morning ritual of decaf and self-help, and while she didn't appreciate the interruption, it wasn't in her nature to turn a customer away.

When she opened the door, the woman thrust a card in her face. Well—how about that? This wasn't just any early bird. No, this early bird was a reporter for a regional newspaper, one that rarely covered gallery events. It looked like Madeleine's emerging feminist artists were about to get some free publicity.

"I'm here to follow up on the incident that occurred on Sunday afternoon," the reporter began. "An argument between Nina Powell and real estate developer, Rupert March."

"Oh, that," Madeleine scoffed, recalling the unpleasant scene. "The story's hardly newsworthy. Just a family squabble about his daughter's artwork."

The woman frowned. "No, ma'am. Judging from a video someone sent us last night, it was more than a squabble." To prove her point, she held out her phone and ran footage of the confrontation. "I'm here to discuss Mr. March's interactions with the deceased."

The deceased? The words made no sense. "I'm sorry," Madeleine said. "Who exactly is 'the deceased?'"

The early bird drew back, a look of astonishment on her young face. "Nina Powell, of course."

Madeleine scoffed at the answer. "That's absurd. I spoke

to Nina just yesterday afternoon."

"No, ma'am. There's no mistake. Nina Powell was murdered last night. Strangled, from what I understand."

Madeleine's thoughts flew back to Sunday's encounter. "There was a disagreement," she admitted. "The situation was awkward and unpleasant but…"

She fell silent, her thoughts oddly out-of-focus. Could it be true? She'd intentionally sworn off the news. Had she missed something. "I'm sorry," she said, her thoughts tangled. "I was unaware of—I mean, this is the first I've heard about…" The words died in her throat.

"How would you describe the confrontation?" the reporter continued. "Did Rupert March use racial and sexist slurs when he confronted Ms. Powell?"

"I didn't hear what he said," Madeleine stammered. "The gallery was crowded, and …"

"So, he might have used racial and sexist slurs?"

"It was a chaotic situation. I was too far away to hear. Now if you'll excuse me…"

"Ma'am, I'm sure our readers will be interested in your…"

Madeleine closed the door in the young woman's face. Nina Powell. Murdered? It wasn't possible.

Heart pounding, she stumbled through the gallery and collapsed at her desk. Nina had helped curate the exhibit on Sunday. She'd recommended nearly half of the artists represented in the show. And now? No—it couldn't be.

Madeleine snatched up her phone, entered Nina's name and stared in horror at the screen. While she'd been quietly sipping decaf and congratulating herself on her successes, the entire region was absorbing the news of Nina's death. No—not just her death. Her murder. She searched for further news. "No suspects yet," a reporter announced, "but Ms. Powell's ties to an upcoming police corruption trial suggest a possible motive."

Her thoughts flew to the reporter she'd just spoken to.

Where there was one, there were bound to be others. And not just reporters, but swarms of curiosity seekers, converging on the gallery in search of gossip. There was no way she could speak to them—not in her present frame of mind.

She turned to her keyboard. "*Closed,*" she typed. "*Will Reopen Tomorrow.*" Grabbing the page from the printer, she raced to the front of the gallery in time to see a news van glide up to the curb. Hah! If those fools thought she was going to answer their questions, they were sadly mistaken.

She taped the sign to the door, locked the gallery behind her and raced down the alley toward the space where she'd parked her car. "A word with you," a reporter screeched from somewhere behind her. "Did you witness Sunday's altercation between Rupert March and Nina Powell?"

Instead of responding, Madeleine dove into her car and started the engine. Undaunted, the reporter approached the vehicle, pounded frantically on the driver's side window and then jumped back, startled, when Madeleine careened out of the space and down the alley. As she approached the street, she saw yet another news van easing into a spot along the curb.

Her heart fluttered against her ribs, wild and frantic like the flailing wings of a trapped bird. For a moment the world seemed off-kilter, the shops, buildings, pedestrians, all of them swaying in a jumble of shape and color. *Don't pass out,* she told herself. *Take a deep breath. Calm down. Concentrate.*

And then reality came into focus—bright and undeniable. Nina Powell was dead. Not just dead, but murdered. How was this possible?

Five

The beginnings of a newsletter stared at Brooke from her laptop. She needed to get it edited and laid out by the end of the week, but instead of sticking to the task, she went online for the hundredth time to check for news updates.

She'd already seen last night's footage of herself being escorted out of the school. She didn't care to see that again, so clicked on a recently uploaded video of Rupert March shouting at Nina Powell in an art gallery. To Brooke's surprise, the gallery in question belonged to Madeleine Hewitt, a close friend and colleague of her late husband. Karl's final exhibition at the Hewitt Gallery had been a sad one—a retrospective of his life's work, curated after his death.

Further stories offered a look into Nina's life. Her childhood commitment to social justice. Her studies in New York where she explored ways of using art to further the causes in which she believed. Her freelance work after college. Her advocacy for victims of human trafficking. Her death at 33 at the beginning of what would have been her third year at Sussex Academy.

From there, Brooke hopped onto a livestream already in progress—a news conference featuring the county DA, a tall, red-faced individual who stood at the podium backed by a handful of cops. His answers were brief and to-the-point. The victim's time of death? Between 7:30 and 8:00 on Monday night. Cause of death? Strangulation. Security camera footage? None. The system failed right before school started. Replacements parts were held up by supply chain issues. Suspects? None as of yet. Was racism a factor? Possibly. It was too soon to tell.

Next was a newly uploaded clip that showed a cutesy reporter standing in front of yellow police tape with Sussex Academy looming in the background. "It's clear by now that Nina Powell was strangled to death," Cutesy told her viewers. "But our sources tell us that the killer made two small puncture wounds on her neck. While these wounds in no way contributed to her death, they raise troubling questions about a possible motive. Ms. Powell was designing sets for a fall production of *Dracula*. Were the wounds intended to suggest the mark of the vampire, and if so, what message was the killer sending?"

Brooke stared at the screen. The mark of the vampire? Did those puncture wounds tie Nina's murder to the play? If so, what was the connection? As the director of *Dracula*, Brooke had a right to know—for her own safety and for the safety of the kids in her care.

She picked up her phone to call Detective Burleigh and put it down again. This wasn't like last year when she'd been front and center in the investigation into Karl's death. Back then the detectives had kept her in the loop. Now they didn't have to tell her anything. If she asked, they'd assure her that everything was under control, and that would be the end of it.

But the detectives didn't have to be at the school every night, directing a play with a cast of freaked-out students. That was her job, and she had no idea how to mentor these kids through the crisis that by now was ripping at the hearts of the entire school community.

She pictured faculty members in the lounge during prep periods, their heads close together as they sipped coffee and swapped tidbits of information. The teachers knew the students. They knew the administration. They knew the gossip and the rumors—the behind-the-scenes details of life at Sussex Academy. And Brooke knew nothing. All she had in the way of context were the shreds of information she'd picked up on the news and the three messages she'd listened to last night—Nina's appointment at Zack's Auto Body, dinner at Don Giovanni's and a vaguely threatening message from a guy named Jay. She was on the outside, looking into the darkness and seeing nothing—not even shadows. If she was going to function in her new role, she needed to shed light on last night's experience. But how was that possible when she knew no one at the school? Well, almost no one. Most of her former colleagues had moved on.

An idea sprang to mind, and seeing no other way to address the frustrating limitations her circumstances imposed on her, she turned off her laptop, left the apartment and rode the elevator to the ground floor.

Twenty minutes later she sat behind the wheel, her eyes fixed on the boxy, stucco exterior of Zack's Auto Body Shop. She took a moment to consider the risks involved in venturing inside to ask a few questions. When there didn't seem to be any, she got out of the car and crossed the street.

A buzzer welcomed her into Zack's waiting room, a dark, dreary place furnished with plastic chairs and a lopsided coffee table stacked with back issues of *Car and Driver*. The air smelled of cigarette smoke, chemicals and paint, and from a radio above the counter, a strident male voice warned about the goals of United Nations Agenda something-or-other.

Brooke took a seat and after a couple of minutes, a dark-haired guy appeared through a swinging door, introduced himself as Zack and pointed to the radio. "Rupert March. Ever listen to him?"

She shook her head.

"Well, maybe you should. There's a lot of crazy stuff going on these days. Things you might not notice until you take the time to look." He wiped his forehead with his sleeve and regarded Brooke through narrowed eyes. "You look familiar. I could swear I've seen you somewhere."

"I don't think so."

"No—I mean it. You look familiar. Really familiar. Have we met?"

"Not that I'm aware of. I'm here about a phone message someone left for a woman named Nina Powell."

The guy eyed her suspiciously. "You a cop?"

She shook her head.

"A reporter?"

"No. I'm directing a play at the school where Nina worked."

He smacked his hand against his forehead. "That's why you look familiar. I saw you on the news last night. Okay—now it all makes sense. Nice lady, Nina Powell. I couldn't believe it when I heard she got—you know." He put his hands on his neck like he was being choked.

"I understand she had an appointment here yesterday afternoon. Did she show up?"

He nodded and bit by bit, the story came out. Zack's business had a contract with the police for hauling away wrecks. That included Rachel Leventhal's Bronco that they'd dragged up from the embankment where she'd crash-landed just a week ago. According to Zack, Rachel was out cold, but it was a wonder she was alive—that's how bad it was.

"Anyway," he concluded, "Nina seemed to think the accident was suspicious, like maybe somebody tampered with the engine or the brakes. I told her we're a body shop and we don't deal with mechanical stuff. If she had questions, she should talk to the police."

Okay, so that was interesting. Both Rachel and Nina were involved with *Dracula*—Rachel as director, Nina as set designer. Rachel was on life-support. Nina was dead. Was there a connection?

Brooke recalled the breathy message from Jay. "Does a guy named Jay work here?" she asked.

Zack shook his head.

"How about someone whose name starts with J?"

He pointed to the name patch on his shirt. "There's only me, Steve, Frank, and a coupla' part-timers. Why do you ask?"

"Nothing important. Just something that crossed my mind."

When it became clear that Zack had nothing to add, Brooke thanked him, returned to her car and drove to the up-scale shopping center where Don Giovanni's Greco-Roman Trattoria was located. While a newcomer to the Lehigh Valley, the restaurant had already established a reputation for world-class cuisine served with a generous helping of opera. As could be expected, the parking lot was crowded, and since it was lunch hour, it was unlikely that the owner would be willing to drop everything to talk to a random stranger. Brooke needed a reason for this visit, and her desktop publishing and editing business would do the trick.

No one was in the vestibule when she entered. A statue of Mozart stood in one corner of the space while framed portraits of opera greats lined the walls. More compelling were the opening strains of *La Donna e Mobile* drifting from a space to Brooke's right. Glancing into the crowded dining room, she saw a handsome, dark-haired tenor in Renaissance attire. Another server stood by, wearing a long gown with a laced bodice. Apparently Don Giovanni's schtick extended to costumes as well as arias.

After a short wait, a hostess wearing a royal blue Renaissance-style gown emerged through a swinging door. "Welcome to Don Giovanni's," she said from beneath a pile of bottle-black hair. "How many in your party?"

Brooke held out her card. "I'm not here for lunch. I'd like to speak to the owner about a business matter."

"One moment please." The woman took the card and reappeared moments later, with a heavy-set, older man wearing knee-length pants, tights and a jewel-studded doublet.

"Good day, signora," he said, bowing theatrically. "Welcome to Don Giovanni's where opera is always on the menu." He nodded toward the dining room. "Today's tenor just returned from a summer at La Scala. Name a favorite, and Giorgio will be happy to serenade you."

"Thank you, Mr.—" she hesitated, "—Mr. Giovanni, but first I'd like to ask you a question."

The man drew back, his dark eyes sizing her up as though she were an expensive slab of prosciutto. "If this is about promotional materials, I already have someone who handles my publicity. But I'll be happy to keep your card on file in the event your services are required in the future."

"That's very kind of you. In the meanwhile, I'd like to ask you a question. I'm sure you've heard about the murder at Sussex Academy."

His smile vanished. "You are with the police?"

"No, I'm not with the police. I'm…"

He looked again at her card. "You're a reporter!"

"No. It doesn't say reporter. It says…"

"It says *desktop publishing and editing.* You came here to pry into my affairs and publish them for the world to see. I'll speak to the police, but reporters? Never! They are pigs! Swine! Scum of the earth!" He strode over to the door, threw it open and pointed toward the parking lot. "You are not welcome here!"

"But, I'm not a reporter. I'm—"

"I don't care who you are. Arrivederci, signora!"

The door slammed behind her as she hurried to her car. She was disappointed, but after last night's encounter with the press, she understood the restaurant owner's animosity.

She was about to back out of the parking space when the tenor in tights emerged from the restaurant, his eyes sweeping the vehicles in the crowded lot. Spotting her, he waved his hands and darted in her direction, his slender frame weaving in and out between the parked cars.

"I recognized you from the news," he announced somewhat breathlessly. "You're from the school where Nina Powell was murdered."

"That's right. She was supposed to meet someone here for dinner last night. Did she show up?"

"Yeah, but I wasn't her server. Della Schaeffer had one-half of the dining room and I had the other—just the two of us since Mondays are slow."

"The guy she was with. Did you know him?

"Never saw him before. But I could see them arguing and then all of a sudden, Nina bolted out of her seat and stormed out the door." Giorgio paused to glance back over his shoulder. "Listen, the boss'll have a fit if he catches me talking to you, so let me make this quick. Della recognized you when you peeked into the dining room." He thrust a scrap of paper into Brooke's hand. "It's her phone number. She wants you to call her."

Six

The parking lot outside the Beacon Arms was crowded—not with cars, but with reporters. Brooke brushed past them and dodged their questions as she raced for the door. Back in her apartment, she settled into the sofa and called Della Schaeffer's number. When the answering machine picked up, Brooke left a message and told Della to get back to her.

From there she turned her attention to the messages that had piled up during the afternoon. There were dozens, most of them from people she hadn't spoken to in years, all of them asking about the murder. She deleted the messages one by one, but stopped at a voicemail from her 83-year-old Uncle Nelson. He'd seen her on the news and was concerned that he hadn't heard from her. She returned the call, and after a brief rundown of events, he reminded her of their monthly dinner engagement scheduled for the following evening. "I guess that's out of the question until after the play," he remarked.

She paused to give the matter some thought. The meeting with the theater students and their parents would start at 6:15 and last about an hour. She'd probably be exhausted after an emotionally draining day, but did she really want to return all alone to this tiny apartment? After only three weeks, she loathed the place. The only bright spot was that her lease was month-to-month. With any luck, her tenure here would be brief.

"Slide the reservation back an hour-and-a-half and I'll be there," she promised.

The final message was from a guy named Ron Webster who identified himself as the school psychologist. "Unless I hear otherwise," he said, "I'll stop by your place sometime after three to discuss tomorrow's memorial service and grief support workshops."

Brooke glanced at the time. He was due at any second. She took a few minutes to eat a slice of peanut butter toast and was just cleaning up when she heard a knock on the door. When she opened it, a thirty-something guy with short, sandy hair introduced himself.

She eyed him curiously. Steel gray eyes. Narrow lips. A trim, athletic physique and a late-summer tan that hinted at afternoons on the tennis court and the beach. For some reason Ron Webster looked familiar. Where had she seen him before?

"A bit of background before we get started," he said once the introductions were out of the way. He explained that he rotated among five private schools—one each day of the week. Given the trauma of Nina's death, he planned to be at Sussex Academy for the remainder of this week and part of the next as well. "But enough about me," he said. "You've been through a tough ordeal. How are you holding up?"

Brooke thought back over her day. She'd taken control of her situation, learned a few things and felt a lot better for having done so. Surprisingly better, to be honest. But she didn't bother explaining. Instead, she told him she was doing okay, considering the circumstances.

"Those circumstances are the reason I stopped by," he told

her. "After a shock like the one you've just experienced, it helps to discuss your feelings."

Brooke said nothing. Her feelings were her own, and sharing them with complete strangers, while helpful to some, was distressing to her.

"Feel free to speak about your ordeal," he urged. "Now, or at any time in the future."

When she said nothing, he tried again. "I'm ready to listen any time you'd like to talk. You witnessed something terrible and it's only natural that you'd want to discuss the experience with an empathetic listener."

Instead of opening up, she felt herself retreating. Who did Ron Webster think he was, invading her space and expecting her, on cue, to spill her guts? That wasn't her style. She turned her gaze out the window and tried to think of an excuse to get rid of him.

Her animosity vanished when he started talking about the students. This man had the wellbeing of three-hundred traumatized ninth through twelfth graders to think about. He wasn't being nosy. He was just making sure that Brooke's state of mind wouldn't negatively affect the kids she'd be working with.

"I'm sure everyone at Sussex Academy—students, teachers, parents—will remember where they were when they heard of Nina's death," he continued, "not to mention where they were when the murder probably occurred."

"I was with the cast," Brooke murmured, thinking back to the events of the prior evening. "We were up on the stage, reading through the script and getting to know each other while just a few doors away…" She shuddered at the thought.

"I was at home," he said, "hosting a Cub Scout event with my wife. There I was, dressed as a Native American and whooping it up around a bonfire in our back yard, while at the school…"

He fell silent. Both of them were having trouble completing their thoughts.

"How can I help?" Brooke asked.

"For starters, I hope you're planning to attend tomorrow's memorial service."

"Of course."

"And the grief support workshops in the afternoon?"

Brooke hadn't planned on hanging around for group therapy with a bunch of strangers. All those tears and hugs and tortured emotions would resurrect memories of Karl's death.

"It would mean a lot to the students," Webster spoke up. "But more importantly, it might give you some context about the school and the issues the kids are facing."

Context. That's exactly what she'd been trying to find. "I'll be there," she agreed.

"Excellent." Nodding his approval, Webster reached into his briefcase and brought out a schedule for the following day. A second page listed the names and backgrounds of the grief counselors he'd assembled to guide the afternoon activities. They were, he assured her, experts in their fields.

Experts—really? Brooke wondered what made them experts. Raw, gut-wrenching experience, or reading books, taking notes and passing the exam at the end of the semester.

Webster glanced at his watch. "I was hoping we'd have time to discuss Amy March's situation, but something came up at the last minute and I have to cut this short. Am I correct in assuming that you and Amy will be working in close proximity for the next several weeks?"

"That's right. I'm the director; she's the stage manager. My assistant, you might say.

"I thought as much. Without going into detail, let me just say that Amy's a deeply needy kid. If you'll stop by my office after school tomorrow, I'll give you some tips about guiding her through this crisis."

"That's very thoughtful of you."

"I have the students' best interests at heart. And yours as well."

As Webster rose to his feet, it dawned on Brooke why he looked familiar. "I know who you are! You're running for political office."

"That's right. County commissioner. I'd appreciate your vote."

Before Brooke could respond, someone banged on the door. When she excused herself to answer it, a scowling Detective Burleigh greeted her from the hallway. His expression lightened when he noticed Ron Webster, but as soon as Webster was gone, Burleigh reconstituted the scowl.

"I just paid a visit to Zack's Auto Body Shop," he snarled. "The owner informed me that someone who fit your description stopped by earlier this afternoon with questions about Nina Powell and Rachel Leventhal. Was that person you?"

Brooke was stunned. She'd never dreamed that news of her innocent foray would get back to the detectives. "Yes, but…"

He held a card in front of her face. "Do you recognize this?"

The question was rhetorical. Of course, she recognized it. It was her business card.

"The owner of Don Giovanni's Trattoria said you used this to weasel your way into a conversation about Nina Powell. Is that also true?"

"I asked a few questions. No more than a journalist might do."

"But you're not a journalist, are you?"

Another rhetorical question. The detective already knew the answer.

"Do you know what your problem is?" he asked.

She wasn't sure. She'd had many problems since Karl's death, and couldn't imagine which one the detective might be referring to.

"Your problem," he continued, "is that you won't leave well enough alone. A year ago, you had everything at stake in the investigation, but now? Now you're on the sidelines, and that's where I want you to stay."

"I didn't mean any harm. I just wanted some context for what happened Monday night."

"Oh, really? You want context? I'll give you context. A cold-blooded killer marched into a school and strangled a woman to death while just a couple of doors away, a bunch of kids were sitting around reading a play. How would you like it if because of your misguided interference, a sociopathic killer went free?"

Brooke didn't answer. Were journalists worried about such things? If anything, their questions were a lot nosier than hers, and as far as she knew, nobody sent cops to their homes to deliver lectures.

"Here's what I want you to do," Burleigh continued. "If you notice anything fishy, don't look into it yourself. Pick up the phone and call me. Do you understand?"

She nodded and waited for him to leave. But he didn't. Instead, he stood by the door, his eyes probing her face in a way that felt intrusive. "You feeling all right?" he asked.

The question took her by surprise. Didn't she seem alright? She thought she was managing pretty well, given the circumstances, and she told him as much.

He didn't seem impressed. "Stumbling on a dead body is a pretty distressing experience," Some folks go to pieces right off the bat. Others bottle up their feelings and get knocked for a loop days or weeks later—a delayed reaction, you might say. That happens a lot with people who look out for others in a crisis—like you with the March girl and her mom. So maybe all your galivanting today was your way of handling things—a coping mechanism, I guess you'd call it. But enough is enough—understand?

When she nodded, he smiled for the first time. "Believe me, Ms. Roberts, we have your best interests at heart. It's our job to keep you safe, and your job, on the other hand, is to stay out of our way."

Seven

Ted had considered calling Tuesday night's presentation *The Rise of Neo-paganism in Post-Christian Culture.* If he'd done that, nobody would have shown up. Instead, he called it *The Old Gods Are Back!* and thanks to the catchy title and some graphics borrowed from Marvel Comics, he was expecting a crowd on this balmy evening in early September.

As he'd hoped, a large audience gathered in the sanctuary of the strip-mall church he regularly attended. Many of the faces were familiar—he saw them every Sunday when he wasn't on the road—but there were a decent number of strangers eager to hear about the "old gods." Ted's approach to the subject wasn't particularly original. A look at the internet revealed tons of videos, podcasts and books devoted to analysis of the fallen angels, giants and mighty men of old presented in the opening verses of Genesis 6. But original or not, the material he was about to present was controversial and guaranteed to spark debate—like most of the topics he presented. Ted specialized in controversy, and the subjects he analyzed—occultism, secret societies, UFOs, etc.—tended to draw unconventional types who typically avoided churches, in strip malls or elsewhere. He'd learned something in his years of studying the scriptures. Evangelism could get messy.

The lecture went well with a lot of people lingering for the Q and A and a few requesting follow-up conversations. Once the sanctuary was empty, Ted gathered his things and headed for the door. He figured that by this time he was alone in the building—the security guards were out in the parking lot keeping an eye on things and they'd lock up when Ted left. But to his surprise, a petite African American woman was waiting in the narthex. She appeared to be in her fifties, judging from the sprinkling of gray in her tightly cropped hair, and she seemed tired as she stood at the door looking out at the night. When she turned to him, however, her eyes were bright with intelligence and warmth.

"Regina Ray," she said, extending her hand to shake his. "I enjoyed your lecture. You gave me a lot to think about."

"That was the goal. I'm glad I hit the mark."

"Well, you did. The subjects you discussed are of great importance to me—for a variety of reasons." She paused as though weighing her words. "But that's only part of the reason I came here tonight"

"And the other part?"

"I have a favor to ask. If you're free tomorrow morning, I'd very much like for you to attend a private memorial service where I'll be speaking."

He eyed her curiously. Her words were perplexing, the invitation mysterious. Why was she asking a complete stranger to attend a random memorial service, and a private one at that?

"I don't understand," he said. "Who's being memorialized?"

"Nina Powell. I assume you've heard of her."

Heard of her? He'd followed Nina's story all day, and at this point, could recite the details backwards and forwards. But it wasn't just his investigative instincts that had kept him glued to the unfolding narrative. Brooke was somehow mixed up in the Nina Powell saga, and more than once he'd gazed at his phone, wondering whether or not to call her. He'd refrained, but just barely.

"Of course, I've heard of Nina Powell," he told the woman. "But she and I never met, so why exactly am I being invited to her memorial?"

"The answer will become clear after the service. Once you and I have had a chance to talk."

Okay, so this was intriguing. A woman he'd never met before was asking him to drop everything and attend a high-profile memorial service. To top it off, she wanted a follow-up conversation. He'd been planning to work on his next podcast, but his curiosity was aroused—big time—and his usual routine would have to wait. "I think I can work you in," he said.

"Wonderful. The service is being held at Sussex Academy, the school where Nina taught. Attendance is limited, so you'll need to show a digital invitation at the door."

They spent a couple of minutes fooling with their phones, and once the invitation showed up in Ted's email, Regina reached into her bag and pulled out a business card. "I neglected to mention that I'm the pastor of Nina's church."

He glanced at the card. Yep. That's what it said. *Reverend Regina Ray*.

"And I also neglected to mention that I prefer to be called Reggie."

"Reggie. Got it. Anything else I should know?"

She averted her gaze. He sensed agitation. Uncertainty. There were things she wanted to say, but couldn't. Instead of rushing to fill the silence, Ted waited for an answer. When none was forthcoming, he continued to wait. She'd speak when she was ready.

"Yes," she finally said. "There is something else you should know. I came here tonight because I need your help."

"I see. And how can I help?"

She glanced toward the church's double doors and the darkness beyond. "I've fallen from grace," she murmured, her voice barely audible. "It's been a long fall, from a very great height, and I'm asking you—no, begging you—to help me find my way back."

Without waiting for comment, she turned and walked into the night.

Eight

Morning noises filtered into the apartment. The hum of traffic. The clanking of cans as a trash truck lumbered down the alley. A bird chirping a wakeup call. Brooke reached from beneath the covers and groped for the remote. A touch of a button and a news anchor appeared on the TV screen. Not local this time, but cable.

"Only a week ago," the anchor said, "Theater Teacher Rachel Leventhal was critically injured when her vehicle went down an embankment. Is it a coincidence that Rachel Leventhal is Jewish; Nina Powell, African American? Has someone steeped in racial hatred decided to purge minorities from this prestigious school? Or are there other explanations for the tragedies that have struck Sussex Academy? Whatever the case, the outrage is building—at the police, at local government and at society as a whole.

The outrage the anchor referred to became visible as Brooke approached the campus for Nina's memorial service. Angry protestors crowded the shoulders and spilled onto the pavement, demanding justice for Nina and an end to police corruption, police brutality and police in general. Brooke slowed to a crawl and then slammed on the brakes to avoid plowing into a guy in ragged jeans and a torn tee-shirt who darted in front of her. When she tapped the horn, he raised his middle finger and let loose a stream of expletives. Nice. Would he have been happier if she'd hit him?

The crowd thickened closer to the school, and so did the police and media presence. A cop stopped her at the entrance to the campus, and when Brooke flashed her ID, he waved her on to another cop who pointed toward the faculty lot at the back of the building. Another cop ushered her into an empty space next to a motorcycle—a massive black Harley with a decal of Thor's hammer on the gas tank.

The sight coaxed forth a memory, not of Thor's hammer but of another Harley. The day was much like this one, the sun bright and the sky streaked with thin, white clouds. She'd stood on the curb while her dad tucked his pony tail beneath his helmet. *"Watch out for your mom while I'm gone,"* he'd told her. He revved the engine and leaned down to kiss her goodbye. She was ten years old when she watched him disappear from view, and she hadn't seen him since. Was he dead or alive? To this day she had no idea.

The memory faded as she entered the crowded fine arts lobby. Students, dressed in muted colors rather than the traditional Sussex Academy uniforms, huddled together in teary-eyed groups while parents, teachers and staff congregated on the sidelines, dabbing their eyes and exchanging embraces. "We're all distressed," she heard Headmaster Dr. Pierce say to a plump woman in a black dress. "Rest assured we're making every possible arrangement for your children's safety."

"Brooke Roberts!" a woman's voice trilled. "I was hoping I'd run into you."

Turning, Brooke saw Amy's mom careening toward her in a pink suit, pink stiletto heels, pink earrings, pink lipstick, pink blush and pink nail polish. Mascara-caked lashes protruded from her eyelids like duck feathers from an oil spill, but all that makeup failed to disguise the puffiness beneath her eyes, the vestiges of recent tears.

She reached out and clasped Brooke's hand. "I'd like to thank you for helping my little girl through that horrible ordeal. Lately Amy's been obsessed with death—and now this. Did you see her art project? Baby clothes and blood? What was she thinking? Children are so troubled nowadays—and why? We devote our lives to making them happy, but in the end they're more mixed-up than ever. They don't know who they are, or what they are, and their attempts at finding out get more bizarre with each passing day. And then this murder. It's too terrible for words."

She cast an anxious glance at the people funneling into the auditorium. "For all we know, the murderer is one of us. A parent, a student, a teacher—someone here in the crowd."

Brooke started to respond, but the woman kept talking.

"Last night I begged Rupert to pull Amy out of school. 'For her safety,' I said. 'We'll home school her; we've done it before.' But he said, 'No—we have a mission at Sussex Academy, and a duty to see it through.'"

Brooke nodded, unable to get a word in edgewise.

"Did Amy tell you she's diabetic? Two shots of insulin every day. And she doesn't eat right unless one of us follows her around and watches every bite she puts in her mouth. That's why home schooling would make so much more sense—for all of us."

She drew Brooke closer. "This *Dracula* play," she said, her voice lowered. "The one you're directing for poor Rachel Leventhal. Could you possibly choose something else? Something less disturbing and more appropriate for young people?"

Brooke was surprised by the question. "Vampires are pop culture icons—audiences love them."

"Why is that?" Mrs. March persisted. "Why are people fascinated by undead creatures that haunt the night? And why is Sussex Academy encouraging this preoccupation? It doesn't seem right. Think about changing it, won't you?"

Brooke was determined to put the matter to rest. "I don't know if you've ever directed a play, but with the clock ticking down to opening night, there's barely enough time to do this show let alone choose another."

A frown passed over the woman's bright pink lips. "Then promise me you'll keep an eye on Amy. You'll let me know, won't you, if she's having any difficulties?"

"Of course."

As Fern walked away, another familiar face stepped up to take her place—one Brooke hadn't seen in nearly a year and one she certainly hadn't expected to see today. Other than the suit and tie, Ted Roslyn looked exactly like he'd looked last fall. Tall and sinewy with scraggly brown hair. A sculpted nose. A grin that lit up a chiseled face. Dark eyes that gazed at her from beneath a broad forehead. And the suit? He wore it well.

"What in the world are you doing here?" she asked once he'd elbowed his way through the crowd.

He shrugged and looked around. "A stranger came up to me last night and asked me to put in an appearance. A bit of a mystery, to be sure. And you? How did you end up in the middle of things?"

She explained her situation and gave a nod toward a student standing on the sidelines. "I'm directing *Dracula*. That kid over there is our leading man."

Ted glanced at the teen who stood alone, scowling as he watched the crowd. "Typecast?"

"Could be, but I don't know for sure. Monday night was the first rehearsal—the first time I met the cast and crew. Throw in the murder, and it's pretty overwhelming."

"You've got yourself a real challenge, no doubt about it."

He reached inside his jacket and drew out a card. "You probably trashed the last one I gave you, so here's another. If you feel like talking, give me a call and we'll have coffee."

She glanced at the card as he walked away. *Ted Roslyn: Dispelling the Darkness Ministry.* It brought back memories of the terrifying journey they'd shared last September. Should she call him so they could catch up? No. There was no point in resurrecting memories she wanted to forget.

She tucked the card in her bag, and as she entered the auditorium, she spotted Amy standing alone against the back wall. The garish clothes were gone, replaced by a simple, loose-fitting black dress, white tights and a tiny red rosebud pinned above her heart. The hideous black eyeliner was gone as well, but the alabaster foundation remained, accented today with a weird shade of blue-gray lipstick. The effect was one of otherworldly beauty. Amy was a statue. A granite angel. The kind you see in cemeteries watching over the graves.

Seeing Brooke, she waved and came over to join her. "Can I sit with you—please?"

Brooke felt something tug at her heart as she gazed at this sad-eyed kid. "Of course, you can sit with me. We're in this thing together."

They found seats in the back, but they'd barely gotten settled when a tall, swarthy individual strode past. His jet-black hair and mustache were neatly trimmed, and his black suit clung to his body with the precision of a military uniform. As he headed down the center aisle, people rose from their seats to shake his hand while others looked away and frowned.

"My dad," Amy whispered. "Can you believe he had the nerve to show up today?"

"He's your father. He needs to be here."

"It's just a show. Everybody knows he hated Nina."

Rupert March stopped near the front to speak to a heavy-set individual with thinning gray hair. The man looked familiar, but something about him seemed off. The suit—that was it. The last time Brooke had seen this person, he'd been wearing tights, puffy pants and a jeweled doublet, his eyes breathing fire as he threw her out of his restaurant.

"The owner of Don Giovanni's," Amy said, her gaze following Brooke's. "He and my dad are like this." She crossed her fingers to show what she meant. "Oh, and he's also the school board president. My dad helped get him elected."

As if sensing Brooke's gaze, Petrakis glanced up and their eyes met. She turned her face away, but it was too late—he'd seen her, she was sure of it. She took a second look. Yes, he was staring at her, his eyes narrowed above a frown.

She was spared further scrutiny when Headmaster Alan Pierce took the podium and introduced the grief counselors who'd be leading the afternoon workshops. Among them was a tall, thirty something woman whose round glasses gave her a smart, bookish appearance. "The Owl Lady," Amy whispered. "She's the guidance counselor but nobody goes to her for guidance. Watch out what you tell her because her mouth is as big as her glasses."

Once the opening remarks were out of the way, Dr. Pierce introduced the featured speaker. Reverend Ray's eulogy focused on Nina's work on behalf of trafficked women and children, her fund-raising efforts to create a safe place to shelter them, her art workshops designed to help women gain self-empowerment and her dedication to the students at Sussex Academy. When she finished, she opened the floor to those who wished to share tributes. Brooke was surprised when Amy rose from her seat and walked to the front of the auditorium.

"Nina was the most wonderful person I've ever met," she began, her voice not much more than a whisper. "She encouraged people to use art to express the things they couldn't express through words. But more than that, she was the type of teacher who'd do anything to help her students."

Brooke wondered what the "anything" was in Amy's case.

"A lot of you have asked what it was like to see Nina in that storage closet. Think of your best friend. Think of a person who's done more for you than anyone in the world. Think of someone you could trust with your deepest secrets. And then think of what it would be like to find that person lying dead on the floor. Think about that, and please don't ask me any more questions."

The room was silent as Amy stepped away from the microphone. When she sat down, Brooke squeezed her hand and felt it trembling.

There were other tributes—lots of them—and it was nearly noon when Dr. Pierce dismissed the audience and told the students to report to homeroom where they'd receive instructions about the afternoon's grief seminars. Amy said a tearful goodbye in the fine arts lobby and headed down the hallway, a solitary figure among the other girls who congregated in groups of three and four. Did she choose to be alone, or was she an outsider—the girl the other girls excluded? Brooke recalled the plywood panel with the bloody baby dresses. Was that really a statement about the plight of girls in our culture as Amy claimed, or was it a cry for help from a desperately unhappy young woman? Brooke suspected the latter.

Someone tapped her on the shoulder and she braced herself for questions, not from reporters this time, but from curious parents who'd seen her on the news Monday night. While "no comment" didn't seem like the right thing to say in this setting, she was determined to convey the same message in somewhat more tactful terms. But when she turned around, it wasn't a nosy parent who greeted her.

"Don Giovanni!" she gasped.

The schoolboard president laughed at her dismay. "Ah yes, in my youth I was quite the lady's man, much like the infamous Don Giovanni. But now? Now I'm a faithful husband, a proud father and a doting grandfather." He bowed at the waist. "Donatello Petrakis at your service." He righted himself and smiled. "Petrakis—because my father was Greek. Donatello—because my mother was Italian. You might say that I represent the glory that was Greece and the grandeur that was Rome."

Brooke couldn't help but return the smile. The man who'd been so hostile not even 24 hours earlier now seemed utterly charming. And a tad wacky, as might be expected from someone who greeted the public every day in tights, puffy pants and jeweled doublets.

"When we spoke yesterday," he continued, "I had no idea you were an employee of this hallowed institution, let alone the Good Samaritan who'd offered support to Amy March and her mother in their hour of need. Had I known, I would have treated you with the respect you so richly deserve."

He brought her hand to his lips and kissed it. "Accept my humble apology, Signora."

"You don't have to apologize," Brooke said, amused by the theatrics. "You thought I was a reporter. I know how they can be."

"Then you'll understand why I spoke disparagingly of our encounter to the detectives. Once I learned the truth, I retracted every vile thing I said about you."

He reached inside his suit jacket, brought out an envelope and handed it to her. "Dinner for two at Don Giovanni's Greco-Roman Trattoria, where opera is always on the menu."

"Thank you, Mr. Petrakis. But you don't need to…"

"Please. My name is Donatello. Don, if you prefer. And you don't have to thank me. It's the least I can do."

He was about to leave, but hesitated. "May I offer a word of advice, Signora?"

"Of course."

"Curiosity killed the cat. Take heed that it doesn't kill you."

Nine

Amy clung to Brooke through the afternoon's workshop, her demeanor much like it had been during the detective's interview on Monday night. Lips sealed. Eyes fixed on the floor. Shoulders slumped. Head bowed so that her pink and purple hair fell forward to shield her face. Another student remained silent as well. Erik Rimmer, aka Count Dracula, sat through the entire session, refusing to participate and sneering at those who did.

The session began as might be expected with tears, hugs and exclamations of horror. Once things calmed down, the grief counselor invited the students to share the things they'd admired about Nina. The list was a long one. Nina was awesome. Beautiful. Gutsy. Funny. An inspiration. A shining light. But as the afternoon progressed, Nina's halo began to fade. She had favorites. She was pushy and opinionated. She designed her art assignments to promote her political agenda. Her spiritual agenda as well—too many projects about goddesses.

The counselor didn't seem bothered by a few sour notes. "Working through our negative feelings for the deceased is part of the healing process," she informed the fifteen teenagers and Brooke. "We can admire Nina while still being aware of her all-too-human frailties."

From there the grief counselor led the students on a guided tour of the seven stages of grief. The tour began at shock and denial and proceeded in a straight line to acceptance and hope. But instead of being encouraged by the counselor's promise of a light at the end of the tunnel, the students did a U-turn back into shock and denial and continued downhill into the dark, twisted world of murder, school shootings and the countless scary things kids have to deal with these days. When the bell rang, they shuffled out in downcast silence, but by three-fifteen, they were back on the sports fields, practicing for upcoming games.

In the office, Brooke bumped into Reverend Ray, the woman who'd delivered Nina's eulogy. After a few introductory remarks, the reverend took Brooke aside and gave her a printed invitation to Nina's invitation-only funeral on Friday. "We had to do this because of the crowds," she explained. "The service will be broadcast to people outside the church, but we don't have room for everyone in the sanctuary. And we certainly don't want unruly people causing an uproar. Take my card as well. If things get rocky and you need a listening ear, feel free to call. I mean it now. Don't be shy."

Once the reverend departed, Receptionist Jocelyn Fisher checked School Psychologist Ron Webster's appointments on her computer screen. "He's booked for the next two hours. Parents. Students. Faculty. Everyone's in meltdown mode." She found a fifteen-minute opening at five, and once that was settled, Brooke went to the teacher's lounge to pass the time until the appointment. By now, the faculty would have left for the day—or so she hoped—and she was looking forward to an hour-and-a-half of peace and quiet.

She opened the, door, ready to kick off her shoes and collapse on the sofa, but to her dismay, the room was crowded with teachers, all of them chatting noisily. Upon seeing her, coffee cups froze in midair, chatter ceased and a deafening silence descended. The situation was painful. They knew who she was, but she knew no one. She was a stranger and an outsider. A colleague but not a colleague. A curiosity who'd stumbled into their midst.

And then a familiar face separated itself from the sea of strangers. A face she remembered from years ago. A face she'd hoped never to see again.

Librarian and Information Specialist Jane Acker was a tall reedy woman with dark, piercing eyes, short frosted hair, a sharp nose and a thin slit of a mouth. She approached Brooke, a coffee mug in one hand and the other extended in greeting. "Brooke Roberts," she gushed. "How wonderful to have you back among us after all these years. But under these circumstances?" She gave a shudder, and kept talking. "A gang of us are heading out for happy hour. Not that this is a happy day—just the opposite—but's that's what they call it, and that's where we're going. We'd love for you to join us, wouldn't we?" She turned to the others for support and was rewarded with nods and smiles.

"Some other time," Brooke said, conscious of the many eyes studying her. "I have an appointment at five and a meeting afterward."

Jane frowned at those words, but Brooke was more than grateful for an excuse to escape the information specialist and her minions. She'd learned something in her two years at Sussex Academy—the information Jane Acker specialized in had more to do with her colleagues' private lives than with the subjects they taught.

Brooke was about to make an exit when she caught sight of a second familiar face—the teacher who'd comforted Amy in the art studio. His gaze met Brooke's, and he nodded a silent greeting. She returned the greeting and hurried from the room.

Now that the faculty lounge was no longer an option, she needed to figure out how to pass the time until her appointment with Ron Webster. There'd be no privacy in the waiting area in the office, and there was no point in going home only to turn around and come back at five. That left the woods bordering the campus. She'd escaped there often in the days and weeks following her mother's suicide. It was a safe bet that, like then, she'd find the solitude she craved.

Leaving the building, she crossed a bright swath of lawn and entered a darker, cooler world. A trail led to a pond where she used to sit back in the day, tossing pebbles in the water and watching tadpoles skitter back and forth. Today, the tadpoles were gone, and the pond that teamed with life in early spring had become a mosquito-infested mud hole, rank with algae and decaying leaves. No comfort to be found there.

She abandoned the festering pond and followed the trail to a grove of pine trees. Needles blanketed the ground, their pungent fragrance wafting into the air and awakening a memory of her dad—the second time that day that she'd thought of him. "Keep your eyes on the ground," he used to tell her on the long nature walks they'd shared. "Hoof marks, scat, paw prints and bits of feathers and fur are nature's way of telling you who walked the path before you came along." Her eyes swept the terrain as she continued on her way, but there was nothing of interest. Just an eagle feather caught in the brush and a clump of smaller feathers left behind by a hungry predator.

Farther along, the trail branched off in two directions. She hadn't ventured this far in the past—her prep periods hadn't been long enough to allow serious exploration. Choosing the right-hand path, she continued in that direction until a familiar sound met her ears—vehicles passing nearby. That was surprising. She'd ventured farther from campus and closer to the road than she'd realized.

A few more yards and the trail opened to a clearing that in turn emptied directly onto the road leading to the school. The clearing wasn't very large—about the size of an SUV or minivan. She eyed the space with interest. The path she'd just followed connected the school to the clearing and then to the road. Had Nina's killer parked there on Monday night so he could sneak, unseen, through the woods and enter the art studio by the side entrance?

She looked around for evidence to support the idea, but if there'd been tire tracks in the clearing or footprints on the path, they were gone now, washed away by the rain on Monday night. She thought of the police prowling the area with their flashlights. What, if anything, had they found?

The question had no answer—at least not one she was privy to—but it kept nagging at her as she retraced her steps and returned to the school. Halfway down the hall, she stopped at the sound of angry voices erupting from a classroom to her left.

"Facts, please," a male voice shouted. "Or don't you care about facts?"

"Hah!" a deeper voice shouted back. "You, of all people, have the audacity to talk about facts? You wouldn't know a fact if you tripped over one."

"And you would?"

"Of course, I would. Unlike you and your colleagues, I deal in facts every day. But since you claim to have a fondness for facts, there's one you would do well to address."

"Oh, really? Like what?"

"Like the fact that you're too familiar with your female students. Way too familiar. And don't think the administration and the school board haven't noticed!"

The classroom door flew open and Rupert March strode into the corridor. He took a moment to brush a wrinkle from his impeccably tailored suit, and then, turning, noticed Brooke standing there. He hesitated a moment before reaching out to shake her hand.

"Ms. Roberts," he began. "I'm glad our paths have crossed. I owe you a debt of gratitude for the kindness you showed my daughter after that terrible incident Monday night."

"I didn't do much," Brooke responded. "Amy and I went to the art studio to see Nina's set designs for the play, and then…"

"Ah, yes—the play," he said, cutting her off. "I was surprised when Rachel Leventhal selected *Dracula* for the fall production and even more surprised when the administration approved it. Who in their right mind would think that a play about vampires is appropriate for high school students?"

Brooke laughed at the question. "It's perfect for high school students. The script we're using takes a stylized approach that should be lots of fun."

"Fun? You're joking, aren't you?"

Brooke shook her head. "No. *Dracula* is a classic story that…"

He held up a hand to silence her. "We are living in perilous times, Ms. Roberts. You need look no further than the daily news to realize that our children are being targeted by dangerous individuals who seek to exploit their vulnerabilities. Ms. Leventhal made an unwise choice when she selected this particular vehicle for the school's bicentennial celebration, and while I wish her a speedy recovery, I see no need for you or anyone else to perpetuate her mistakes."

With that, he turned and strode off in the direction of the administrative offices.

"Well, well, well," a man's voice chimed in. "You've just had your first encounter with Rupert March. If you're lucky, it'll be your last."

The speaker was the man Brooke had noticed in the faculty lounge. He had a kind face. Handsome too, with brown eyes and hair the color of honey. His casual appearance—khakis, a denim shirt and a tie, loosened now at the neck—was a stark contrast to Rupert March's crisply tailored suit.

He reached out and shook her hand. "I'm Chris Van Auken."

"And I'm…"

"Brooke Roberts. I know. You were with Amy in the studio when she found Nina's body. You're filling in for Rachel Leventhal. You taught here years ago. And you're probably wondering why Sussex Academy is nothing like it was back then."

"To be honest, I haven't noticed. Not with everything else going on."

"Then it's a good thing our paths have crossed. There's a lot I could tell you if you're interested."

"I am but first…" She checked the time. She had twenty minutes until her appointment with Ron Webster. "Sure. Fill me in on what I've missed."

He glanced up and down the hall. "Let's relocate to my classroom. The building's crawling with spies."

He ushered her into a bright airy space decorated with maps and history-related posters, several of which displayed pantheons of ancient gods and goddesses. An image of the Hindu god Shiva hung on the wall across from the door. "I am Shiva," it proclaimed. "Destroyer of Worlds."

He took a final look up and down the hall before closing the door. "Where to begin?" he wondered aloud. After thinking about it for a few seconds, he smiled and raised an index finger. "We'll start with uniforms. I guess you've noticed our students are wearing civilian clothes?"

"Yes, but I assumed that was just for today with the memorial service."

He shook his head. "Thanks to my efforts—and the efforts of a few of my colleagues—uniforms are a thing of the past. Along with certain other outdated prep-school protocols."

"Such as…?"

"Such as stuffy lectures. Such as teaching to the test. Such as bowing to the opinions of dead white men and the traditions they spawned."

Warming to his subject, he paced the room, his remarks punctuated with elaborate gestures and peppered with educational buzzwords. Asynchronous learning. Extended reality. Student-centered classrooms. Gamification. A revolution was underway, he told her. The old guard was dying, and a new, enlightened age was being born.

"And then…" He stopped pacing and turned to her with a frown. "And then Rupert March enrolled his daughter here and—bang! He started raising a ruckus, and before long, he'd convinced alumni and donors that our academic standards were tanking because of what he calls "radical social experiments." But his big power play came last spring when he got Don Petrakis elected school board president. Since then, the two of them have been on a crusade to undo years of progress and return the school to its classical roots."

"Classical roots have a lot going for them," Brooke remarked, remembering the literature classes she'd taught years ago. "I loved the curriculum back in the day."

Van Auken took a step back and appraised her through narrowed eyes. "Are you telling me you're on Rupert March's side?"

She laughed at the question. "I'm not on anybody's side. I'm only here in the evenings. Once the play closes, I'll be gone."

He continued to study her, his expression skeptical. "You're sure March and Petrakis didn't pull strings to get you hired? They've been doing that, you know. Screening candidates to keep rabble rousers off the payroll."

"Not to worry. I'm here because Dr. Pierce was desperate to find someone who knew enough about theater to throw a play together by opening night. I'm the only one he could find at a moment's notice."

The answer must have been satisfactory because Van Auken resumed his performance, complete with grandiose gestures. He explained that under March's influence, a decade of work was being systematically undone. Schoolboard meetings had turned into battlefields. Alumni and donors, troubled by news of declining standards, were withholding funds. The school's finances were in freefall just as payments for the new fine arts wing were coming due.

"How's Dr. Pierce handling all this?" Brooke asked, curious as to how the headmaster was navigating the storm.

"Good question. When I shared my frustrations, he said, 'Chris, these are delicate matters at a difficult time in the life of our school. Be patient and handle Mr. March with diplomacy.'"

He grabbed an inflated plastic globe from a bookcase and threw it on the floor. "Here's what I think of Dr. Pierce's diplomacy!" With that, he stomped on the globe and kicked it across the room where it crash-landed, deflated, beneath Shiva, Destroyer of Worlds.

Brooke watched the incident with something between amusement and alarm. The outburst was over-the-top, but, from the sounds of it, so were the tough times at Sussex Academy. Throw murder into the mix, and it was no wonder people were on edge.

"Sorry," Van Auken muttered. "I should learn to keep my mouth shut. You just happened to catch me at a bad moment, in a bad day, in a really bad week." Sighing, he strode across the room to a closet next to his desk.

"It's okay," Brooke assured him. "I'm sure everyone in the school is having a bad day."

"Yeah, but they didn't see what you and I saw on Monday night."

He looked back at her and something seemed to pass between them. They'd shared a terrible experience that night in the art studio, and that experience seemed to bind them together in ways she couldn't quite explain. Flustered, she averted her gaze, and when she looked back, he was pulling a motorcycle helmet out of the closet. She thought of the Harley in the faculty lot. She'd just identified the owner.

There was a knock on the door and a girl poked her head in the room. "Sorry to bother you, Mr. Van Auken. I've tried and tried, but I can't find the answer to the question you asked in class. Can you help me?"

He put his helmet on the desk and pointed to a chair. The girl yanked a textbook out of her backpack, and when she sat down, her black leather miniskirt wriggled up her thighs. Van Auken leaned over her shoulder, his head nearly touching hers, and as she shifted her weight, her leather skirt wriggled a bit more, like a serpent writhing up her legs.

Brooke left without saying goodbye. Chris Van Auken had made a lot of noise about March's outdated opinions, but when it came to the allegation of being too familiar with his female students, he'd managed to ignore the subject entirely.

Ten

The office was buzzing when Brooke arrived for her appointment with Ron Webster.

"Emergency schoolboard meeting in five minutes," Receptionist Jocelyn Fisher whispered. "We're hemorrhaging donors. All this negative publicity couldn't come at a worse time."

The phone rang and Jocelyn eyed it with loathing. "That thing hasn't shut up all day. Frantic parents. Nosy alumni. Tightwad donors who think the sky's falling. They're right of course, but we're not supposed to let on."

She snapped the phone from its cradle. "Sussex Academy," she barked into the mouthpiece. "Ms. Fisher speaking. How may I help you?" She covered the phone with one hand and nodded toward a closed door beyond her desk. "Ron's with a student. They should be done shortly."

Brooke took a seat and paged through one of several brochures lying on the coffee table. The pictures were glossy, the text descriptive. Who wouldn't want their child to attend a school like this one? Perfect facilities. Perfect curricula. Perfect teachers. Perfect administrators. Perfect everything—as long as you overlooked impending bankruptcy and murder.

A door opened, and a young girl dressed in black, as most were today, stood in the opening. "Thank you, Mr. Webster," she sniffled. "You've been a big help."

Webster nodded for Brooke to join him in his office, a space barely large enough for shelves, a desk and a couple of chairs. A photo on the bookcase showed him on a racing bike, his hands raised in triumph as he crossed the finish line. Another showed him hitting a tennis ball while a third showed him swinging a golf club. Yet another portrayed the whole family: Webster with his politician's smile; his wife, an attractive blond in a conservative navy suit and pearls; and their children—a baby girl and two boys who looked to be about eight and five.

"Nice family," Brooke remarked.

"Thanks. I'm rather fond of them."

A stack of board games took her eye. *Proud to be Me. Emotional Bingo. Night on Stress Mountain.*

"Students often have difficulty opening up to adults," Webster remarked, following her gaze. "Games put them at ease, but as you can imagine, board games are pretty much passé these days. That's why I've devoted a chunk of my spare time to developing computer games for use in therapeutic settings. The first one should be on the market early next spring."

"Impressive," she remarked.

"I like to keep busy. And speaking of busy, I'm expecting a call at any moment, so let's cut to the chase: Amy March. While I can't go into specifics—confidentiality and all that—I can at least give you a sense of what you'll be dealing with.

He launched into a list of Amy's issues. Trouble relating to her peers. Extreme moodiness that often interfered with meaningful social interactions. Hostility toward authority. A tendency to seek the companionship of nurturing adults such as Nina and to a certain extent, Rachel Leventhal.

"My advice, Webster concluded, "would be to establish professional boundaries right from the start. You're a teacher, not a friend. Maintain your distance."

"Amy's my stage manager. Brooke reminded him. "She'll sit next to me every night at rehearsal. How am I supposed to put distance between us?"

"That's why we're having this conversation. If boundary issues become a problem, let me know, and we'll develop strategies to help you navigate. Or, since I'm typically here only one day a week, you can always share your concerns with Guidance Counselor Gretchen Coates.

"And that," he said, "brings me to a sensitive matter Dr. Pierce asked me to…"

His cell rang and he glanced at the screen. "My campaign manager. I'll just be a minute."

The minute stretched into several as Webster paced back and forth, his voice lowered and the phone pressed to his ear. Brooke overheard snatches of a conversation about promotional billboards. The call concluded with a decision to use the photo on the bookcase—the one of Webster winning a bike race—and another of him at a Cub Scout event.

That settled, he clicked off and sat down again. "That took way longer than I'd hoped. Where were we?"

"You mentioned a sensitive matter."

"Oh, yes. The board is requesting that faculty and staff refrain from public discussion of socially sensitive issues related to Nina's murder. Sexism, racism, hate crimes, hate speech—the sorts of things the media keeps harping on."

Brooke eyed him curiously. "Is this for PR purposes or because these problems don't exist at Sussex Academy?"

He glanced at his watch and frowned. "The answer's complicated, but in the interest of time, let me assure you that Sussex Academy has a no-tolerance policy for any kind of discrimination, whether expressed verbally or through hurtful actions. Our policy statements make that abundantly clear. Realistically speaking, however, every school has students who seek attention by offending others. Sussex Academy is no exception to that rule."

He rose to his feet to indicate that the discussion was at an end. "This has been a tough day," he said, his tone friendly and supportive. "Hang in there just a bit longer. It's almost over."

▾ ▾ ▾

The meeting in the auditorium got off to a rocky start.

"We understand your concerns," Headmaster Dr. Pierce shouted over the roar of theater students and their parents. "And we share them."

"Oh really?" yelled someone's mom. "Then how do you explain this?" She held up a newspaper headline. *Vampire Haunts Historic Prep School!* "I didn't hear anyone mention this in the memorial service."

"I'm scared," a teenage girl whimpered. "Really scared." She placed a protective hand on her neck. "What if one of us is next?"

"We're all scared," the girl's dad echoed. "What do you say we postpone the play until the killer's behind bars."

"Better yet," a mom chimed in, "the whole school should go virtual starting right this minute."

"But those marks on Nina's neck," moaned another mom. "How do you explain them?"

"It's the curse of Dracula!" a student shouted, and his friends responded with cheers and laughter.

Dr. Pierce glared at the young man. "It's nothing of the sort. The marks on Ms. Powell's neck were puncture wounds made by a pointed object. We have that on good authority from the forensic pathologist, so there's nothing to worry about on that score."

"Nothing to worry about?" a dad roared. "A demented killer strangled a teacher and made fake vampire marks on her neck, and you're telling us there's nothing to worry about?"

"What I mean," Pierce called out over the ensuing din, "is that you have nothing to worry about where vampires are concerned. The marks are puncture wounds made by a sharp instrument. But please—we're here to discuss our plans for keeping your children safe."

He explained that on most evenings play practice wasn't the only activity in the building. There were school board meetings, committee meetings, basketball in the gym, kids returning from away games, and so forth. Safety in numbers, in other words.

Once that was out of the way, he introduced Tom, the Rent-a-Cop, a retired police officer in a gray and black uniform with a holster at his waist to show he meant business. Tom explained that he'd be patrolling the halls each evening, inspecting classrooms and poking his nose into secluded nooks and crannies. And yes—that included the auditorium and the backstage area with its prop room, costume room and dressing rooms. At no time were any students to be alone in the halls or the parking lot. If they needed to leave the auditorium for any reason, they should call Tom to provide an escort. At nine every night he'd supervise them as they went to their cars.

This seemed to reassure the parents, and the meeting wrapped up on a much calmer note than the one on which it had begun. Once everyone was gone, Brooke visited the prop room to inventory the items collected so far. There wasn't much to see. A crucifix. A vial that would contain holy water. A fake plant that would pass as wolfbane. And a plastic bat that would drop from the fly space every time Dracula raised his cape and flapped out the window. She made a note to talk to the tech crew about rigging the wires—the bat drop had to be perfect.

A few seconds off and the entire show would be ruined.

Her inspection complete, she locked up, and as per directions, placed a call to Tom. He showed up a moment later, glad, he said, to be of service. As they walked to her car, he assured her that he'd keep her safe and emphasized the point by patting the gun at his waist.

Brooke felt the tension melt from her shoulders as she left the campus behind. The day had been full of challenges, but she'd handled them like a pro. She'd spoken to School Board President Don Petrakis, and not only had they mended fences, he'd given her a gift certificate—dinner for two at his upscale restaurant. She'd faced Jane Acker and her colleagues and had refused to be dragged into Jane's network of gossip and intrigue. She'd made a friend and hopefully an ally in Chris Van Auken who'd clued her in on the changing landscape at Sussex Academy. She'd established a working relationship with School Psychologist Ron Webster who'd promised support in dealing with Amy. And she'd stood her ground with Rupert March who'd fled from her presence. Not fled, exactly, but he'd shut his mouth and stalked away. Small victories, to be sure, but they added to a sense of wellbeing as she sped into the night.

At a little after eight, she arrived at Peggy's Tavern, an out-of-the-way inn where she and her uncle met once a month for dinner. The parking lot behind the tavern was packed with vehicles—an unusual sight at this hour on a weeknight—and she was forced to take a spot far from the door. She hurried toward the colonial-era establishment and was greeted in the vestibule by the maître d', an older gentleman named Walter. Given the number of cars outside, Brooke was surprised to find the dining room nearly deserted and when she asked, Walter explained that an event was underway in the second-floor banquet area. A large affair, he said, and his comment was backed up by a sudden burst of laughter from on high.

Uncle Nelson was waiting for Brooke at their favorite

table. As usual, he looked distinguished in a dark suit, crisp white shirt and striped tie, his preferred mode of attire, even on casual occasions. He rose to greet her, his blue eyes sparkling from behind a pair of wire-rimmed glasses that in turn glistened in the candlelight. She planted a kiss on his cheek and sank wearily into the Windsor chair across from him.

In spite of her fatigue, it wasn't long before they were deep into the whodunit of Nina's murder. The conversation continued in that vein through the salads and well into their entrées, but faltered when she described her visits to Zack's Auto Body and Don Giovanni's.

Her uncle put down his fork. "It's one thing to be an armchair detective," he said, his voice uncharacteristically stern. "It's a different matter altogether to interfere in a police investigation."

"But I wasn't interfering. I was looking for context. An understanding of life at Sussex Academy."

He responded to that remark in much the same way Detective Burleigh had responded—by scoffing at its foolishness when weighed against the obvious dangers. "Be patient, my dear," he said, his expression softening as he reached across the table to stroke her hand. "This isn't a PBS mystery where the investigation is wrapped up in 90 minutes. It could end tomorrow or it could drag on indefinitely."

Brooke acknowledged the truth of his words, and the conversation continued pleasantly from that point. No more discussion of the murder—just small talk about books, movies and the Bach Choir's upcoming season.

"Speaking of Bach," her uncle said. "A friend of mine from the choir claims to be an expert on vampire lore." He fished a card from his pocket and handed it to Brooke. "Give him a call sometime. He might give you some clever ideas to use in the play."

"*Professor Rodney Cavendish,*" Brooke read aloud. "*Vampire*

Expert Extraordinaire," She laughed at the choice of words. "Not just a vampire expert, but an extraordinaire one at that."

"Rodney's admittedly eccentric," Uncle Nelson said with a smile. "But don't let that deter you. I think you'll find him a welcoming diversion from the weightier matters at the school."

Brooke stuck the card in her bag and stifled a yawn.

"It's late, my dear and you've had a long day," her uncle said. "I hope you don't mind foregoing coffee and dessert."

"Not at all. Can I drop you off at your apartment?"

"I've already arranged for an Uber. Go home now, and get some rest."

They found the Uber idling outside the front door. Brooke gave her uncle a kiss on the cheek, and once the car disappeared in the distance, she walked to the parking lot behind the tavern. By now the lot was nearly deserted, and her Outback looked forlorn beneath the trees at the edge of the property. As she hurried in that direction, a chill breeze grazed the back of her neck, and a dog howled from somewhere nearby. She peered into the darkness, and seeing nothing other than the trees, her thoughts shifted from the dog to Nina's killer. A few stealthy steps, a few quick moves, and the ligature would have been around Nina's neck. She imagined the pressure increasing. The ligature tightening. Nina's lungs screaming for air. Tiny capillaries bursting and bleeding into the whites of her eyes.

She brought her hand to her neck and thought of the puncture wounds that suggested the mark of the vampire. Why did the killer add that detail? What message was he—or she—trying to convey?

The dog's howling resumed, louder this time. Closer too, or so it seemed. Was it about to attack, or was it sounding a warning? Was someone hiding behind a tree, watching Brooke approach? She glanced back at the tavern. She'd never thought to ask Walter to walk her to her car—it wasn't his job to provide an escort, and besides, there'd never been danger before. There probably wasn't danger now—just her imagination getting the best of her. Or maybe this was the delayed reaction Detective Burleigh had told her about—repressed horrors rising up from where she'd buried them.

She thought about running back to ask for help, but quickly discarded the idea. Running would only make the dog give chase. Instead, she reached in her pocket for her keys, pushed the unlock button, and within seconds was behind the wheel with the door locked. The engine started with a hum, but instead of feeling a sense of relief, her thoughts spiraled back to the conversation at Zack's Auto Body. Nina thought someone tampered with Rachel Leventhal's SUV. Why? What was going on at Sussex Academy that Brooke didn't know about?

She shook off the questions. She was tired—exhausted, to be honest—but she'd soon be back in her apartment with the door bolted and the double chain locks fastened in place. She'd listen to music—something soft and soothing that would lull her to sleep.

She shifted into drive, but instead of gliding forward, the car shimmied to one side and thudded noisily on the pavement. She recognized the symptoms. A flat tire.

Sighing, she got a flashlight out of the glove compartment and shone the light toward the surrounding trees. Seeing nothing to fear—not a wild dog or a crazed murderer—she stepped onto the pavement and aimed the light at the driver's side tires. They were both fine.

A different sight greeted her as she walked around the car. Not one flat tire, but two. One was a chance occurrence. Two meant someone flattened them on purpose.

Eleven

Detective Radley knocked on the door and waited. He and the boss had stopped by Reverend Regina Ray's townhouse just a few minutes ago, and when she wasn't there, they'd decided to try their luck at the church. He knocked again and after a few seconds, she answered. Seeing them on the steps, her smile faded. She'd been expecting someone else, she told them, but if they'd wait a minute, she'd call the person in question and reschedule.

Once that was done, they followed her down a narrow flight of stairs to her basement office. On the way, they passed rooms set aside for the church's day care center and Nina Powell's art workshops. When Detective Burleigh asked to see the latter, the reverend unlocked the door and stood aside so they could enter a space crowded with collages, paintings and crazy sculptures made from throwaway junk.

"Redemption," the reverend said in way of explaining the statues. "Women take the broken, ruined pieces of their lives and mold them into something beautiful."

Beautiful—really? Freakish was more like it, at least in

Radley's mind.

They left the studio and entered the office at the end of the hall. As usual, Radley took notes and chimed in with an occasional question while Burleigh handled the bulk of the interview. For the most part it was a good system. It kept the subject of the interview from feeling overwhelmed, and it allowed Radley to pay attention to body language and facial expressions as well as details of their surroundings. Later he and the boss would analyze the exchange.

The reverend described Nina Powell as wonderful. Amazing. Brilliant. A guiding light. And so forth. But instead of the broad gestures you might expect when someone's singing somebody else's praises, Reverend Ray sat with her arms folded tightly against her body. She occasionally broke the pose to fidget with a ring or rub her hands together or toy with an earring in her left ear, but mostly she took too long to answer, like she was scripting her comments before speaking them.

The boss's cell rang in the middle of a question, and he stepped out of the office to take the call. After a minute or two, he beckoned for Radley to join him. There'd been an incident involving Brooke Roberts. Something about a couple of slashed tires. A car was dispatched to the scene, but Burleigh wanted Radley to follow up while he stayed behind to finish the interview.

"Go over the questions the team discussed earlier," the boss said, his voice lowered. "And be sure to reinforce the message I delivered yesterday. The one about staying out of our way."

Fifteen minutes later, Radley arrived at Peggy's Tavern and found Brooke in the rear parking lot with a couple of cops and the maître d', an older, hand-wringing sort of guy who seemed bewildered by the situation. "I've worked here thirty years and nothing like this has ever happened," he moaned. When asked for details, he explained that a party on the second floor had broken up at around 8:30 after which there were only a handful of cars in the lot. As far as he could recall, Brooke left the building sometime after 9:15. That gave the slasher only a brief window of opportunity to do his work.

Radley thanked the maître d' for the information and turned to Brooke for a rundown of the evening's events. She'd stayed at Sussex Academy for a meeting. She'd met her uncle around eight. When she discovered the slashed tires at approximately 9:30, she dialed 9-1-1 and ran back to the restaurant. The cops arrived soon afterward and called a tow truck.

"Tell anyone where you were headed tonight?" he asked once the details were clear.

She shook her head.

"Anyone follow you from the school?"

"Not that I noticed."

He turned to the responding officers. "We'll need to impound the vehicle and have it checked out—top to bottom."

"You can't do that," she protested. "I need it back as soon as the tires are replaced. I have a meeting tomorrow afternoon and rehearsal at six."

He tried not to laugh—sometimes smart people could be so dumb. "What good are two new tires if somebody messed with your engine? How'd you like it if your brakes failed on some dark, lonely road."

She stared at the Outback as though calculating the risk, but this time she didn't argue.

"I'll give you a lift home," he said. "We'll have a loaner delivered in the morning."

When the tow truck materialized, Radley watched the car get loaded on the back and vanish into the night. After some back and forth with the officers, he held the door to his unmarked sedan, and Brooke slid into the passenger seat.

For the most part, it was a silent ride to her new address, and that was just as well because he had a lot to think about.

The investigation was turning into a monster—a gigantic squid with grasping tentacles, or a hydra lashing out in all directions. There were, after all, plenty of folks who had a reason to kill Nina Powell. Crooked cops. Human traffickers. White supremacists. And those were just the headline-grabbing possibilities. Others were less sensational. An angry colleague. A friend smarting from betrayal. A jilted lover. A family member with a deep-seated grudge.

And that brought him back to the vampire mark on her neck. What was that about and what did it suggest about the killer's motive?

"Turn right at the next light," Brooke said. A few more turns and they arrived at Brooke's apartment. She didn't argue when he invited himself up for questions, but even so, he wished the boss were there—official policy was to do things in twos to avoid accusations of impropriety. In this instance, the recording device in his pocket would have to suffice as evidence of his honorable conduct.

The third-floor apartment was a tiny dump of a place, especially when compared to the timber frame he remembered from a year ago. Now, that was a house, complete with open-beamed ceilings; two massive stone fireplaces and enormous windows that looked out over acres of forest. It was the kind of house he'd like to own someday. But this place? Not exactly his idea of home sweet home.

Brooke seemed to sense his critical appraisal because she offered a hasty explanation. She'd sold her house in the woods. She was shopping for another place. This apartment complex was the only one that offered a month-to-month lease, and this was the only unit available.

Once that was out of the way, Brooke offered him a seat on the sofa, and when he asked if he could record the interview, she nodded her approval. So far, so good.

"It's pretty obvious what went down tonight," Radley

began as she settled into a chair across from him. "Someone heard you'd been snooping around yesterday, and they sent a warning. This time it was your tires. Next time...?"

He watched her face. Yeah, she'd gotten the message—loud and clear. Safe to say, she wouldn't be sticking her nose where it didn't belong. Or so he hoped. He'd seen her in action a year ago and suspected she'd need repeated warnings to keep her on the straight and narrow.

"So, let's talk about the things leading up to the tire incident. Anybody upset with you?"

She considered the question. "Yesterday the owner of Don Giovanni's kicked me out of his restaurant. We cleared things up after the memorial service, but he left me with a warning."

"What kind of warning?"

"Curiosity killed the cat. Make sure it doesn't kill you."

"Sounds like good advice. Anyone else?"

"Fern March wants me to cancel the play and so does her husband. They seem to think that vampires are a bad influence on their daughter."

That wasn't surprising. Radley had learned a few things about Little Miss March since that interview on Monday night. For starters, she and the kid who played Dracula had sabotaged the prom last year by dressing as vampires and proclaiming themselves King and Queen of the Undead. Some of the students thought it was funny, but most were furious that Amy and Eric stole the spotlight and ruined a special evening that was supposed to be about springtime in Paris.

She's different, the students told Radley. *She's obsessed with vampires and goddesses. But mostly she's sneaky and conniving, and we never know what she's thinking.*

None of that was surprising, He'd had the March kid pegged for trouble the moment he'd laid eyes on her. She was a pretty thing, a fact that her weird makeup, ugly clothes and creepy jewelry couldn't hide. Smart too. He could tell by the way she seemed to tune everything out while actually taking everything in. She was calculating and crafty—a manipulator and a liar if he was reading things right. Juvenile detention centers were full of kids like Amy March.

He resumed his questions. "Anybody in the cast and crew ticked off at you?"

"Not so far. They don't know me yet and I don't know them, except..." She hesitated a moment. "The kid who plays Dracula disappeared for 25 minutes during what was supposed to be a ten-minute break. He seemed pretty annoyed when I sent another kid to find him. But that's hardly a reason to slash my tires."

A couple of cast members had already tipped Radley off about Count Dracula disappearing for 25 minutes instead of ten. They claimed he'd been out in his SUV, listening to music and sulking over Amy March who'd recently put the kibosh on the summer fling they'd shared. Maybe it was true. Maybe Rimmer was nursing a broken heart after being dumped by a teenage hottie in black clothes and creepy makeup. But his absence coincided with the time of Nina's death, and that's why the team was keeping an eye on him.

He didn't tell Brooke any of that, nor did he tell her that it wasn't unusual for people to omit details under the stress of a first interview. Better to let her think she was in trouble for the omission.

"If you've been withholding anything else," he said, his eyes fixed on her in a way he hoped was intimidating, "now's the time to cough it up."

She said there was nothing, and even though he didn't quite believe her, he moved on to other matters.

"The teacher who went into the closet Monday night," he continued. "Chris Van Auken. Can you describe his demeanor when he saw the deceased?"

The question seemed to surprise her. "He was upset. Like

all of us."

"Did his reaction seem sincere?"

"Of course, it seemed sincere. Why wouldn't it?"

"No particular reason. Was his shirt clean when he entered the closet? Before he touched the victim, I mean?"

"I didn't notice."

The answer was what he'd expected. The puncture wounds on the victim's neck had produced just enough blood to draw attention to the phony vampire mark. But traces of blood had shown up on Chris Van Auken's shirt, and that begged the question: what was his real reason for rushing into the closet? Was he checking for a pulse as he claimed, or was he trying to mask the evidence of blood stains acquired earlier that evening?

The crime scene had provided little in the way of evidence. During the day students got art supplies off the storage closet shelves and put them away at the end of class—scores of muddled fingerprints attested to the fact. After school the custodian mopped the floor in the studio and the closet, and when the forensics people checked for evidence after the murder, all they found were fibers and residue from the custodian's mop as well as a bit of hair, fiber and fingerprints from Chris Van Auken. Otherwise, the closet floor was clean. Too clean. There should have been something to tie a perp to the scene, but there wasn't. It was as though a sleek, hairless creature had slithered into the studio, wrapped itself around the victim's neck, and disappeared without a trace.

"Funny," Radley mused aloud. "It was like the perp was some kind of reptile,"

No sooner had the words escaped his lips than he silently cursed his stupidity. He was revealing details he shouldn't, and the boss would be ticked when he listened to the tape and caught the blunder. Radley cast a glance at Brooke. She seemed too distressed to pick up on what he said, and since he wanted her to stay that way, he got up from the sofa, walked to the windows and looked out at the alley and the rickety old fire escape snaking up the back of the building. "Make sure you keep the windows locked," he said sternly. "You never know who might crawl up the fire escape and pay you a visit. Especially if they think you've been snooping around and asking questions."

That did the trick. He could tell she was scared. Really scared. Safe to assume she wouldn't be interfering in the investigation.

He said goodnight and promised to have a loaner delivered by ten the next morning. Down in the parking lot he cursed himself for the reptile blunder and then he brushed it off. There wasn't much Brooke could do with the information, but he'd been sloppy and the boss would be sure to rub it in.

Twelve

Ted looked at his watch and frowned. Eleven o'clock and still no call from Reggie Ray. He'd been sitting in this coffeeshop, waiting for a phone call for over an hour and he was pretty sure what she'd say. That it was late. That she was exhausted. That they'd have to postpone their meeting. Meanwhile, Ted still had no idea why he'd been invited to Nina's memorial service.

His phone rang, and when he snatched it up, Reggie was full of apologies. The conversation with the detectives had lasted longer than she'd expected. She wouldn't blame Ted if he wanted to postpone. That would, however, mean putting off their conversation until after Nina's funeral on Friday. In other words, if they didn't meet tonight, they'd have to wait until Saturday.

Ted opted out of postponing, and within fifteen minutes he was standing outside the church in Bethlehem's Southside, just blocks from the site of the former steel mill. When he knocked, Reggie unlocked the door and led him into the sanctuary, a silent, dark space lit only by the glow of a street light spilling through a stained-glass window above the altar. The jeweled image was a familiar one: Jesus holding a lamb while sheep grazed at his feet.

"I'm glad you made it to the memorial," she said. "I wanted you to get a sense of Nina's influence. She was a powerful figure in our congregation."

"Sounds to me like she was a powerful figure everywhere she went."

"True enough. She made her mark, that's for sure."

"And that's what you wanted to talk about?"

"Only in part. I wanted you to stop by so I could discuss…"

Her phone squealed and she rolled her eyes at the interruption. "Forgive me. A pastor never knows when a call might be urgent." She turned her face away and lowered her voice, but Ted had no trouble hearing what she said.

"Of course, I remember who you are. You were with Amy March on Monday night." She listened for a moment. "No need to apologize. I gave you my card and said you should call."

Ted stared in amazement. That was Brooke on the phone. He'd given her his card as well, but she hadn't called him. She'd called someone else instead.

"Slow down," the pastor said. "I can't understand a word you're…" There was a pause before she spoke again. "Someone slashed your tire? Two tires? How awful." She mouthed the words "excuse me" in Ted's direction, slid out of the pew and walked toward the front of the church, the phone pressed to her ear. While he couldn't hear what she said, he could read her expression when she turned around. Empathy. Concern. Support. All the things he would have offered Brooke—and more—if he'd been given a chance.

The call lasted nearly ten minutes. "Sorry about that," Reggie said as she stuck the phone in her pocket. "Now where were we?"

Ted wasn't sure about Reggie, but he knew exactly where he was—on the porch outside a timber frame in the woods. Brooke had just opened the door, her eyes wide with fear. He'd stayed late into the night, talking about this and that until exhaustion won out over fear. She was in danger again, but she'd called someone else. She didn't need him anymore.

"I asked you here," Reggie said, bringing him out of his thoughts, "to discuss my fall from grace."

Of course. Reggie's fall from grace. That's what she'd said last night, and that's why he was here.

He forced Brooke out of his mind and listened instead to Reggie's story. It began, as most stories do, with a bit of background. This church building had once been home to a mainline denomination, but over time it evolved into a more ecumenical, interfaith direction. When the former pastor moved on, the congregation began a search for a dynamic, progressive leader with a strong feminist orientation. Reggie was only too happy to accept the position when they offered it to her.

Nina's family attended the fellowship, and as pastor, Reggie had watched the gangly 14-year-old blossom into a beautiful, outspoken young woman who'd gone to art school in New York and returned with a vision for merging art and political activism. The goddess lay at the heart of Nina's vision—not a specific goddess, but any number of female deities who coalesced into one great mother of us all. Her enthusiasm was contagious, and soon Reggie began weaving teachings about the goddess into her weekly sermons. The goddess, as Reggie saw her, was a metaphor—a powerful symbol to guide women in their spiritual journey.

The response had been overwhelming. Growth. Hope. Revival. Not the tent-meeting revival of yesteryear, but a revival of optimism for women who'd been beaten down for too long. But what had begun as a metaphor gradually evolved into something more in the minds of the worshippers.

"I never intended for women to pray to the goddess or make shrines to her in their homes," Reggie said softly. "And I certainly never intended for the teenagers in Nina's workshops to sneak into the sanctuary late at night, light candles and whisper incantations to their favorite goddesses."

"Kids did that? Wasn't the building locked?"

"It was, but apparently Nina'd been unlocking the door at night and letting them in—without my knowledge or consent. I found out about it two weeks ago when Rupert March burst into my office and demanded to know why the church was sponsoring occult ceremonies as a youth activity. I was stunned when I heard the accusation, but later when I confronted Nina, she laughed in my face and said I was overreacting. That it was innocent fun. That the girls were exploring new paths and trying out new ideas. That it was all part of growing up.

"Needless to say, I was furious with Nina for going behind my back," Reggie continued. "But it didn't take long for things to come into perspective. The blame for what happened there in the sanctuary lay with me. Those goddess ceremonies were an outgrowth of ideas I'd set in motion."

She went on with her story. Her father, now deceased, had been a pastor, and she'd grown up with a single goal in life—to follow in the footsteps of the kind and powerful man she adored. She'd gone to college and then to seminary, but the things she'd heard there were vastly different from the things her father taught from the pulpit. Rather than exegeting the Bible's ancient texts, her seminary professors dissected them, repudiating their history and allegorizing their message until all traces of the supernatural were torn from the pages.

Angels—gone.

Miracles—never happened.

The resurrection—a myth.

And life itself? The result of chemicals coalescing by chance in a primordial swamp.

She described a time, not so terribly long ago, when feminist spirituality walked hand in hand with reason, and science was their god. And then something began to stir. A trembling in the earth. Clouds racing across the sky. Ravens cawing from the trees. The goddess rising from her grave.

"I thought those ancient deities were dead and buried in the pages of children's books and literary anthologies," Reggie continued. "But like you said in your lecture, the old gods are back—or so it would seem."

She sank back against the pew, her gaze fixed on the image of Christ as the Good Shepherd. "It's a nice old window, don't you think?"

It was. It could use a little work—a crack split the Lord's left cheek and another threatened to amputate his right arm at the elbow. Another divided the sheep into two groups, like on Judgment Day—although, to be fair, that was about sheep and goats, not sheep and sheep. But in spite of the damage that came with age, Ted liked the comforting feeling the image evoked, and he liked the atmosphere of this old church building. There was an English feeling to the place, and it made him feel like he'd stepped back through history to a simpler time.

"We had a building inspector here in July," Reggie continued. "He gave us 90 days to fix the window or replace it with something else. If we failed to do either, he'd revoke our occupancy permit. We worked hard to raise the money—bake sales, car washes, flea markets, a silent auction. With the funds in hand, the committee met last week to finalize the details. The next morning, I was informed of their decision. Instead of repairing the window, they'd voted to replace Jesus with the goddess."

She looked at Ted, and he could sense the weight of anguish bearing down on her. "How is it possible that after two-thousand years, the Lord is no longer welcome in His own house? And how in the world," she continued, her voice trembling, "did I allow it to happen?"

Thirteen

The phone call to Reverend Ray had been the impulse of a moment. A desire to hear a human voice. To have someone tell her she was safe, even if she wasn't. And now she was alone, the windows staring at her, their dark eyes keeping watch. Someone was out there in the night, someone who knew where she worked, what car she drove, and where she lived. "It's like the perp was some kind of reptile," Detective Radley had said. The words conjured up a sleek, slithering, hairless being, a comic-book creature by day, but a monster at night.

She drew the curtains, turned out the light and thought of the hours that lay ahead. She wouldn't make the sofa into a bed. Not tonight. Instead, she'd sleep on it the way it was, and she'd sleep as she was, fully clothed and ready to flee—with her shoes on, just in case. She got a blanket out of the steamer chest, pulled it over her and lay on her side, her gaze fixed on the curtains and all the terrors of the night that lay behind them. She recalled the nameless faces that had stared at her throughout the day. Parents with their questions. Teachers in the faculty room. Students eyeing her with curiosity. Had one of them slashed her tires?

Hearing a noise, she threw off the blanket, bolted to the window and parted the curtains. Just an inch—no more. A streetlight shone on the fire escape and on a dumpster, half-full of rotting trash. No one was there.

She returned to the sofa, and tried to get comfortable. When the effort proved futile, she sat up and drew her knees to her chest. This was just like those lonely nights after Karl died. Paranoia, she'd told herself at the time. But it wasn't paranoia. Someone had been watching her then, and another someone was watching her now.

She thought of the woods she'd visited earlier in the day. The trees towering overhead. The pine grove with its fragrance. The clearing near the road—the one big enough for a car. Had Nina's murderer parked there Monday night? And what about tonight? Had someone been waiting there? Someone who knew she'd be leaving the school after the meeting in the auditorium? She pictured herself driving by the spot, oblivious to a vehicle inching out of the shadows and following at a distance.

But maybe she hadn't been followed—not in the ordinary sense. Maybe someone planted a tracking device on her car. If that's what happened, the police would find the device during their inspection. Unless, of course, it had already been removed by the person who'd planted it. Or unless the person who'd planted it was a cop.

She sat up a bit straighter. Were the media's insinuations true? Did a cop kill Nina to shut her up, and was that cop warning Brooke to stay out of the way? Is that why Detective Burleigh stopped by on Tuesday? Was he really worried about her bungling his investigation, or was he worried about the opposite—that she'd put the pieces together like she'd done a year ago? Was that why Jason Radley came up to the apartment tonight? Were he and his boss protecting a colleague? Or worse—were they protecting each other? If so, whom could she trust?

No one—that's who. Not until the case was solved. And then what? How could anyone be sure the police were charging the right person?

Further questions came at her in the darkness. Was Nina's crusade against human trafficking a local story or something bigger? Traffickers worked in networks stretching across regional boundaries. While many of these traffickers sprang from the dregs of society, the brains of the operations were often powerful, well-connected people—individuals you'd never suspect of being involved in something so vile. But a powerful person wouldn't murder Nina—not on his own. He or she would hire a hit man to do it for him.

Another noise sent her racing to the window. Someone was creeping up the fire escape, someone sleek and slithery—she was sure of it. She parted the curtain a crack, just enough to see the metal stairs. No one was there.

She returned to the sofa and huddled beneath the blanket, exhausted but afraid to sleep for fear of being caught off guard. Every now and then she'd drift off, only to be jolted awake by a noise—real or imagined. The hours dragged by, each minute an eternity. And then, with the first light of dawn, fear vanished like a fever breaking after a long illness. A sense of relief flooded over her, but just as she dozed off, the phone rang.

The caller was Receptionist Jocelyn Fisher, phoning on behalf of Guidance Counselor Gretchen Coates. Gretchen would like to meet with Brooke an hour before the six o'clock rehearsal. Brooke searched her mind for a face to match with the name. That's right. Gretchen Coates. The Owl Lady. The tall woman with the round glasses.

The call was followed minutes later by a call from Uncle Nelson. He'd enjoyed their time together, he told her. Brooke said nothing about the slashed tires—no need to add to her uncle's worries. He ended by reminding her to make an appointment with his friend from the Bach Choir, and when the conversation ended, Brooke placed a call to the *Vampire Expert Extraordinaire.* Dr. Cavendish's schedule was packed at the moment, a secretary told her, but he could meet with her in two weeks. She agreed to the arrangement and made a note of the time.

At ten, a pair of cops stopped by with a loaner vehicle, and a while later, Brooke headed out the door for an appointment with the director of a nonprofit organization seeking an editor for their bi-annual newsletter. She left with renewed determination to focus on her editing business—something she could control—unlike the murder investigation that was completely beyond her control.

She bumped into her neighbor, Maggie Jenkins, in the parking lot outside the Beacon Arms. Maggie, a tall, skinny woman in her mid-thirties, made her living buying up things at yard sales and flea markets and selling them online and at antique malls.

"You're still alive," Maggie said, her tone icy. "Too bad you never bothered to return my call."

Brooke thought back to the pile of phone messages she'd deleted two days ago. "Sorry. Things have been chaotic. Overwhelming to be honest."

"Like I've never heard of chaotic and overwhelming? Like I wasn't ready to stand by in your hour of need?"

"I said I'm sorry."

Maggie shrugged it off. "Forget about it. What's done is done." She ran her fingers through her short, spiky hair. "Do you like the color? It's a new look for me."

The color Maggie referred to was yellow. Not blond, but yellow, as in daffodils, taxis and children's raincoats.

"Nice," Brooke said.

"You mean it?"

"Sure. It's interesting."

"Bernie, thinks so too," Maggie remarked, referring to her

significant other, a former pro-wrestler. "And by the way, if you're free Saturday morning, he and I are going to an estate sale. Wanna' join us?"

Brooke couldn't picture Bernie wanting her tagging along. "Three's a crowd. I'd be in the way."

"Bernie won't mind. He likes you. And besides, he wants to hear about the murder as much as I do."

That clinched it. Spending Saturday morning with the two of them would be the equivalent of spending happy hour with the Sussex Academy information specialist and her minions.

"Maybe another time."

"Suit yourself," Maggie said with a shrug. "I'll catch ya later."

▾ ▾ ▾

At five o'clock, Guidance Counselor Gretchen Coates ushered Brooke into her office, a white shoebox of a room devoid of artwork, photographs or personal touches. Gretchen's desk was a sleek, L-shaped structure made from plexiglass and stainless steel. The matching chairs were equally sleek with cushions that seemed to float magically above curved stainless-steel frames. A set of coordinated plexiglass shelves held a smattering of books, but there were no tchotchkes to add a note of whimsy and no plants to suck up the CO_2. Not even a coffee mug to indicate that a human being occupied the space.

Settling behind her desk, Gretchen brushed a piece of lint from the uncluttered surface and adjusted her owlish glasses. Once that was done, she folded her hands and got down to business. "Dr. Pierce asked me to meet with you to discuss the problem students you'll be working with during the next few weeks."

Problem students? Brooke didn't like the sound of that. There'd been no word of "problem students" when she'd agreed to take this job.

"We'll begin with Amy March," Gretchen said, her tone succinct and professional. "Her freakish makeup, her obsession with vampires and her Neanderthal social skills are part of a costume she wears to let us know that she's nothing like her literary namesake. While she's highly intelligent, she refuses to complete assignments for teachers she doesn't like. Since she hates most of them, her grades are abysmal. She's extremely needy with erratic mood swings that run the gamut from moping child to angry rebel, to alluring temptress. Her neediness exerts pressure on everyone who interacts with her, and while Nina didn't seem to mind serving as her mentor, she allowed things to go too far. That's why I'm speaking to you today—to advise you to avoid making the mistakes Nina made."

The words were troubling. Nina acted as Amy's mentor and Nina was dead. Was there a connection? Brooke brushed the thought aside. After last night's episode with the slashed tires, she was reading too much into just about everything.

"While our faculty and staff empathize with Amy's issues," Gretchen continued, "we've learned to maintain boundaries. Sadly, Nina wasn't as cautious as the rest of us. In fact, I recently learned that she'd been scheming to help Amy run away from home this coming January—the day after her eighteenth birthday. Mr. March discovered the plan right before school started and demanded that Nina be fired. She was murdered before the board had a chance to review the matter.

"Another incident occurred about the same time," Gretchen continued before Brooke had a chance to comment. "Over the summer Amy convinced Nina to open up her church for weird, occult rituals involving goddesses and who-knows-what-else. Her dad found out about it, and his reaction was what you might expect. And here's the reason I'm telling you all this. With Nina gone, Amy's on the prowl for another mentor. That might be you, so be prepared. And be prepared for her father to scrutinize every move you make."

This was not what Brooke wanted to hear. None of this was in the contract she'd signed. None of it.

"And that brings us to our next problem child, Count Dracula."

Gretchen extracted a thick folder from a drawer and dropped it on her desk with a thud. "Erik Rimmer's conduct reports from last year," she said, rifling through the contents. "We have similar files from his freshman and sophomore years, and I expect more of the same before he graduates. He's been diagnosed at various times with attention deficit disorder, borderline personality disorder and oppositional defiant disorder. The latest is addictive personality disorder, which he uses as an excuse to justify his pornography habit. We're not buying into it, so if you catch him looking at nasty videos on his phone, confiscate the phone and bring it to the office so Dr. Pierce can deal with it. What Erik does out of school is his business, but we've got a standard to maintain. And a word to the wise. Erik's IQ is extremely high—in the same range as rocket scientists, nuclear physicists and criminal masterminds. Sadly, he favors the latter."

Brooke let that sink in. She wasn't directing a play. She was chaperoning the inmates at a lunatic asylum. "If he's so difficult," she asked, "why did Rachel Leventhal give him the leading role?"

The question elicited a smirk. "Erik's mother donated a large sum of money toward our new auditorium. And when I say large…" she rolled her owlish eyes, "I mean enormous. Because of his mother's generosity, Rachel felt pressured to give Erik the part. On the bright side, the type casting's perfect. He's sinister, devious and arrogant. Everything you'd want in Count Dracula."

Brooke didn't find the remark particularly reassuring.

"There's something else you need to be aware of," Gretchen continued, "Apparently Amy and Erik were an item over the summer. She dumped him before school started and he's pretty ticked off about it. It could make for interesting dynamics as the play moves forward."

Terrific, Brooke thought to herself. More challenges to make a complicated situation even more complicated.

Having made her point, Gretchen put the folder back in the drawer—no need to clutter up the desk. "Moving on to other matters," she said, her manner brisk and efficient, "since Nina's death, the gossip mills have been working overtime. You're bound to hear all sorts of wild speculation, so rather than running to the detectives with every bit of news that crosses your path, Dr. Pierce would like you to share it with me. Afterward, I'll pass the information on to Dr. Pierce who will pass it on to the detectives.

"The reasons for this policy should be obvious. First of all, we don't want to inundate the detectives with multiple reports of the same rumors. The second reason relates specifically to your situation. You're on campus only a few hours each evening while I'm here all day. I'm in a far better position to separate nonsense from credible information that should be passed up the chain of command."

Brooke didn't respond. She had no idea what criteria Gretchen would use to determine which rumors got reported and which ones didn't. Furthermore, she had no way of knowing if Gretchen's rendition of things would be accurate or if she'd slant the details before they reached official ears. But even though Brooke had no intention of following through on this absurd request, she decided to put it to a test.

"As it just so happens," she said nonchalantly, "I've already picked up some interesting gossip. I don't think it's related to Nina's murder, but as you said, I'm in no position to judge."

Gretchen eyed her curiously. "What sort of interesting gossip?"

"It's probably not worth mentioning, but yesterday I happened to overhear Rupert March accuse History Teacher Chris Van Auken of being too familiar with his female students. Is it true?"

Gretchen's eyes widened behind her owlish glasses. The reaction lasted only a few seconds, but it was long enough to catch a glimpse of something messy behind the Owl Lady's minimalist façade.

She recovered quickly. "Not only is Chris too familiar with his female students, he's too familiar with his female colleagues. He winks and whispers and flirts, and the women flirt right back whether it's at a faculty meeting or at a school event with parents, students and schoolboard members present. He turns his classes into parties with the way he clowns and jokes around, and while most of the students love him, they're too young to realize that he's basically an irresponsible, immature egomaniac. Long story short, Chris is your best friend one day, and the next day he's gone. If he casts his roving eyes in your direction, consider yourself warned. He's not to be trusted."

The meeting wrapped up quickly after that. On the way to the auditorium, Brooke thought about Gretchen's odd request—not the warning about Chris Van Auken's roving eyes, but the suggestion about playing whisper down the lane with rumors related to the murder investigation. She thought about the chain of command—Gretchen to Dr. Pierce to the detectives. The idea was ridiculous, but it raised an interesting question. What exactly were the headmaster and the Owl Lady trying to hide?

Fourteen

Fern March was waiting when Brooke arrived in the fine arts lobby. Today's outfit was a silver-flecked navy pant-suit, red lipstick, matching nail polish and an array of red, white and blue bracelets that clattered when she threw her arms around Brooke in a tearful embrace.

"It's a nightmare, isn't it?" she moaned. "For all of us, but especially for you and Amy." She released Brooke, her eyes wet with tears. "Believe me, Ms. Roberts, if you'd known my daughter just a few years ago, you wouldn't recognize her today. She was such a sweet child with blond curls and cute little outfits. But now? Now she's sullen and rebellious, and she wanders around in hideous black rags she picks up at thrift shops. And her jewelry? Ghastly. Absolutely ghastly."

Brooke didn't want to be rude, but tonight was the first re-hearsal since Nina's murder, and she wanted to be on time. "I understand your concerns, Mrs. March. But I can't talk now. Not when I've got a rehearsal to run."

Fern grabbed her arm to keep her from leaving. "Rupert and I tolerated Amy's pink and purple hair—it's just a fad, we told ourselves. We tolerated the hideous outfits and the weird jewelry and the makeup. But vampires? She's obsessed with them. Vampire movies. Vampire books. Vampire websites. Last year she went to the prom with that Rimmer boy—both of them dressed as vampires. You'd think her teachers would discourage such things, but instead, Rachel Leventhal chose *Dracula* for the fall production. What in the world was she thinking?"

Brooke recalled Gretchen's warnings and Ron Webster's as well. Maybe Amy wasn't the only one with whom she needed to set boundaries. Maybe the same applied to Amy's mom. "If you're worried about your daughter's obsessions, you should consider getting her professional help. And if you don't want her to be my stage manager, tell me now so I can find someone else."

Fern waved a hand dismissively, setting the bracelets clattering and clanking. "She would never agree to it. She spent the entire summer helping Rachel collect props, including a coffin an undertaker agreed to loan to the school. We thought that after Rachel's accident Amy'd be uncomfortable working with a new director and would step down. But as it turns out, she's fond of you, and insists on seeing it through. But if the show were cancelled because of what happened to Rachel and Nina, that would settle it, wouldn't it?"

Her frown deepened, revealing a network of worry lines beneath the smooth plaster of her makeup. "First Rachel. Then Nina. It's terrifying, isn't it? All these tragedies occurring so close to my little girl?"

Brooke took a hard look at the woman. What did Mrs. March mean by that? And how far was Mama Bear prepared to go to protect her only cub?

She left Fern fretting in the lobby and headed into the auditorium. Amy was already there, her natural beauty masked by ghoulish makeup, outlandish clothes and macabre jewelry. *Boundaries*, Brooke reminded herself as she sat down next to her. *I need to set boundaries.*

Count Dracula took the stage in the same outfit he'd worn the day before: black jeans, a black tee-shirt and a black leather vest studded with chunks of metal. He kept dropping character to run licks up and down the neck of an air guitar, and when Brooke interrupted to give directions, he responded with wise-cracks intended to amuse his fellow cast members at her expense. Not knowing what else to do, she asked him to stay after rehearsal for a bit of private coaching. She didn't like the idea—not after the things Gretchen had told her—but Erik was the star and she needed to know what he was capable of when not distracted by the other kids. He agreed to the plan and sealed his promise with what was probably a dissonant chord on his invisible guitar.

In spite of Count Dracula's noncompliance, the rehearsal ended on a positive note. The cast members seemed eager to impress their new director, and Amy, while despondent and at times teary-eyed, stuck to the task of taking notes in the prompt book. At nine, Tom-the-Rent-a-Cop showed up to escort the students to their cars while Erik excused himself for a bathroom break. While he was gone, Brooke reviewed Amy's work. In spite of her distress, she'd done an excellent job of capturing the details of the blocking.

The rear door opened, and Brooke turned around, expecting to see Erik. Instead, Chris Van Auken nodded to her from the back of the auditorium. It was easy to understand why the female faculty found him appealing. He was handsome with a winning smile, but there was more to it than that. His natural good looks were enhanced by a rebel attitude and devil-may-care swagger. The motorcycle helmet tucked under one arm only added to his bad-boy charm.

"Mind if I join you?" he asked as he sauntered down the aisle.

He didn't wait for an answer. Instead, he took the seat next to her, and as he got settled, Brooke caught the scent of bergamot and something earthy that suggested the forest after the rain. Interesting—even his aftershave was appealing. Lacing his fingers, he stretched out his arms, revealing a braided leather wristband fastened with a silver clasp in the shape of ravens.

"The ravens of Odin," he said, following her gaze. "Faithful servants who acted as his spies. We've got our share of spies here at Sussex Academy, but they don't report to Lord Odin. They report to Rupert March."

After glancing around, he leaned closer, so close that his knee grazed Brooke's. "A word of advice," he whispered. "Watch what you say around here and who you say it to. And don't believe everything you hear. Like yesterday for example. You didn't mention it, but I'm sure you heard Rupert March accuse me of being too familiar with my female students."

"As a matter of fact..."

He held an index finger to his lips. "Shush. It's a lie. Rupert March cooked the story up to get me fired. Once I'm gone, March and Don Petrakis will replace me with one of their hand-picked lackeys. I don't intend to let that happen, but I can't control the rumors unless I know who's saying what. So, here's what I'd like you to do. Keep your eyes and ears open. If you hear any gossip with my name in it, let me know who said what."

Brooke didn't know how to respond. This was the second time in just a few hours that someone asked her to filter gossip, rumors and innuendo. It was natural, she supposed, to be anxious in the midst of a murder investigation—no one close to the crime wants the spotlight of suspicions pointed in their direction. But relative strangers asking her to cough up information struck her as odd. She thought back to Detective Radley's questions the night before. The bulk of them were focused on Chris Van Auken.

"I doubt I'll hear much," she said. "Not when I'm only

here nights,"

"Maybe you will, maybe you won't. I'm just asking you to be on guard. And by the way," he continued, a smile teasing at his lips. "In spite of March's accusations, I'm not too familiar with my female students. In fact, I prefer women who've been around the block a few times. Older and wiser, you might say. Not that much older, but definitely wiser. Know anyone like that?"

The question was flirtatious, and it called for a playful response. But at the moment, Brooke was incapable of repartee. Instead, she thought of Gretchen Coates's words: *Consider yourself warned.*

"You don't need to hear my problems," he said when she failed to respond to his flirtations. "You've got enough of your own trying to direct a play with Amy March as stage manager and Erik Rimmer as leading man."

Brooke was grateful for the change of subject. "I'm glad you mentioned Erik. We're only two nights into rehearsals, and I'm already finding him challenging."

"Challenging is an understatement. Any other school would have expelled the kid long ago. But since Erik's mom donates beaucoup de bucks, we can't afford to get rid of him. I've spent the last two years mentoring him and his buddies, and believe me, if those guys make it to adulthood without getting thrown in jail, they'll have me to thank."

Brooke heard a noise from the stage. She looked up and saw Erik standing there. How much of the conversation had he heard?

▼ ▼ ▼

Van Auken said goodnight, and once he was gone, Brooke joined Erik on stage. If he'd overheard Van Auken's remarks, he didn't let on, and soon she was coaching him through the elegant, sweeping gestures that were part of Count Dracula's

seductive charm. If he could carry the moves over to the boudoir scene—the one where he looms over Lucy and bites her
neck—they'd have a hit.

"The scene in Lucy's boudoir is critical to your character,"
Brooke explained. "There's a tension in the air as though Dracula's craving not just blood, but…"

"Sex?"

She saw the look in Erik's eyes. What was she thinking,
engaging in a conversation like this, all alone on the stage with
the resident porn addict? "What I'm trying to say," she stammered, "is that you need to develop the inner life of your character. Focus on feelings you've had in the past and bring them
into your performance to make it more convincing. It's called
method acting. Practice it that way, okay?"

"Cool."

He dropped character and went back to running riffs up
the neck of an invisible guitar, but instead of voicing her impa-
tience, Brooke decided to try diplomacy "Do you play a real guitar or just a pretend one?"

"A real one. I'm in a band. 'Blood Rage.' Ever hear of us?"

She shook her head.

"I guess you could say I grew up with music. Mostly Mozart
because my mom swears it makes you smarter. Must have
worked, or so the IQ tests say. She expects me to be a scientist
and follow in her footsteps, but I've got news for her. That's not
going to happen."

"And your dad?" Brooke asked, anxious to keep things
going now that Erik seemed willing to talk. "Is he a scientist
too?"

An odd smile curled at the edges of Erik's mouth, the sort
of smile you might see on Count Dracula's face just before he
raised his cape and turned into a bat. Brooke would have loved
to capture the moment and save it for opening night, but it disappeared as quickly as it came, replaced by an icy darkness in

Erik's eyes—a darkness well-suited to Count Dracula but disturbing in the eyes of a seventeen-year-old kid.

"Are you referring to my father, the brain surgeon?" he asked. "Or my father, the rocket scientist? Or my father, the Nobel laureate? Or whatever genius my mother picked out to create me."

He no longer ran his fingers up the neck of his air guitar. Instead, he turned his face away and stood in silence, his arms limp at his side as if all the air had been sucked out of him. "I'd better go," he said.

He jumped off the stage and was about to leave the auditorium when he stopped and looked back at her. "As far as my father's concerned, I never met him and neither did my mom. He was just some Mensa creep she picked for his superior bloodlines." He gestured at his lean, adolescent torso. "I'm the result."

After that, he fled the auditorium and left Brooke alone to turn off the lights.

Fifteen

On Friday morning, the cops dropped off Brooke's Outback. They'd given it a clean bill of health. Other than the slashed tires, there'd been no damage. Sadly, they could offer no clue as to who'd done the slashing, and thus no assurance that it wouldn't happen again.

An hour later she left the car in an overflow parking lot a few blocks from the church where Nina's funeral was being held. An anxious mood hung over the neighborhood, not just because of the funeral, but because of the riots that were expected to break out as dusk approached. Shop owners had their windows boarded up, and cops were out in droves, setting up metal barriers and shooing people off the streets and onto the sidewalks. The media was there as well, eager to scoop up sensational stories to share with their viewers.

Brooke made her way to the old stone church, and after showing her invitation at the door, she joined the receiving line that stretched to the front of the sanctuary. As the line inched forward, she was struck by a colorful display of papier-mâché masks arranged behind the altar. A glance at the program revealed that they'd been created by women in Nina's workshops. Each mask represented a goddess and a spiritual attribute—strength, courage, wisdom, etc.—that each goddess represented and that the mask-makers hoped to make their own.

At the end of the service, mourners filed out of the pews and joined the protestors, cops and reporters in the streets. The crowd was respectful, their voices subdued and their passions muted as the hearse began its sad journey to the private interment. But once the hearse was gone, the energy shifted, and the fires smoldering in countless eyes warned of a coming inferno.

Brooke headed off to reclaim her car but stopped when someone shouted her name. Turning, she saw Chris Van Auken hurrying in her direction.

"Skipping school?" she asked him.

"Nina and I were close. Real close. Dr. Pierce let me have the day off so I could be here." He glanced back at the church. "I figured there'd be food after the service. Stupid of me, considering the size and the mood of the crowd. But that doesn't keep me from being hungry. Care to join me for a bite to eat?"

Her first reaction was to say no. Since Karl's death, she'd made a point of holding men at arm's length. But she was hungry, and the thought of eating peanut butter and jelly in her lonely apartment wasn't particularly appetizing. She agreed to the plan, and a few minutes later, she and Van Auken entered a nearby greasy spoon and took their place in line with other folks from the funeral. After a brief wait, a hostess showed them to a booth next to a boarded-up window.

Neither of them seemed inclined to dwell on the tragedy of Nina's murder—the emotional testimonies at the funeral had said all there was to say. After exchanging a few remarks on the subject, they moved on to other topics. Van Auken proved to be a nimble conversationalist and before long he was telling Brooke his life story. He'd been a wanderer as a kid. Got into trouble. Got out of trouble. Came into his own in his late teens. Two reasons. Survivalist camp and college. Survivalist camp taught him how to look out for himself. College awakened his thirst for knowledge. He preferred interdisciplinary studies—a smorgasbord of subjects rather than a single main course. He thought of it this way: literature for breakfast. Science and math for lunch. History for dinner. Art for dessert. And later, as Shakespeare so eloquently stated—*if music be the food of love…*

Brooke ignored the sly smile and the flirtations that went with it. Once Van Auken realized she wasn't playing along, he moved on to a discussion of his current passion: exploring his Germanic roots via Viking festivals and reenactments.

He held out his wrist and showed her the armband she'd noticed the night before, the one with the silver ravens. "Metallurgy was a big deal with the Vikings," he explained. "They made tons of jewelry and household stuff, but mostly they made some pretty awesome weapons and armor. And that's why I go to these festivals—for the battle reenactments. There's nothing like hand-to-hand combat to get the blood pumping. Picture it," he said, his eyes gleaming as he leaned across the table. "Swords slicing into peoples' guts. Axes hacking off limbs. Men falling to the ground in agony. And then, once the last drop of blood is shed, we dust ourselves off, raise a mug of ale and shout "skoal!" What could be more fun?"

He lifted his glass and Brooke lifted hers as well. They clinked them together, said skoal and downed swigs of iced tea like they were drinking mead from jeweled goblets instead of iced tea from plastic glasses in a crowded diner.

As it turned out, Van Auken wasn't just an entertaining conversationalist. He was also a good listener, and before long she was telling him about Karl—not the sad details that were always with her. Not the part about his death and all she'd lost with his passing. Instead, she told him about the timber frame house in the woods and the huge windows where she and Karl watched the changing seasons. She told him about stuffing canvases and easels in the back of their van and heading out to paint meadows, riversides and seacoasts. She described their travels, sometimes chaperoning college students, sometimes on their own with packs on their backs and Eurail passes in their pockets. Her favorite spots? Chartres Cathedral. The British Museum. Las Ramblas in Barcelona. Stonehenge, except for the crowds.

Van Auken raised his glass to Stonehenge. "Now you're talking. They don't build them like that anymore."

She laughed. "No, they don't."

"I've always wondered who erected that pile of rocks. Druids? Aliens? A race of giants?

"I have no idea."

"But you've wondered, haven't you?" His eyes sparkled as he asked the question. "Merlin gets my vote. It's as good a story as any."

The conversation continued in that vein—light, witty, entertaining—and they lingered in the booth long after the lunch crowd was gone. When they finally called it quits, Van Auken walked her to her car, and as he left, Brooke again recalled the Owl Lady's words: *Considered yourself warned.*

▾ ▾ ▾

The dying light poured through the Good Shepherd window, splashing puddles of color across the altar and gilding the old oak pews with gold. The funeral was over. Tears cried. Emotions spent. Dust to dust. Ashes to ashes.

Reggie took a seat at the back of the empty sanctuary and gazed at the Shepherd window. It would soon be gone, and already she felt herself grieving the loss. In recent days the window had come to take on new meaning, its message speaking to her heart in ways it never had before. *"The Lord is my Shepherd; I shall not want. He maketh me to lie down in green pastures; he leadeth me beside the still waters. He restoreth my soul."*

In the last two decades she'd strayed far from God's green pastures into a lost and lonely wilderness of her own making. But the Shepherd hadn't left her there. No—He'd come searching and when He found her, He'd stretched out His shepherd's crook to draw her back, lift her up and gather her in His arms. It was like being a child again, pure and bright and happy in her father's church with the choir's voices swelling and filling the air with those wonderful old hymns. *The Lord is My Shepherd. Savior Like a Shepherd Lead Us. The King of Love My Shepherd Is.*

A pang ripped through her heart at the thought of what would soon unfold. In a matter of weeks, the goddess window— a window designed by Nina—would smile down upon the congregation. Prayers would be prayed toward her. Hymns sung. Candles lit. Heads bowed. For generations to come, those who worshipped in this building would see the goddess above the altar and remember the woman who'd created her. Nina Powell. A saint. A martyr. A legend. A goddess who'd briefly dwelt among us. Ironic, wasn't it, that the goddess that would soon replace the Good Shepherd bore a striking resemblance to its creator? But isn't that the way of things? We magnify our presumed better qualities and impose them on God, thereby remaking Him in our own image.

Some major decisions loomed in Reggie's future. She could remain in her current position, weak and compromising and bowing to pressure. Or, she could say goodbye to the goddess and the people who worshipped her and follow the Shepherd wherever He might lead.

She closed her eyes to pray, and in the silence of the empty sanctuary, another possibility presented itself. She could do both. She could follow the Shepherd's leading here in this place and instead of cowering, she could stand firm in the face of mockery and scorn.

Opening her eyes, she met the blind, staring gaze of the goddess masks. They seemed to be laughing at her, just as Nina had laughed when confronted with issues that had arisen in the last few weeks. She recalled that angry moment in her office with Nina's mocking words and harsh laughter echoing from the walls. The memory was so real, so profound, that Reggie could swear she heard that laughter now, rising from the darkness to fill the sanctuary.

No, she realized with a start. The sound wasn't a dying memory. It was real, and it came from somewhere outside the church. As she listened, it grew louder, punctuated at times with loud bursts of profanity. Had the rioting begun?

A search on her phone confirmed her fears. She watched angry mobs turn over police cars. Set trash cans on fire. Throw rocks through store windows. Race into stores and out again, their arms full of merchandise. Meanwhile, protestors continued to march, their cries against police corruption fading into nothingness while madness erupted all around them.

Frightened, Reggie whispered a prayer of gratitude for the sturdy red doors she'd locked and the solid, stone walls that sheltered her. The building was a mighty fortress and it would keep her safe.

A volley of thuds crashed against an exterior wall. Was she as safe as she hoped? Would rioters break down the doors? Would they drag her into the street? Was such a thing possible?

A brick crashed through a section of the Shepherd window and fell to the floor with a thud. Reggie scrambled to her feet, ready to flee. But where would she go?

She sank back in the pew as rocks burst like missiles

through the window. The bombardment continued, and by the time silence returned, all that remained of the Shepherd and his sheep were hunks of twisted lead and a rainbow of shattered glass, sprinkled like confetti on the altar.

Sixteen

orning light crept through the curtains and painted a glowing line on the floor. Saturday at last—the beginning of a two-day reprieve from Sussex Academy. And from everything else as well. Brooke decided to linger in bed until eleven, and after that she'd go into town for lunch, all by herself with no one to make demands on her time or attention. After lunch she'd go to a movie and sit alone in the dark with no one knowing where she was.

But was it safe to go out? A look at the news revealed that the rioting had been confined to the neighborhood surrounding Nina's church. It fizzled out around three a.m. but was expected to heat up again at nightfall and spread into other neighborhoods. "If you haven't boarded up your businesses by now," a police woman warned, "I suggest you get…"

A knock at the door drowned out the cop's advice. Rather than answering, Brooke pulled the blankets over her head and willed the person—whoever it was—to go away. When the knocking persisted, she remembered that her neighbor had asked her to go to an estate sale this morning. She'd said a definite no, but it sounded like Maggie was determined to give it another try. Best not to respond.

The knocking started up again, louder this time. "Anybody home?" a girl's voice called out. "It's me. Amy."

Amy? What was she doing here? *Boundaries*, Brooke reminded herself as she threw off the covers and pulled on a pair of sweats. Both the school shrink and the guidance counselor had told her to set boundaries. The door that separated her and Amy was a boundary. What would happen if she opened it?

She found Amy in the hall, her eyes red as though she'd been crying. The unflattering makeup was gone as were the macabre accessories and weird clothes. Instead, she wore a simple, sleeveless black dress that fell a few inches below her knees. Without waiting for an invitation, she came inside, sank into a chair and slumped forward, her head in her hands and her pink and purple hair tumbling over her bare shoulders. There was a whole lot of drama queen going on here, but even so, the sight tore at Brooke's heart. The girl was in pain and she'd turned to her for support.

Boundaries, the warnings voice whispered. *You need to set boundaries.*

Later, she told the voices. *As soon as I find out what this is all about.*

Bit by bit, Amy's story came out. Her father drove her to school on Friday to make sure she didn't ditch classes and sneak off to Nina's funeral. When she got home, she discovered that her mom had spent the day unearthing the vampire books and DVDs hidden in her closet and beneath the bed. Later, her dad threatened to burn the entire collection, and that led to a huge screaming match that sent Fern March running from the room in tears. Amy, on the other hand, stomped up the stairs, locked herself in her room and spent the night missing Nina. She woke up this morning and told her parents she was going to the library to work on a history paper. When her father said she couldn't leave the house, she said fine—if she flunked history, it would be his fault. He finally caved, and she drove to Brooke's place instead. And now…

"Hold on a minute," Brooke interrupted. "You can't expect me to support a lie. Go to the library right now and work on that paper."

"You were with me when we found Nina's body," she said without looking up. "You know what that was like. Do you really expect me to work on a history paper at a time like this?

Brooke didn't know what to say. She wanted to heed the alarm bells sounding in her head, and yet she couldn't just brush that experience aside like it never happened. She and Amy had shared something horrific in the art studio—something they'd remember for the rest of their lives. Maybe it would be better to work through things now and let boundaries wait until later.

She sat down on the unmade sofa bed. "Okay. Let's talk."

Amy began by pulling a sketch book out of the backpack she'd dropped on the floor. "My art journal," she said "I made it in a summer workshop at Nina's church. It's all I have to remember her by, but if my parents find it, they'll burn it along with my vampire stuff. If I ask a friend to guard it, the pictures will turn up all over the internet. Can I leave it with you? Please?"

Once again Brooke was torn. Art journals were more than sketchbooks. They were mixed-media diaries that took hours to create. What would be the harm in holding onto it until things quieted down?

The alarms clanged in her head. There'd be plenty of harm if the journal contained evidence related to Nina's murder.

When she said as much, Amy clutched the journal against her chest. "Evidence? There's no evidence here—just a bunch of drawings about my life. Private stuff that's nobody else's business. Didn't you keep a diary as a kid? Would you have wanted people looking through it and posting it on the internet?"

Brooke ran a hand through her uncombed hair. No—she wouldn't have wanted anyone pawing through the countless pages of teenage angst she'd written back in the day. But this situation was different. Way different.

"I promise I won't keep it here long. Just until I think up another place to hide it. It's more than an art journal—it's my last connection to Nina. You get that, don't you?"

The request made sense—at least at an emotional level. "One week," Brooke agreed. "You've got one week to get it out of here. After that it's fair game."

She opened the steamer chest that doubled as a coffee table and watched Amy place the journal on top of a pile of sweaters. Once that was done, Amy wrapped her arms around herself and shivered. "It's freezing in here. Could we go somewhere else and talk? I'm too upset to go to the library."

Brooke thought of the boundaries that were becoming shakier by the minute. But seriously, what could be the harm in sharing a heart-to-heart over bagels and coffee? After Amy'd had a chance to vent, Brooke would send her home and that would be the end of it.

"There's a diner nearby," she said. "I'll treat you to breakfast."

"I already had breakfast, so maybe instead..." Amy reached in her bag and fished out a glossy ad featuring bagpipers, Highland dancers and Irish bands. "There's a Celtic festival this weekend. It might take my mind off Nina, and who knows—maybe I'll get some ideas for my history paper on Celtic goddesses. Think of it as research."

Research seemed as good an excuse as any. An hour later they were on the fairgrounds, jostling their way through the crowds. Amy looked lovely in the bright sunlight with the autumn breeze teasing at her hair and her dress swaying as she walked. More than once men paused to cast an appreciative glance in her direction, and at times the smiles she gave them seemed a bit too inviting. But for the most part, she directed her attention to the festival. Her enthusiasm was contagious, and Brooke found herself thinking that maybe this was a good thing. She was getting to know a different side of Amy, one the girl kept hidden from watchful eyes at Sussex Academy. Sharing this time away from the school and away from reminders of Nina's murder was giving them a chance to get to know each other. If a production was to be a success, the director and stage manager needed to function as a team.

They paused to watch caber tossers—muscle bound guys in kilts who hurled logs through the air. When the sound of fiddles beckoned, they joined a crowd gathered around a Celtic band and then moved on to a stage where young girls performed complicated Irish dances. A glitter of silver caught Brooke's eye, and she steered Amy through the crowd to a vendor selling handcrafted jewelry while bagpipes droned in the distance.

After a few minutes Amy held up a Celtic cross. "Do you like this?"

"It'll ward off vampires," Brooke said. "Celtic vampires, anyway."

It was supposed to be a joke, but Amy seemed to take the remark seriously. Instead of laughing, she described an Irish legend about an alluring female vampire name Dearg Due. A second legend spoke of a dwarf named Abhartach who, along with the Romanian tyrant, Vlad the Impaler, inspired Bram Stoker's *Dracula*. There were Scottish vampires as well: the mysterious child vampires of Glamis Castle, the shape-shifting Baobhan Sith of the Highlands and the Gorbals vampire of recent legend.

Her stories finished, Amy put the Celtic cross back and watched the people passing the jewelry booth. She seemed preoccupied as she scanned their faces, as though she were searching for someone in the crowd. "I wonder if they're here," she murmured.

"Celtic vampires?" Brooke asked. "I haven't seen any."

"No, silly—my father's spies." Turning back to the jewelry, Amy picked up a raven pendant and held it to her throat. "I'm sure they're here somewhere, blending in and pretending to enjoy the festival. Meanwhile, they're watching my every move. Yours too."

Brooke put down the piece she'd been admiring and studied the fairgoers. She recalled Chris Van Auken's remark about Rupert March's spies, and she thought of the unknown person who'd followed her from the school and slashed her tires. The memories coupled with Amy's strange narration cast a cloud over the festival while in fact, the sun lit the sky with a ferocious and blinding light.

"Let's call it a day," Brooke said. "We'll grab Chinese take-outs on the way back to my apartment and then you can head off to the library to do what you're supposed to do."

Amy held the raven necklace to her throat and studied her reflection in the mirror. "Give me a sec to buy this. I have a thing for ravens."

Brooke eyed her curiously. Chris Van Auken had a thing for ravens too.

Once Amy'd paid for the necklace, they turned their steps toward the exit and paused on the way to listen to a Scottish ballad about a woman and her demon lover. Amy found the song enchanting, but Brooke thought it was creepy, just like the mood that had settled over this otherwise pleasant outing.

"Enough of that," she said as the song faded. "Let's get going."

Amy nodded in agreement, but instead of keeping pace, she dawdled along the way to watch border collies round up sheep and to study craft items at various booths. Near the exit, she steered Brooke toward a tent selling Celtic trinkets and tee-shirts. "We'll look at this stuff for a couple of minutes, and then we'll leave. I promise."

She seemed distracted as she browsed through the items,

and before long, she moved to the doorway and stood beneath the shadow of the tent flap. From there her eyes swept the crowd, and when Brooke joined her, she pointed to a tall, sturdy guy in a green plaid kilt. His dark, shoulder-length hair was streaked with gray, and it was hard to tell his age. Older than forty-five but younger than sixty was the best Brooke could do.

"Your father's spy?" Brooke asked.

Amy laughed at the question. "Don't be ridiculous. My father's spies don't wear kilts. He's a friend of mine, but I can't let anyone see me talking to him. But if you went over and gave him this…" She slipped a hand into her bag and withdrew an envelope sealed with blood-red wax.

Brooke stared at the object in Amy's outstretched hand. So this was the reason for the trip to the fair. Not the fun. Not the jewelry. Not the pipers or the caber tossers or the dancers or the fiddles. And certainly not research for a history paper on Celtic goddesses.

"I get it," Brooke said. "This entire outing was a set-up to get me to deliver your messages."

"You had fun, didn't you?"

"That's not the point. Who is that guy? He's old enough to be your father."

The girl met her gaze without wavering. "Give him the note. He's expecting it."

"I have to read it first."

"It's private."

"Listen, Amy. For all I know he's planning to cart you off somewhere, and I'll end up in prison for aiding and abetting a kidnapping."

"Okay. Be that way." She tossed her hair and darted over to the man. Once she'd handed him the envelope, she returned in a snit and walked a few paces ahead of Brooke as they continued toward the exit.

Boundaries, Brooke reminded herself as they left the festival. She'd been advised to establish boundaries. Instead, she'd opened her heart to a manipulative, little con artist, and to a world of trouble as well.

▾ ▾ ▾

Amy's petulance wore off by the time they stopped for Chinese takeouts. Back in Brooke's apartment, she settled down at the kitchen table, picked at her egg roll and launched into a list of complaints about being Rupert March's daughter. He was loud-mouthed and pushy, she said, and that blowup with Nina in the art gallery was proof of how awful he could be. It served him right that he started getting death threats after Nina was murdered—lots of people thought he had something to do with it. The threats were getting so bad that he had to cancel business trips and hire bodyguards to follow him around. If things got any worse, Amy would have to leave school and hide out with her parents in a secret place stocked with ammo, food and water—enough to survive for a year. She hoped it wouldn't come to that—no one wants to spend their senior year in a bunker with a pair of idiots like her mom and dad. It was bad enough that her dad was home every night because now she couldn't disable the security system and sneak out like she did when her mom had too much wine and fell asleep in front of the TV.

She held up a chunk of eggroll and stared at something greasy dangling from it. "There's something important I need to talk to you about. It's about me and Erik Rimmer." She glanced over at Brooke. "Don't laugh. Teachers think he's a jerk, but lots of girls think he's hot. Did you know I was seeing him over the summer?"

Brooke recalled her conversation with Gretchen Coates. "I believe someone may have mentioned it."

"Probably the Owl Lady. She can't keep her mouth shut.

Or maybe it was Ms. Acker in the library. She's even worse. But here's what I need to tell you. All last year I had a thing for Erik, but he never seemed to notice me. It was driving me crazy, and then I met a woman in Nina's art workshop who's into magic—spells, potions—that sort of thing. I asked her to make me a love potion, and the next day at lunch, I got Erik to taste it. I didn't tell him what it was, and when he took a sip, he said it was awful and walked away, as rude as ever. I was furious because I'd paid this lady sixty bucks for a stupid potion that didn't even work, but to my surprise, Erik was waiting for me in the parking lot after school. And then he asked me to the prom. So obviously the potion worked—right?"

Brooke tried not to laugh. Kids were crazy these days. "There are plenty of other explanations," she said. "He probably liked you all along and was working up the courage to ask you out. You showed an interest, and he took it from there."

"But that's the point. He didn't like me. I could tell. And here's the part I can't stop worrying about. I think the potion worked too well. I broke up with him right before school started, but he keeps calling and texting and following me around. Every time I look at him, he's staring at me."

"Give him time," Brooke said with a smile. "Before you know it, he'll move on to someone else."

"Maybe. But there's more to the story. Did you know he's addicted to porn? That's not as weird as you might think—lots of kids are. I tried to act like it didn't bother me, but it was giving me the creeps and that brings me to the scary part of the story. When I told Nina about Erik's porn addiction, she said I should honor my feelings and decide what I wanted in a relationship. Did I really want to hang out with a guy whose mind was warped with dark fantasies he expected me to fulfill?

"I didn't, and when I told Erik it was over, he got mad— real mad, like he might hit me. When he asked why I was ditching him, I told him about Nina's advice. And now…" She laid her chopsticks down and looked away. "And now I'm worried that he took it out on Nina. Killed her, I mean—for breaking us up. All because the love potion was too strong."

Brooke didn't know what to say. Erik had been missing for 25 minutes the night of the murder. Did he go to the art studio to have it out with Nina for meddling in his love life? Did an argument turn into something worse?

"Have you told this to the police?"

"Sort of. I couldn't say much because my dad and his lawyers kept butting in whenever the detectives asked a question. And here's something else I keep thinking about. Erik's not the only person I gave the potion to."

Brooke sat up a bit straighter. "Who else, Amy? Not that guy at the festival?"

She laughed at the idea. "No. Absolutely not him. He's way too old. But..." Her gaze shifted to the steamer chest.

"The answer's in your journal, isn't it?"

"Would that matter? I'm allowed to like whoever I want to like, aren't I?"

"Yes, but..." Brooke told herself to calm down. She'd jumped to the conclusion that Amy had something going with the guy in the kilt when, in fact, she probably had a crush on some dopey teenager. But whatever the case, she didn't want a journal full of Amy's secrets hiding in her apartment. Not with a murder investigation going on.

She decided to settle the matter once and for all. "After what you just told me, I have a responsibility to look at your journal—cover to cover. If anything seems fishy, I'll hand it over to the authorities."

"But you said I had a week to find another place to hide it."

"Things have changed. I know more now than I did earlier. Either you take it with you, or I look at it."

"Fine," Amy said with a roll of her eyes. "I'll take it with me since you're being so nasty about it. But just so you know, you're nothing like Nina. You're a coward and a phony like every other teacher at that school."

Brooke didn't bother responding. Instead, she went over to the chest to retrieve the journal but stopped when she opened the lid. It hadn't registered earlier, but the ravens on the cover bore a striking resemblance to the ravens on a certain hand-crafted Viking wristband.

She glanced back at Amy who sat sulking at the kitchen table. "Chris Van Auken," she stammered. "Is that who you gave the potion to?"

Amy's mouth dropped open. "Mr. Van Auken? No. I promise it wasn't him. My father says terrible things about him, but they're just rumors. You can't believe anything…"

Someone knocked on the door. "I know you're in there! "a man's voice bellowed. "Open up or I'll call the police."

Amy stared, wide-eyed, at the source of the racket. "My father. We can't let him find me here."

Seventeen

Amy stopped staring at the door and looked around instead for a place to hide. Finding none, she ran to the window, scrambled over the sill and darted down the fire escape only to stop halfway to the bottom as two men in dark suits came sprinting down the alley. "My father's body guards!" she shrieked.

She reversed course and dove back inside, giving Brooke barely enough time to slam the window and lock it. An instant later, the dark-suited goons were on the landing, shouting, cursing and pounding on the glass. Meanwhile, Rupert March continued his assault on the door. At any moment the windows would shatter or the door would fall from its hinges.

Brooke looked at Amy for a clue to their next move.

"Open the door," the girl said softly.

"You're sure?"

"What difference does it make? He already knows I'm here."

Stumped for alternatives, Brooke turned the deadbolt, slid the chain lock and opened the door. "Aha!" Rupert March shouted as his eyes met Amy's. "Just as I thought! Get your things, young lady, and come with me."

Brooke expected a defiant outburst from Amy. Instead, a look of resignation stole over her face, the sort of look you'd expect from Joan of Arc as the torches touched the kindling. Was this another manipulative stunt, or was that fatalistic expression genuine?

March shifted his gaze to Brooke. "My daughter told me she was going to the library to do research. She lied and spent the day with you instead."

"I can explain. You see…"

He held up a hand to silence her. "There's nothing to explain. The facts speak for themselves. And as for you…" He glared at Amy. "We'll settle this at home."

Brooke glanced over at the window and the bodyguards who stood on the fire escape. Who did they think they were, standing there making ugly faces at her through the glass? And who did Rupert March think he was, barging into her apartment and shouting orders? And who, for that matter, did Amy think she was, showing up unannounced and dragging Brooke into her family's psychodrama?

Fed up with all of it, Brooke crossed the room and opened the window. Puzzled by her action, the body guards looked at their boss for directions. When he nodded, they thrust their bulky arms and legs over the sill and clambered onto the rug.

"I'll be speaking to the administration about this," March informed her as the guards took their places on either side. "You can expect to hear from Dr. Pierce shortly." With that, he took Amy by the arm and steered her toward the door.

At the same moment, a woman's voice rang out from the hall. "Yo, Brooke, you missed an awesome estate sale this morning. You should have seen all the stuff we…"

Brooke's neighbor, Maggie appeared in the open doorway, followed by her boyfriend, a tall, muscular, massively tattooed former wrestler named Bernie. His smile faded as he looked, first at March and then at Amy and then at the body guards and then back at March. "Unhand that woman," he shouted.

Amy's dad seemed somewhat put off by Bernie's tone of voice. "This isn't a woman," he clarified. "This is my daughter. And who do you think you are, barging into this apartment and telling me how to treat my own child?"

"I'll tell you who I am. I'm a decent human being who recognizes a bully when he sees one. And if I'm not mistaken you're…"

"I'm Rupert March."

"Hah! That idiot on the radio?"

"That's right." A look of confusion clouded March's face. "I'm on the radio, I mean."

"Well let me tell you something, Rupert March. I saw that video of you and Nina Powell in the art gallery. I don't know much about art, but I know a loud-mouthed, misogynist, racist bully when I see one. And here you are again, picking on a defenseless woman." He snorted derisively. "Any decent person would be ashamed of himself"

March somehow maintained his cool in the face of Bernie's insults. "This is a private matter between my daughter and myself," he said, his tone forceful but controlled. "How I handle it is none of your business."

"Is that so? Well, maybe I should make it my business. I'm telling you for the last time to take your mitts off that woman!"

Before March could respond, a smallish guy who works as an accountant on weekdays and as a birthday party clown on Saturdays stuck his head in the door. Alfie must have just returned from a gig—he'd taken off his wig, but his face was a startling white, his eyebrows blue, and his cheeks, nose and mouth bright red. "Can we keep it down in here. I could hear you people shouting all the way down…" When he saw Amy's dad, his mouth dropped open, and he took off like a shot. "It's

Rupert March!" Brooke heard him yell. "The fiend who attacked Nina Powell is right here in the building."

Soon Brooke's neighbors were trying to crowd their way into the apartment. As the noise ratcheted up, a tall, dark-haired guy named Johnny North arose from their midst, a camcorder on his shoulder. Over the years he'd earned the nickname Johnny-on-the-Spot due to the massive number of video clips he submitted to local news outlets. He aimed his camera at Rupert March. "What do you have to say for yourself, Tough Guy?"

A frown crept over March's lips, and Brooke sensed that his composure was beginning to unravel. "This is a family matter," he shouted over the din. "And that's how I intend it to stay."

Johnny pivoted toward Bernie who cleared his throat and took a step closer to the camera. "I entered this apartment and found this man..." He pointed to Rupert March, "...wrenching this woman's shoulder out of its socket." Johnny aimed his camera at Amy who stood passively beside her father, still looking like Joan of Arc except for the pink and purple hair.

"Meanwhile, those thugs over there..." Bernie pointed at March's body guards, "...kept nodding their approval while Rupert March tried to drag this woman out of here against her will. Somebody needs to put an end to his reign of terror, and that's exactly what I intend to do." He turned to the residents and raised a fist in the air. "Are you with me?"

A cheer went up from the crowd.

"We, the people refuse to stay silent!" Bernie shouted. "We the people refuse to tolerate injustice! We the people refuse to be victims!"

Another cheer went up from the crowd, and soon everyone was waving angry fists and shouting, "No more victims! No more victims!"

"This is ludicrous," March bellowed. "I found my child sequestered in this…" he hesitated as though searching for the right word "…in this decaying flophouse among these…" He pointed at Alfie in his clown makeup, at Maggie with her neon yellow hair, at Bernie with his tattoos, and at the others gathered in the room. "Any decent father would remove an innocent child from a place like this."

He turned toward the camera and pointed at Bernie. "This man's allegations are completely slanderous. He'll be hearing from my attorneys in the morning!"

March's body guards drew closer, their hands fluttering near their belts like they were itching to go for their guns. "We'd better get out of here," one of them said. The other cast a worried eye at the crowd. "He's right, boss. They're losing control."

Bit by bit, the guards steered Amy and her father toward the open window and down the fire escape. Bernie and his followers were right behind them, tromping down the metal steps and waving angry fists, while shouts of "No more victims!" bounced off the buildings on either side of the alley. Brooke watched their departure and the near riot conditions down below until, fed up with the entire spectacle, she slammed the window and locked it.

"That was outrageous. Rupert March was only doing what any concerned father would have done under the circumstances."

Maggie nodded but said nothing.

"Can you believe how this turned out?"

Maggie shook her head and remained silent.

"How did things get so crazy so fast?"

Maggie gave a helpless shrug.

Brooke took a closer look at the expression on her neighbor's face. "Are you okay?"

Maggie nodded. "I've never seen anything like this. Have you?"

"No. I can honestly say I never have."

"Wasn't he incredible?"

"Who?"

"Bernie," she whispered.

They stood together at the window, watching as Maggie's hero and his followers disappeared around the corner.

"Oh Brooke," Maggie sighed. "I think I'm in love."

▾ ▾ ▾

Later that night the two lovebirds joined Brooke for the news. Maggie and Bernie snuggled together on the sofa to watch the 45-second clip the local station edited out of Johnny's lengthier footage. Maggie stared at the screen, and when it was over, she turned her star-struck gaze upon her champion.

"That was incredible, Bern."

"I meant every word of it."

"You were so powerful."

"You felt it too? I haven't had a rush like that since the last time I wrestled on TV."

"Soon the entire world will know what I've always known—that you're a hero."

They kissed, and for a moment Brooke felt like an intruder in her own apartment.

Bernie pulled himself away from Maggie's lips. "Maybe we oughta' leave and—you know—go back to my place."

"Let's go to mine," she countered "I just washed the sheets. The purple satin ones I picked up at the Goodwill Store."

"Your place then."

Maggie glanced at Brooke. "Do you mind? I hate to leave you alone on a Saturday night."

"Go. Being left alone would be wonderful."

Eighteen

A sheet of plywood covered the opening where the Good Shepherd once stood. The service would start soon, but without that familiar image to focus on, Reggie was having trouble collecting her thoughts.

To be fair, it wasn't just the absence of the window that had her stomach tied in knots. A weekend of riots had left neighborhood properties destroyed and businesses looted. And now, in the midst of anarchy and chaos, she had a sermon to deliver.

She'd struggled long and hard to find the words for this first message since Nina's death. In the end, she'd decided to focus, not on Jesus, the Good Shepherd, but on Moses who'd shepherded God's people through the wilderness. She knew ahead of time how the congregation would react to the shift in messaging. It wouldn't be pleasant, but hours of prayer had prepared her to accept the inevitable.

Hearing footsteps in the narthex, she rose from the pew and stood at the entrance to greet those filing in. At a few minutes before ten, she took her accustomed seat at the front of the church and glanced toward the pulpit and the notes she'd placed there earlier. Should she deliver her message as written, or should she wait a few more weeks until the grief and horror of Nina's death subsided? It would be easy to toss together some off-the-cuff remarks. A word of comfort from the Psalms. A bit of wisdom from Proverbs. A time of sharing for those who mourned. A message of encouragement for those affected by the riots. A service like that would be deeply satisfying to those who sought solace. Is that what she should do?

She closed her eyes and breathed a prayer for guidance. No. She wouldn't capitulate to public pressure. There'd been too much of that in years gone by.

Once the singing ended, she took her place in the pulpit and looked out at the sea of faces. Her voice wavered as she blundered through the opening prayer, but the energy shifted when she directed the congregation's attention to the papier mâché goddess masks behind the altar.

"These masks were created by women in Nina's workshops," she began. "Some of their names are familiar. Aphrodite. Isis. Demeter. Kali. Ishtar. Others are more obscure: Ixchel, Mayan goddess of the moon. Yemaya, African goddess of the sea. Sky Woman, mother goddess of the Iroquois. Erzulie, Haitian goddess of love.

"We are gathered here this morning, to seek comfort in the midst of grief. To find healing in the midst of pain and courage in the presence of fear. But more importantly, we are gathered here to consider a familiar message spoken for the first time thirty-five hundred years ago. The words rang forth that day in a blaze of fire and in the presence of the holy angels, and the message remains true these many years later."

She looked at the faces of the goddess worshippers and she looked at the masks they'd made, and then she spoke the words of the Lord: *"Thou shalt have no other Gods before me."*

▼ ▼ ▼

The Sunday morning talk shows—the local ones—were full of the incident in Brooke's apartment. She watched the footage play out, and once the clip ended, a panel of talking heads appeared on the screen.

"The authorities should put that poor child in protective custody," a woman opined. "For her own safety."

"Did you see the expression on her young face?" another asked. "Such obvious suffering is heartbreaking to watch."

"And what about the way Rupert March tore into Nina Powell in the Hewitt Gallery," someone chimed in. "A day later she was dead. What was that about?"

"I'll tell you what it's about," answered a shrill voice. "The man is a racist, a misogynist and a tyrant. Will someone explain how he keeps getting away with it?"

The broadcasters' remarks didn't exactly match Brooke's recollection of yesterday's events. Where they'd seen a raging tyrant, she'd seen a man struggling to keep his cool in deteriorating circumstances while at the same time dealing privately with death threats, worries about his family's safety and exasperation about his daughter's many deceptions. The only time March had shifted from reasonably calm to visibly angry was when Bernie incited the crowd to shout slogans and wave their fists. In response, March accused Bernie of slander and threatened him with lawyers. That—of course—was the clip this channel and the others kept playing.

The skewed portrayals of yesterday's events raised questions in Brooke's mind about the footage shot in the Hewitt Gallery. Had it been selectively edited as well? If so, what else about Rupert March was being misrepresented? Was he really the monster the networks claimed?

Go to the source, Brooke's father used to tell her back when she was way too young to appreciate the advice. In this case, going to the source meant taking a deep dive into March's radio shows and podcasts. The thought wasn't particularly inviting.

Since Karl's death, Brooke had steered away from controversy. Heartbreak and loss had been challenging enough.

And now?

She found the website and chose an episode at random. The one she selected turned out to be a discussion of the World Economic Forum's influence on international policy. The presentation raised disturbing questions, but through it all, March's arguments, while fiery and impassioned, were hardly the ravings of a lunatic. His comments seemed logical and well-researched, and she'd learned more than she'd expected to learn. But to be fair, one podcast was hardly representative of the whole. Scrolling through the episodes, she chose another with a related theme. She was just settling into the subject when her phone alerted her to an incoming text:

"I saw the video of you and Rupert March, Chris Van Auken wrote. *"We need to talk. Can I interest you in coffee?"*

▾ ▾ ▾

A few hours later, Brooke entered the boarded-up coffee shop and saw Van Auken at a corner table, his eyes glued to his phone. He didn't seem to notice as she went to the counter to place her order, and he didn't look up as she made her way to the table with a mug of decaf.

"You startled me," he said when she sat down across from him. "You must have sneaked in the back way."

She pointed to his phone. "You're just like the kids. They can't tear themselves away from those things."

"Guilty as charged. But what do you expect? I'm basically a kid at heart." He showed her what he'd been looking at—the Rupert March footage shot by Johnny-on-the-Spot. "The whole thing's hilarious, but that's beside the point. What I want to know is how in the devil did it happen?"

Brooke took a sip of her decaf and thought back over yesterday's events. "To be honest, the whole thing started with the history paper you assigned. Amy told her dad she needed to go to the library to work on it. Instead, she came to my place."

"A history paper?" Van Auken asked, an eyebrow raised. "Let me break this to you gently. There's no history paper. Amy lied. That's what she does. You fell for her lie, and now her dad has you pegged as a bad influence. That's not a good spot to be in."

Brooke turned toward the window and stared at a flaw in the plywood. Just a short time ago, Dr. Pierce had made everything seem so simple. Seven weeks to direct a play, he'd told her. The cast was already chosen. Costumes ordered. Volunteers lined up to build the sets. It would be easy, breezy.

"I don't blame Rupert March for seeing me as a bad influence," she said wistfully. "I made some pretty stupid mistakes. I guess I should call and apologize."

"Hah! You think that will change anything? It won't. Not now that you're on his bad list. And that's why I sent you that text. If March makes your life miserable—which he will—and if you find yourself needing a shoulder to cry on..." He tapped his left shoulder and grinned. "Feel free to make yourself at home."

There he was, flirting again. It seemed to come naturally to him, this ability to shift from deadly serious to light-hearted in a split second.

"Thanks, but I have no intention of crying on anyone's shoulder. Not over Rupert March or anyone else."

He raised his tiny espresso cup in a toast. "That's the spirit. But if Rupert March doesn't get to you, believe me, his darling daughter will. Her name comes up frequently at faculty meetings. The operative word when dealing with Amy is 'boundaries.' I suggest you set a few."

Brooke let out a sigh. "Ron Webster gave me the same advice. And so did Gretchen Coates."

"But you didn't listen, did you?"

"I wanted to listen—really—but Amy came to me in tears and it seemed only right to offer support. After that, things somehow slipped out of control."

Van Auken smiled knowingly. "That's how it always goes with Amy. A sympathetic ear. A kind word. A heart-to-heart talk. And then, before you know it, things slip out of control. Meanwhile, she's wriggling her way into your life, and once she puts down roots, you can't get rid of her. Not without a fight."

Brooke eyed Van Auken curiously. Had Amy wriggled her way into his life and had things slipped out of control? If so, how had that played out? Her gaze drifted to the ravens on Van Auken's armband. They stood next to each other, chest feathers touching and faces turned away—like spies, alert to their surroundings. The ravens were mirror images of the ravens on the cover of Amy's art journal. Were the similarities coincidental or was there a deeper meaning? Did Amy have a thing for Van Auken? Is that why her dad was accusing him of being too familiar with his female students? Did Rupert March suspect something he couldn't yet prove?

"What I'm trying to say," Van Auken went on, "is that while Amy's needy, she's also manipulative. She's cooperative as long as teachers go along with her whims. When they don't, she gives them nonstop attitude. Striking a balance can be tricky. If you need advice in dealing with her, don't hesitate to ask."

He drained his cup and placed it on the saucer. "Enough school talk. I don't know about you, but I'm sick of staring at plywood and longing for open skies. My bike's right outside the door. What do you say we go for a ride?"

The offer was tempting. It had been a long time since Brooke had been on a bike. An odd thing, considering it was a normal mode of transportation when she was a child. She re-called putting on her kid-sized helmet and climbing on the back of her dad's Harley. Sometimes they'd ride to an ice cream stand along the river. Other times they'd leave the bike in a lot near the Delaware Canal and go hiking on the towpath. As they walked, her dad would point to trees and say their names: *Northern Red Oak. Black Walnut. Sweetgum. White birch.* She remembered signing out a book about trees from the school library. Later, she'd surprised her father with all the names she'd learned. But it wasn't just trees. There were birds, flowers, butterflies, and at night the constellations whirling overhead. A universe of beauty waiting to be named and catalogued.

"A penny for your thoughts," Van Auken said.

She came back to the present, confused by the feelings the memories evoked.

"I know why you're hesitating," he said with a grin. "You're afraid of motorcycles."

"No, it isn't that."

"You can't fool me. I know a scaredy-cat when I see one. Well, let me assure you…"

"I'm not afraid," she snapped, annoyed at him for misinterpreting her thoughts. "It's just that…"

And then she fell silent because there were no words to explain what she'd just experienced. She was back there again, watching her dad ride off to join his biker buddies for a stargazing party in Arizona. Later, his friends told the police that he'd wandered off in the desert one night and never came back. The cops pursued every lead, but in the end, they'd come up empty handed. Brooke thought she'd put those years of pain and loss behind her, but all at once they came rushing back.

"You okay?" Van Auken asked, his brown eyes studying her from across the table.

She rose to her feet. "I think I'd better be going. Thanks so much for the things you shared."

She headed for the door, anxious to get away, but he was right beside her, his gaze tender as he walked her to the car.

"This has been way too much too handle," he said as she slipped behind the wheel. "Nina's murder. Count Dracula's rotten attitude. Amy's goofiness. Rupert March showing up at your door and acting like a jerk. Go home and get some rest. And don't forget…" He smiled and patted his left shoulder. "The offer still stands."

Nineteen

The man's face was weather-beaten, and his hooked nose looked like it had seen more than its fair share of fights. A scraggly, gray beard matched strands of hair escaping a red bandana, and the tattoos blanketing a pair of bulging biceps had a distinctly Nordic flavor. Ted recognized Odin's spear. Thor's hammer. And runic symbols—lots of them.

"Mr. Flynn?"

"Just Flynn."

They shook hands and Ted slid into the booth, curious to see where the conversation might lead. His video series on the old gods had apparently hit a nerve with this crusty, old character, and after some email correspondence, they'd agreed to get together for coffee. Ted never knew what to expect when he met with strangers he encountered online, and that's why he'd scheduled a face-to-face in this crowded, well-lit truck stop. There was safety in numbers.

Once the coffee was delivered, they got down to business. Flynn explained that he had roots in Norse paganism. It was earthy like him. The faith of his fathers, so to speak. Not that he literally worshipped the ancient gods and goddesses. Instead, he revered the spiritual practices drawn from the myths and legends of his ancestors. And then he stumbled on Ted's Genesis 6 videos. He had questions and he wanted answers.

As he spoke, a hostess led a teenaged couple past the booth. The girl glanced at Flynn and her eyes widened. "Those tattoos." she whispered to her male companion. "Is that guy a racist?"

Her companion took a quick glance. "More than a racist—he's a Nazi."

The remark wasn't meant to be heard, but Ted had heard it, and he could tell Flynn had as well. In less than a nanosecond, Flynn was out of the booth. "What did I hear you say?"

The boy backed up a step or two. "I didn't say a word."

"Oh, but you did. You insulted my heritage. That's something I don't take lightly."

The kid didn't answer, whether from defiance or fear, it was hard to tell.

Flynn took a step closer. "Would you like to apologize now, or would you prefer another way of settling the matter?"

Ted braced himself for what seemed inevitable. He pictured Flynn grabbing the kid by the shirt, hurling him against a table and triggering a chain reaction that would end up with fists flying, tables tipping over and chairs soaring through the air. At some point, some idiot would pull a gun and the carnage would begin.

Thankfully, none of that happened. Instead, the boy mumbled an apology, and Flynn stepped aside to allow the young couple to pass.

"I get a lot of that," he said as he eased back into the booth. "It's the tattoos. People take a look at the runes, and instead of assuming I'm Scandinavian, they figure I'm a Nazi. Ridiculous, but that's how it is."

While Ted didn't condone Flynn's strong-arm tactics, he

knew exactly what he was referring to. Back in the day, the Nazis had co-opted various Norse runes as symbols of Aryan supremacy. Contemporary Neo-Nazis continued the misappropriation, leading to misunderstandings and unpleasant scenes like the one that had just unfolded.

Flynn drained his mug and signaled the server for a refill. "You'd like to think Nazis are a thing of the past," he said, once the coffee was poured. "But these creeps keep refusing to die. In fact, just the other day a friend told me about a neo-Nazi training compound in the woods not too far from here. Interestingly, he claims they recruited some kids from that stuck-up prep school. You know—the one where that activist lady got killed."

That was news to Ted. He'd been following the Nina Powell story pretty closely, and while there'd been lots of speculation about the murder being a hate crime, this was the first time he'd heard of a connection to actual neo-Nazis.

"The media keeps squawking about a racial angle to the Nina Powell case," Flynn continued. "And then you find out they've got neo-Nazis roaming the halls of the school where she was murdered. Makes you wonder, don't it?"

Indeed, it did, and Ted was still wondering as the conversation shifted to other topics. It was still on his mind an hour later when he gave Flynn a Gospel of John and told him to stay in touch. And he was still thinking about it the next morning as he jogged past the row houses in his Allentown neighborhood. He usually listened to a podcast while he ran, but this morning he was preoccupied with the things Flynn had told him.

He returned home and climbed the stairs to the spare room where he kept his weights. After fifteen minutes of heavy lifting, he took a shower, got dressed and stared at his computer monitor. He had a video to edit, but he couldn't get this neo-Nazi business out of his mind. Were the rumors true? Were there really Nazi students wandering the halls of Sussex

Academy? He wanted answers—it wasn't his fault that he'd been born with an investigative journalist's nose for a story. Back in his newspaper days he would have found a contact inside the school, someone smart who'd be willing to funnel information in his direction. Ironically, he had just that sort of contact—Brooke. But would she be willing to talk to him? A year ago, she'd made it clear that, while she was grateful for his help, she didn't want him hanging around. But things had changed in the last twelve hours. He'd gotten hold of information she'd probably find interesting, and she in turn, might have information he'd find interesting. This would be a business exchange, plain and simple. I'll tell you this, if you tell me that.

That decided, he picked up the phone and punched in her number. The phone rang—once—twice—three times. He was just about to give up when a voice answered. Not the voicemail voice he'd dreaded, but Brooke's voice—alive and in person.

There was a bit of awkwardness as he stumbled through the hellos and how-are-yous, but once that was out of the way, he got down to business. "There's some totally weird stuff going on at that school where you work," he informed her.

The remark was greeted with silence. "Totally weird stuff at Sussex Academy? Gee—I hadn't noticed."

Okay, so he'd made a dumb opening statement and invited her sarcasm. "What I'm trying to say is that I've heard a few things I think you'll find interesting. Can you meet me for coffee?"

More silence. "Can't you just tell me over the phone?"

"Sorry. This information requires a face-to-face. Today, if possible."

The silence returned, but to be fair, he understood the reason for her hesitancy. She was afraid of ending up in a nightmare scenario like the one last fall. Or maybe she hated him and was determined to avoid him at all costs. Whatever the case, he was disappointed, but not surprised, when she said she was busy. He countered by saying this was important. Really important because it involved students from Sussex Academy.

"Students from Sussex Academy" must have been the ticket because later that afternoon, he stood in front of a chalkboard in a boarded-up coffee shop. He decided on a Spiced Pumpkin Latte and once the barista whipped it up, he took it to the same table where he'd waited for Brooke a year ago. He'd been sleep-deprived that day and barely able to keep his eyes open, let alone frame a coherent sentence. Today he was alert and on top of his game except for a sense of trepidation at the thought of seeing her again.

He reminded himself of the purpose of this meeting. An information swap. No more. No less. He and Brooke lived in different worlds. There was exactly zero possibility of a relationship. Not now. Not ever.

Even so, he sat up a bit straighter when she walked in. Last fall he'd named her Sad-Eyed Woman of Mystery, and while she was no longer sad-eyed, she'd never shaken the aura of mystery—at least in Ted's mind. He sensed that there were secrets she kept, not just from him, but from everyone. To be fair, everyone has secrets, but hers seemed deeper somehow, as though an alternative person lived inside her, one she protected with her life.

He rose to greet her, and when he offered to treat, she said thanks anyway, but she'd buy her own coffee. He insisted—after all, she was here because he'd invited her. When she refused again, he watched her walk to the counter and return with a mugful of something hot and steaming. And then, just like a year ago, she sat down and he was thrown off balance when he looked into her blue-green eyes.

Twenty

Brooke's hands clenched the steering wheel. Not because of the traffic—there was hardly any—but because of the things Ted had just told her. Could it be true? Were neo-Nazis lurking among the students at Sussex Academy? Might they have had a hand in Nina's murder? Or, as was more likely, was this just another example of the outrageous stories Ted liked to tell? When she'd asked him to provide students' names, he couldn't. Instead, he told her to keep an eye out for kids wearing Norse symbols. The symbols might be indicative of Nazi sympathies or they might be totally innocent—it was hard to tell.

The idea was ludicrous. Did he really expect her to take inventory of the tattoos, jewelry and tee-shirts every kid was wearing? The *Dracula* cast and crew represented only a small fraction of the student body. How was she supposed to account for the rest of them?

The stories got wilder as Ted described a neo-Nazi compound somewhere in the area. When Brooke asked about the location of this compound, he said he didn't know. A friend would get back to him with the information. Once he had the address, he'd pay a clandestine visit to find out what went on there. Really? A clandestine visit to a Nazi compound? The statement proved what she already knew. Not only was Ted a religious fanatic; he was also a reckless daredevil. Last year it was demons. This year—Nazis.

She should have excused herself at that point, but she'd hung around to finish her latte. And that meant listening to stories about Nazi SS Leader Heinrich Himmler and his search for occult ritual objects mentioned in Norse mythology. Among them was Thor's hammer, which, in Himmler's delusional brain, was no ordinary hammer, but a high-tech weapon, capable of delivering earthshattering devastation. And not only that—the symbolic representation of Thor's hammer was the swastika.

So, of course, the first thing Brooke saw when she arrived at Sussex Academy was Thor's hammer on Van Auken's Harley. Why had he put it there? Was it because he loved all things Viking, as he claimed, or was there a darker explanation? She laughed at the thought. There was no way Chris Van Auken was a Nazi. The thought was ridiculous. But that's the effect Ted's ideas had on a person. He made you see things you never would have thought to look for.

But to be fair, what did she really know about Chris Van Auken? And what did she know about any of the people who walked the halls of Sussex Academy—students included? When she'd asked Ron Webster if racism was an issue at the school, he'd given some vague response about rebellious kids doing whatever they could to challenge social norms. Was he trying to keep her from learning about Neo-Nazis in the student body? Was there a possibility that these students were involved in Nina's murder? Was Webster helping the school keep a lid on information that might further damage its image?

These questions weighed heavily on Brooke's mind as she

got out of the car and entered the building. Amy was already in the auditorium, her eyes fixed on the prompt book. Today's outfit was a black mini-skirt, a baggy red tee-shirt and a belt made of miniature plastic skulls connected by metal chains. Her blue eyes seemed to vanish beneath gobs of thick, black liner, her lips glistened blood-red against her pale face and she barely resembled the girl Brooke had gone to the Celtic festival with on Saturday.

"How did things go at home?" Brooke asked as she slid into a seat. "I hope your dad wasn't too tough on you."

Amy sat up straighter and brushed a strand of pink and purple hair from her face. "He shouted and stomped around for a while, and then he took away my car keys for a month except for school and rehearsal. Things calmed down while we ate dinner, and then he went nuts all over again when he saw the video clip on the news. He got even crazier when I couldn't stop laughing at the guy with the clown makeup and that crazy, tattooed guy who kept waving his fists and shouting 'No more victims!'"

"So, he wasn't *too* upset?"

She laughed at the question. "Oh, he was pretty upset, but mostly at you. He says you're turning out to be a bad influence, and Sussex Academy must have been desperate to hire someone who lives in a cheesy apartment building with a bunch of derelicts and weirdoes. To make a long story short, I don't think he likes you very much. And I'm pretty sure he called Dr. Pierce to tell him to fire you. But don't worry. He'll get over it—he always does."

There was the matter of the art journal to discuss. But at the moment, Brooke had a rehearsal to run. Count Dracula surprised her by being charmingly seductive, but he wasn't the only one who was charmingly seductive. Chris Van Auken showed up as the kids were taking a ten-minute break.

"Feeling better?" he asked.

Brooke nodded. "Sorry about the meltdown yesterday. I don't know what came over me."

"Don't be so hard on yourself. You've been through a lot, and you're entitled to a meltdown. And by the way, the offer for a bike ride still stands. And so does the shoulder to cry on."

She ignored the remark and after some small talk, he said goodnight and stopped at the front of the auditorium to joke around with the kids gathered on the stage. Definitely not a Nazi, Brooke decided as she watched the way Van Auken interacted with them. And not too familiar with his female students either. He was a popular teacher whose good looks and friendly nature made kids like him.

Rehearsal proceeded smoothly, and at nine, Tom-the Rent-a-Cop showed up to escort the students to their cars. Brooke was just about to leave when a voice rang out from the back of the auditorium. Turning, she saw Dr. Pierce heading down the aisle. He gestured toward a seat, and when Brooke sat down, he did as well.

"Rupert March phoned me over the weekend," he began. "He told me his daughter lied about going to the library on Saturday and spent the day with you instead. Later, you encouraged your friends to publicly humiliate him."

"Part of that's true," Brooke confessed. "But I had nothing to do with the people who showed up and made a scene." She offered a brief explanation of events and when she finished, Pierce fell silent, his hands steepled beneath his chin.

"You realize the position this puts me in," he said after a moment's thought. "Mr. March is demanding that I ask for your resignation, and while I sympathize with his concerns, the idea is frankly impossible. There's no way I can find another director at this late date, even if I wanted to. Which I don't."

"Let me apologize to him," Brooke offered. "It's the least I can do."

"I doubt that will do much good—not with the pressure

he and his family are under at the moment. I'll tell him I spoke to you, and I'll offer an apology on your behalf. But to be fair, you're the one who deserves an apology. It was never my intention to ask so much of you."

He rose to his feet with a sigh. "I have no problem with your work. I've heard nothing but favorable reports from the students and their parents." He started up the aisle and turned back. "Before I leave, a word to the wise. Keep your distance from Amy. She's known to be clingy."

Brooke watched the headmaster walk away. How in the world was a director supposed to keep her distance from the stage manager? The request was impossible.

Back at home she put on some water for tea, and as she waited for it to boil, her gaze wandered across the room to the steamer chest in front of the sofa. Amy's art journal was still inside, and so far Brooke had resisted looking at it. Amy had agreed to take it with her on Saturday, and she would have done so if her father hadn't shown up when he did. Under the circumstances, it seemed only right to revert to their original plan. Amy had one week to get it out of here.

When the phone rang, she put the subject out of her mind. The caller was someone named Della Schaeffer, and while the name sounded familiar, Brooke couldn't quite place it. And then it came to her. Della Schaeffer. The server who'd waited on Nina Powell at Don Giovanni's. The one who'd asked Giorgio to give Brooke a note with her phone number scribbled on it. Brooke had called and left a message, but in the chaos of the last week, the matter had slipped from her memory.

After a bit of small talk, Della explained why she'd hoped to speak to Brooke. She'd watched the news the night of Nina's murder and she'd seen the footage of Brooke outside Sussex Academy. From that moment on, she'd sensed a mysterious connection between the two of them. After all, she (Della) was the last person to see Nina alive and Brooke was the first to see her dead. That explained the connection, not just to each other, but to Nina as well. Della hoped that she and Brooke could get together soon to explore the paranormal implications of that connection—maybe through a séance or a channeling session.

The idea was crazy, but rather than saying as much, Brooke tactfully steered the conversation in a more helpful direction. Della confirmed what Giorgio had already said, namely that Nina met some guy for dinner that night. They got into an argument, but Della couldn't tell what it was about because they shut up whenever she approached the table. She did, however, get a pretty good look at the guy. He was Nina's age or a bit older. Good looking in a laid-back way. Tall, but not overly so. Light brown hair—not short, but not long either. He was wearing khakis and a denim jacket over a button-down shirt. Oh, and there was a helmet with a Harley logo on the seat next to him.

Brooke drew in her breath. Della had just described Chris Van Auken. He'd never mentioned having dinner with Nina just hours before her death. Why had he kept that information to himself?

Twenty-one

Van Auken was back at break on Tuesday, chatting up the girls and joking with the guys. There was one like him in every high school. He was the teacher the girls had crushes on and the guys tried to emulate. The teacher kids liked to be around, in part because he'd never grown up.

The ten-minute break flew by with no opportunity to broach the subject of his dinner with Nina. He showed up again on Wednesday, and after a few minutes of kibbitzing with the kids, he took Brooke aside and asked her to join him for coffee or a drink after rehearsal. She thought about accepting but decided against it. While she'd love to delve into his reasons for keeping quiet about the incident at Don Giovanni's, she didn't want to encourage his flirtations.

He was back on Thursday night, and this time he bypassed the students at the back of the auditorium and ambled toward Brooke. "Since you turned me down last night, I decided to try a different approach." He held up a thermos. "Coffee in the parking lot under the stars. It's decaf, so I don't want to hear any excuses about caffeine keeping you up all night."

Brooke was about to say no—being alone in the dark with the resident Don Juan didn't sound like a good idea. But on second thought, the setup was perfect. They'd sip decaf, she'd ask questions and once she had answers, she'd leave. She accepted the invitation, and he sealed the deal with a high-five.

He was back at a little after nine. "I've got it covered," he told Tom-the Rent-a-Cop who showed up to walk Brooke to her car. Tom acknowledged the arrangement with a wink and went off to complete his rounds.

Van Auken held the door at the rear of the building and escorted Brooke outside. The night was warm for mid-September, the air heavy with the scent of freshly mown grass. Off in the distance crickets chirped a whirring song, while across the parking lot, moths fluttered around a pole lamp that cast a puddle of light on the macadam.

He sat down next to Brooke on the stoop and poured decaf into a couple of foam cups. While they waited for it to cool, he talked about the play. She was doing a terrific job. The students liked her—he couldn't blame them for that. Yes, Erik was difficult, but to be fair, the kid had tons of issues, starting with his overworked, high-profile mom who never had time for him. She was a hematologist—aka a blood doctor. Funny that the blood doctor's son was playing Dracula. Maybe she'd donate real blood so they wouldn't have to use the fake stuff in the play. Just kidding, ha, ha. Brooke shouldn't waste time worrying about Erik's attitude—it was an act—a defense mechanism. Someday he'd surprise them all and return to the school as their most prominent alumnus—a musician, a neuroscientist, a Nobel laureate—someone important. Erik might be a headache, but Rupert March was the guy to watch out for—a fascist dictator in panic mode now that his nasty temper and misogynistic attitudes were being exposed for the world to see.

"There's nothing more dangerous than a fascist dictator in panic mode," he continued. "But take it from me: March is more afraid of you than you are of him."

"I seriously doubt that."

"It's true. He's intimidated by strong, beautiful women."

"I'm not either."

"Of course, you are."

"No, I'm not."

"Yes, you are. You're strong, and you're beautiful. What's there to argue about?"

"Stop it. You're flirting. You're always flirting."

"Am I?" he asked.

"Compulsively. When you talk, you flirt."

"I don't mean to."

"Yes, you do. It's obvious."

"I object. All I'm doing is making polite conversation. Is that so terrible?"

Brooke ignored the question. It was getting late, and this back and forth would go on forever if she let it.

Van Auken seemed to read her mind. "Now, don't go crying about how late it is. You can't leave until I show you something." He got out his phone, scrolled through a bunch of pictures and stopped at an image of a Viking in battle gear, his face hidden by a helmet inscribed with runes. "That's me underneath all that metal. Scary, huh?"

"Totally scary. I wouldn't want to meet up with you in a dark alley."

His expression was gentle as he gazed at her. "Funny, but I feel just the opposite about you. A dark alley. A candlelit bar. A parking lot beneath the stars. Any one of them works for me." And then he grinned. Always clowning. Always flirting.

She ignored the remark and he resumed scrolling through his pictures. "Here I am at a festival last month without the helmet and the body armor." He looked exactly as Brooke might have imagined. Bare-chested. Muscular. And appealing. Chris Van Auken was definitely appealing.

He moved on to photos of rugged guys brandishing swords, knives, axes—all kinds of weapons. Next were winter scenes of sturdy folks in fur-trimmed capes and boots, ale-drinkers gathered around campfires and costumed vendors selling weapons, jewelry and crafts. An image flew by of a woman clinging to Van Auken's arm. She looked familiar, but the picture was gone before Brooke could identify her. And then she realized who it was. The Owl Lady. The round glasses were a dead giveaway.

"Was that Gretchen Coates?" she asked.

Van Auken laughed at the question. "Gretchen Coates? Get serious. We don't allow guidance counselors at Viking festivals."

He swept through several more images and stopped at one of a redhead in a moss-green gown. The girl was lovely with wisps of fiery hair escaping a braid that fell just below her shoulders. "I can picture you like this. Independent and free-spirited, with a touch of sadness in your eyes." He scrolled to another image and grinned. "And I can picture you like this as well." The woman in the photo stared back at Brooke, a shield in one hand, a sword in the other, an expression of savage fury on her face. "That's the real you. A force to be reckoned with."

Brooke supposed she should be flattered, but she wasn't. Van Auken's praise meant nothing. It was all a game, and she was tired of it. It was time to take control of the conversation, find out what she needed to find out, and be on her way.

"Before I leave," she said, "there's something I need to ask you."

"Ask away."

She hesitated, uncertain how to shift gears from frivolous to deadly serious. Seeing no other way, she dove right in. "I heard that you were with Nina a few hours before she died. That you had an argument at Don Giovanni's and she ran out in a huff."

His smile faded. "Who told you that?"

Brooke wasn't about to reveal her source. "It doesn't matter who told me. Is it true?"

"People have arguments. Nina and I had one. It's no big deal."

"I agree. Except that Nina was murdered a few hours later."

When he said nothing, she continued probing. "It seems odd that you didn't mention the incident. We've had plenty of time to talk about it."

"Why would we talk about it?" he asked, his tone abrasive. "It's my business, not yours."

"Maybe so, but I have a right to know who I can trust around here and who I can't."

"What's not to trust? I gave you a head's up about the issues at the school. I told you about Rupert March and his schemes. Did you think I was lying?"

She didn't answer. She'd wondered if Van Auken was lying. Especially when it came to Amy.

"I see where this is headed," he continued after a few seconds of silence. "You think I killed Nina."

"I didn't say that."

"But you're thinking it, aren't you?"

"I asked why you didn't tell me about having dinner with her the night she died. It's a simple question, and I'd like a simple answer."

Scowling, he flung the contents of his cup on the macadam and watched the spray sparkle in the moonlight. "Here's a simple answer for you. Party's over. Time to go home."

When she didn't respond, he rose from the stoop, yanked her to her feet and stared into her eyes. "Get this through your head," he snarled, his face inches from hers. "I didn't kill Nina. And in case you're still wondering, I'm not too familiar with my female students either."

He released her with a shove and pointed toward her car.

"Leave. Now."

Brooke could feel his eyes following her as she opened the door and slid behind the wheel. And he was still staring when she glanced in the rearview mirror and backed out of the space next to his Harley.

Two questions were uppermost in her mind as she left the campus behind. Why did Van Auken lie about the photo of Gretchen Coates at the Viking reenactment? And why did he bring up accusations about being too familiar with his female students? Why conflate that with Nina's murder unless there was a reason to do so?

Twenty-two

Detective Jason Radley threw his pen on the desk and stared in the direction of the noise. How was a guy supposed to concentrate with all that racket going on? Earplugs—that was it. He needed earplugs.

The buzz of angry voices grew with each passing minute. "Overtime pay isn't adequate," a cop complained. "We should be getting hazardous-duty pay as well," shouted another, and Radley was inclined to agree with him. In just a few hours these men and women would put on riot gear and take to the streets for another night of dodging bricks and bullets. Nowadays, wearing a uniform was the same as hanging a target on your back, and at times Radley felt guilty that his job allowed him to show up for work in civilian clothes.

He took a swig of the nasty sludge that passed for coffee. It left a bad taste in his mouth, just like the 24/7 drip, drip, drip of rumors claiming that Burleigh's people were dragging their heels on the Nina Powell investigation. The media kept working the story about cops protecting their own, and as far as Radley was concerned, these rumors were responsible for the onslaught of smashed windows, overturned cars and dumpster fires. Things would continue in this vein until a suspect was behind bars, and that's why the higher-ups were piling on the pressure. It was time, they said, to put an end to the gossip and attach a face to the crime.

The state attorney general had a different take on the matter. Alarmed by media hype about police corruption, he'd dispatched a team of snoops to investigate. As a result, cops tiptoed around headquarters, watching every word they said and hoping nothing in their backgrounds would pop up to make them look bad. Others lay awake at night, worrying that some dumb remark posted years ago on social media would show up to cancel their careers. Meanwhile, formerly friendly colleagues eyed each other with suspicion, seasoned cops talked about early retirement, and to put it mildly, morale was at an all-time low.

The griping ceased when footsteps in the hall announced Detective Burleigh's arrival in the building. The footsteps passed Radley's cubicle, and a few seconds later the boss's office door opened and slammed shut. He was testy these days—irritable and sarcastic and an entirely different person from the guy Radley thought he knew. The whole team felt it, and you could sense the tension in the briefing room when he called them together. But the other team members weren't paired up with him day in and day out like Radley was, and they didn't have to put up with the painful silences that had taken the place of collegial banter.

Sighing, he picked up his pen, drew a circle on a sheet of paper and wrote a name in the middle. Amy March. She knew things she wasn't telling—he could tell by the shifty way she responded to questions. That wasn't unusual for teenagers. Most of them had worlds of secrets they kept from the adults in their lives. But Amy was trickier than most, and her flaky emotional makeup made her tough to interview. That and the fact that her father insisted on having his attorneys present at each meeting. No wonder the little vixen kept her trap shut.

Radley wrote down a second name and drew a line to connect it to Amy's. Erik Rimmer's twenty-five-minute absence from rehearsal the night of the murder gave him plenty of time to kill Nina Powell. He blamed Nina for breaking up his hot, summer fling with Amy March, and given Rimmer's temperament, it was easy to imagine him going to the art studio for a confrontation, only to have it spiral out of control. Racism could have played a part as well. Rimmer was reputed to have such tendencies, but when asked, he told the detectives that people said that about him because he refused to let the school brainwash him into seeing everything in terms of race and gender. He was proud of his bloodlines, he'd insisted—at least on his mom's side since he didn't have a clue who his father was. The fake vampire mark was a bit harder to explain. Why in the devil would Count Dracula leave a calling card at the scene? Rimmer was too smart to do something that stupid, and yet there was always the chance that doing so had given him a perverse thrill. But the biggest complication was that fact that there'd been exactly zero physical evidence to connect him to the crime.

Not so with history teacher Chris Van Auken. He'd left behind traces of hair and fiber when he'd rushed into the closet, and there were traces of the victim's blood on his sleeve. He'd been in an on-again, off-again relationship with Ms. Powell for nearly two years—sometimes romantic, but not so much of late. The night of the murder, they'd met for dinner at Don Giovanni's. The purpose of this meeting, according to Mr. Van Auken, was to confront restaurant owner and schoolboard president Don Petrakis about a policy he kept refusing to address at board meetings. The confrontation never happened because Mr. Van Auken and Ms. Powell got into an argument about her tendency to get too involved in her students' personal lives. She responded with a hissy fit and stormed out of the restaurant.

But was that really what the argument was about? Had Nina Powell learned something that would support rumors of Chris Van Auken being too familiar with his female students, and did she confront him with that information at dinner? He claimed that he'd left the restaurant and returned to the school to work on something in his classroom. Was that true, or did he go back there knowing Ms. Powell would be alone in the studio, giving him the perfect opportunity to silence her before she could expose the truth about his interactions with the young ladies of Sussex Academy?

A third line connected Headmaster Dr. Alan Pierce to Amy March. He'd been hired with a mandate to modernize Sussex Academy, and he'd responded by bringing in fresh new blood with new ideas. These new ideas had sounded good on paper, but hadn't proven so in practice. Long story short, the school was falling apart under his watch. Lousy test scores. A massive financial melt-down. Students in open rebellion. Donors disappearing. And other crises, too numerous to mention.

Matters reached a tipping point right before school started when Rupert March demanded that Nina Powell be fired for her part in a plot to help his daughter run away from home. While Pierce agreed that Ms. Powell had overstepped her bounds, he was caught between the proverbial rock and a hard place. The public adored Nina and saw her as a saint for her role in exposing the dirty cops with ties to human traffickers. Firing her prior to the upcoming trial would have unleashed a wave of outrage at a time when the school was struggling to rebuild its image. But if Nina were dead—martyred by some unknown assailant—Pierce's problems would be solved.

So, did he bump her off? Everyone has their breaking point and Pierce was obviously teetering on the edge. The only hitch was the vampire mark on the victim's neck. It didn't seem likely that someone as meek and mild as Alan Pierce would think of a detail like that, and yet, you never know what people will do when pushed beyond their limits.

There were other potential suspects with ties to Sussex Academy, and in a few minutes Radley and the boss would head back for a third interview with Librarian and Information Specialist Jane Acker. She'd been a motherlode of information, and while he was anxious to hear what she might have to say, he wasn't looking forward to Burleigh's silence on the rides to and from the school. Maybe the boss was reacting to pressure from the higher ups, or maybe he'd had it with the DA poking his nose into everybody's business, or maybe it was something personal he was holding back.

Whatever it was, it made Radley uneasy, not just because things were uncomfortable between the two of them. No—it went deeper than that. All this talk about dirty cops had planted suspicions in Radley's brain. Suspicions that were making him lie awake at night wondering if he could still trust the guy he'd trusted for so long.

Twenty-three

Storm clouds hovered overhead as Brooke hurried to the farmers market in the center of Easton. Judging from the crowds, she wasn't the only person who'd shown up early on a gloomy Saturday morning in hopes of beating the rain. A long line stretched in front of her at her favorite produce stand, and while she waited, she reviewed Thursday night's conversation with Van Auken. When pressed on the matter of his dinner with Nina Powell, he'd done a complete one-eighty. Why had he reacted so strongly? And why had he made a point of insisting that there was nothing going on with him and his female students? Is that what he and Nina Powell had been arguing about at Don Giovanni's?

"Next," the vendor shouted. Once she'd paid, Brooke gathered her purchases and left the booth. She thought about heading home, but in spite of the humidity and gloomy skies, a festive mood hung over the square. Her cramped apartment seemed like a prison cell when compared to the market with its colorful displays of home-grown and home-made merchandise, and she was glad she'd thought to stick a collapsible umbrella in her bag. She'd take her time and head back only when the rain became a downpour.

She stopped to buy a jar of spicy mango salsa, and as she chatted with the vendor, someone called her name. Turning around, she saw Information Specialist Jane Acker making her way through the crowd, her hand raised in greeting. Brooke considered fleeing—she had no desire to talk to Jane. But it was too late. They'd already made eye contact.

Jane rushed over and gathered her in an unwelcome embrace. "I'm so glad we've connected at last," she gushed as she released her. "It's hard to believe you've been at Sussex Academy two whole weeks and we still haven't had a chance to catch up. But now's as good a time as any, don't you think?"

Brooke had no desire to spend even a second with the Sussex Academy information specialist. In the days following her mother's suicide, she'd mistaken Jane's questions for compassion, only to learn that everything she'd told her in confidence had become public knowledge within hours. There was no way she'd let that happen again.

"I know the perfect place for a chat," Jane continued. "A bakery just a few blocks from here. Coffee's on me."

"Thanks, but…" Brooke caught herself before an excuse slipped out. It had just occurred to her that two could play Jane's game. She forced a smile to her lips. "Coffee would be lovely. And you're right. It's been a long time. Too long."

Soon Jane was steering her through the busy market, past stores and restaurants boarded up with plywood. As the first raindrops began to fall, Jane opened a door and ushered Brooke into a dimly lit space, fragrant with the aroma of coffee and chocolate. Pastries beckoned from a display counter along one wall and candles on each of eight small tables warmed the room with their glow. After ordering, Brooke and Jane found seats and made small talk while waiting for their lattes to be delivered.

Or, to be accurate, Jane made small talk. The heat and humidity were oppressive, but the rain would bring cooler temperatures. Autumn was upon them, and while she wouldn't miss the scorching temperatures, it was hard to say goodbye to summer. Already she was longing for the beach. And for flowers. She hated the thought of her garden turning brown and withering in the cold.

The chatter stopped when the server deposited their order on the table. "This seems just like old times in my office," Jane said once the server vanished. She took a sip of her latte and licked the foam away with a swish of a catty tongue. "You remember those cozy conversations, don't you?"

Remember? How could Brooke forget? She pictured the tiny room behind the circulation desk. Carts of books waiting to be shelved. A flickering candle in a glass jar. A plate of Scottish shortbread cookies. Mugs filled with Earl Grey tea. A setting conducive to friendly intimacy while being just the opposite.

"It's such a shame we fell out of touch," Jane continued. "I thought of you so often after your husband's death. I tried to reach out on several occasions, but you never got back to me."

Brooke felt her shoulders tighten. Karl's death was off-limits, especially to Jane. She looked longingly toward the door and wished she hadn't agreed to this conversation.

"You must be lonely," Jane persisted. "What's it been now—over a year?"

"That's right. But I'd rather not discuss it."

"I understand completely. I only mentioned it because most people view a year as the proper period for mourning a husband's death. The custom began, I suppose, with Victorian widows. Imagine wearing black for twelve, long months and then all of a sudden being free one day to face the world in bright colors. A perfect way to announce that you're circulating again—don't you think? Nowadays, the signals aren't nearly as clear.

"Which brings me to a question I've been dying to ask. What's this I hear about you and Chris Van Auken? He's handsome, isn't he? Charming too." She sat back to watch Brooke's reaction. "Don't look so surprised. I'm referring, of course, to a private tete-a-tete behind the school a few nights ago. Could it be that love is in the air?"

Brooke stifled the urge to get up from the table and walk out the door. How did Jane know about that? She recalled the events of that evening. Had students overheard Van Auken asking her to join him after rehearsal? No. It must have been Tom-the-Rent-a-Cop. Who better for Jane to draft into service than the guy who snooped around the building every night? Brooke would have to watch her step around Tom in the future.

But for the present, she needed to answer Jane's questions. If she agreed that Van Auken was handsome and charming—which he was—Jane would soon be entertaining her colleagues with tales of love and passion. On the other hand, denying the obvious, namely that Van Auken was indeed handsome and charming, would awaken Jane's suspicions. Neither option was acceptable.

"He's a lot of fun," Brooke remarked off-handedly. "But I can't imagine anyone taking him seriously. In fact, I have it on good authority that he's not to be trusted where women are concerned."

Jane rose to the bait like a hungry trout. "And who, may I ask, is this 'good authority'?"

Brooke hesitated, not because she didn't have an answer, but because she knew that her reticence would fuel Jane's curiosity. "I shouldn't name names. It doesn't seem right."

"Nonsense. Your story's safe with me."

It wasn't—there wasn't a story in the world that was safe with Jane.

"Go on," the information specialist urged. "Who told you

he's not to be trusted?"

"I guess it wouldn't hurt if…" Brooke allowed her voice trail off. "No. I shouldn't."

Jane rolled her eyes and leaned across the table. "Oh, for heaven's sake. Just tell me already."

Brooke knew that the longer she dragged this out, the more interested Jane would become. "Okay," she said after an excruciatingly long pause. "Since you asked, Van Auken's name came up last week in a conversation with Guidance Counselor Gretchen Coates. She seemed rattled when I mentioned him."

Jane threw back her head and laughed. "Rattled? I'll bet she was rattled. Gretchen and Chris used to be chummy. Very chummy. Uncomfortably chummy, if you know what I mean."

Brooke thought again of the picture on Van Auken's phone. The one of Gretchen clinging to his arm at a Viking re-enactment. Why had he lied about it?

"They tried to keep things hush-hush," Jane continued, "but you know how school gossip is. Nothing stays hidden for long. Of course, Chris denies there was ever anything between him and Gretchen, but I know better."

Soon the details came pouring out. Gretchen had been carrying on with Van Auken in secret for over a year when Nina came on board. From then on, it was Chris and Nina sitting to-gether at school events. Chris and Nina laughing in the halls. Chris and Nina plotting and scheming in the faculty lounge. Chris and Nina falling silent whenever Gretchen entered the room.

"What made the situation so beastly," Jane continued, "was that Nina and Gretchen were close friends. Nina knew that Gretchen was over the moon for Chris, but that didn't stop her from moving in on Gretchen's territory. Oh no—whatever Nina wanted, Nina got, make no mistake about it. But her fling with Chris didn't last long. She got tired of his games, and I can't say I blame her. Chris is charming if all you're interested in is a laugh or two. But just try to get close to him and see what happens. He'll back away every time. He's everyone's best friend until you touch a nerve, and then he's gone. When he shows up again, it's back to fun and games."

She reached across the table and placed a manicured hand on Brooke's arm. "I've got a little secret for you. Chris Van Auken is hiding something, and I think I know what it is."

Brooke didn't bother asking for an explanation. She knew from experience that Jane Acker was constitutionally incapable of holding back a juicy story.

"So, one day last spring," Jane continued after a pregnant pause, "Chris happened to mention something about attending survivalist camps as a teen. I naturally assumed he'd been an Eagle Scout, but when I said as much, he laughed and brushed off the remark. 'Eagle Scouts could never survive the SEAL-Team-Six-level training I endured as a kid,' he told me. When I asked him to explain, he changed the subject and started clowning around like he always does. I was curious as to why he was being so evasive, so I decided to look into the matter for myself. I did an internet search, and do you know where I ended up?"

Brooke shook her head.

"I ended up on the Department of Justice website. And do you know what I discovered?"

"Tell me."

"I discovered that so-called "wilderness experiences" do a better job of reforming incorrigible youth than traditional juvenile detention centers. The revelation was shocking. Did Chris get in trouble as a kid, and did a judge consider him incorrigible? Is that why he attended survivalist camps? And if so, what were his crimes? And more importantly, was he really reformed, or is there something in his nature that can't be reformed? The man's quite capable of violence—just look at those Viking reenactments he's so proud of."

She sat back in her seat, her manicured fingers drumming on the table. "You can't begin to imagine how frustrating this has been. Juvenile records are sealed to the public, and while I've tried to get the detectives to cough up some answers, they've been no help whatsoever. Don't you think his colleagues have a right to know if Chris was an incorrigible youth? If that were true at one time, is it still true today? Or, if he's been reformed, does his shady past explain why he insists on mentoring kids like Erik Rimmer and his friends? Is that Chris's way of paying off a debt to society, or is something else going on when he meets these boys for coffee and video games? I've tried to get answers, but the students involved won't talk and…"

A noise trilled from Jane's handbag. "My phone. Give me a sec to see who it is." As she listened, her eyes grew wide and she ran a hand through her short, frosted hair. "I'm so sorry. No—don't cancel. I'm only five minutes away."

"A hair appointment," she said as she gathered her packages and scrambled to her feet. "And now I have to run, just as I was about to fill you in some nasty secrets about life at Sussex Academy."

And that quick she was out the door, taking the nasty secrets with her.

Twenty-four

The gallery was closed on Mondays, but Madeleine Hewitt was at her desk anyway. The windows were boarded up and the doors locked, making it easy to hide from those who stopped by. The majority of visitors these days weren't here to see the feminist art exhibit, but to pester her with questions about Rupert March's confrontation with Nina Powell. By now the story was old news, but that didn't stop people from feigning interest in the works on display before revealing the real reasons for their visit. But maybe this unwelcome notoriety was a blessing in disguise. All publicity is good publicity, someone once said.

She stared at the stack of paperwork that had accumulated while she'd been dealing with nosy questions from the public and the press. The stack would only get bigger if she didn't deal with it. She opened an envelope and fished out a bill, but her thoughts were elsewhere.

Last night, she and Sid had been at it again. It started, as did most of their fights, with his drinking, and quickly segued to infidelities of years gone by. There were the usual accusations and ultimatums, and it ended where it always did: money. She'd naively assumed that their future was secure. That their finances were on solid footing. That she'd have no trouble getting the loans necessary to expand the gallery and open another in New York.

Those dreams were gone now, and she desperately needed to talk to someone—not just about her finances, but about her dying marriage and about a world that was slipping crazily out-of-control. She'd thought about contacting a therapist, but she'd been down that road before with less than satisfying results. She knew several art therapists, but they were friends, and she didn't want them involved in her personal business. Her friends and colleagues knew nothing of her situation, and that's how she wanted it to stay—at least for now. Friends were loyal to a point, but they easily forgot their loyalties when the gossip wheels started turning. And the self-help books she'd relied on? Totally useless. She pulled the latest one out of a desk drawer and after rifling through it, tossed it in the waste paper basket. There—she was done with that author and with others as well.

Her gaze drifted to the card Reverend Regina Ray had given her. The reverend had been at the gallery during the upheaval with Rupert March, and she'd reached out to Madeleine after Nina's murder. She'd told her to call if she needed a listening ear, but so far Madeleine hadn't followed through. She knew that Reggie's church members faced life-and-death challenges on a daily basis, and it was hard to believe that the reverend would have much sympathy for a white, upper-middle class woman mourning the loss of financial security. But the falling apart of a marriage and the disillusionment and heartbreak that followed? Surely, she'd have compassion for that.

Madeleine picked up the phone and put it down again. How was any of this possible? Up until now she'd lived a golden life. She and Sid had two handsome sons, two lovely daughters-in law and five beautiful grandchildren whose college funds they'd promised to endow. They were a shining couple. Well-connected in the community and respected by their many friends and colleagues. Sid had preferred not to retire from the university where he'd taught for over 35 years—supposedly because he loved his work and his students. In reality, he needed the income.

Toughen up, she told herself. She'd faced crises before and had come through them with flying colors. But none like this. Never anything like this.

The phone rang, but she paid scant attention to the message rattling in the background. At least until a sentence caught her ear. "I'm interested in a piece called *Little Women*," the speaker said. "Please call me at…"

Madeleine snatched up the phone. Yes, the caller was inquiring about Amy March's artwork, and she seemed disappointed when Madeleine explained that while she'd had several offers, the item wasn't for sale. Even so, the caller raised the most recent bid by a thousand dollars. Notoriety, she said. The provenance of the piece and the story that went with it made it highly desirable. The call ended with Madeleine promising to notify her if the status of the artwork changed.

Afterward, Madeleine sent Amy a text—the fifth one so far describing interest in her work. Once that was done, she dove into the items on her to-do list and was still at it two hours later when the buzzer sounded from the front of the gallery. She let out a sigh. Someone—a reporter or a nosy neighbor—hoping to wring the last bit of dirt from the story of Rupert March's confrontation with Nina.

Glancing up at the monitor, she saw, not a reporter but Fern March. What was she doing here? The gallery was closed today, and Madeleine wasn't about to make an exception for this woman who, judging from her frown, was here to cause trouble. And then she reconsidered. Better to find out what this was about rather than risk an unpleasant scene when customers were around.

She strode to the front of the gallery and opened the door, determined to make quick work of things and send Fern on her way. "Good morning, Mrs. March," she began, her voice icy. "What brings you here this morning?"

Instead of answering, Fern, sniffled once or twice, looked sadly at Madeleine, sniffled some more, and then, to Madeleine's surprise, she threw her arms around her, nearly knocking her off her feet. A jumble of words escaped Fern's lips, but their meaning was lost in an avalanche of sobs.

Madeleine cringed at the histrionics—this was so not her style. She was about to push Fern away, but kinder spirits prevailed. "Come inside," she said as she gently extricated herself from the woman's embrace. "We'll sit in my office and once you're settled, you can tell me what this is about."

Nodding, Fern reached in her bag and pulled out a tissue. "I'm so embarrassed," she whimpered. "I never intended to make a scene, but something came over me and now..." She fell silent as she followed Madeleine to her office and sank into a chair. "Rupert doesn't know I'm here," she said, dabbing at her eyes and setting her gold bracelets jangling. "Promise you won't tell him."

Madeleine laughed at the remark. "There's no danger of that. Your husband and I travel in different circles. I doubt our paths will cross."

"But they will. Sooner, rather than later."

The laughter died on Madeleine's lips. It was bad enough finding Fern on her doorstep. But Rupert March? The thought was too terrible to contemplate.

"One of the reasons I stopped by," Fern continued between sniffles, "is that Amy said buyers have been calling the gallery to ask about her art project. As much as I despise the thing, I was touched by how happy the news made her. And that's partly why I'm here. I wanted to thank you for helping her through this difficult time."

The words lifted Madeleine's spirits. Amy'd been completely mortified when her father started shouting at Nina, and before the dust had a chance to settle on that incident, Nina was dead. Madeleine's heart went out to Amy, and she was glad the news she'd shared had encouraged her at this difficult time.

"Well then," she said to Fern, "you'll be pleased to know that there's been another offer. We're up to $12,000. Quite a lot for a piece by a high school student."

Fern shuddered and smiled at the same time. "Who would want that ugly thing on their walls?"

"You'd be surprised. One bidder wants to hang it in a university women's center. Another collects feminist art. Others are intrigued by the panel's connection to the Nina Powell story. All this media coverage has made Amy's work well-known and highly desirable."

The remark elicited a frown. "So, you're saying the interest has more to do with the piece's notoriety than with Amy's talent?"

"That's often the case with iconic works of art," Madeleine explained. "Certain pieces appear at a pivotal moment in history and their value increases accordingly."

"It doesn't matter," Fern said with a shrug. "Rupert will never allow it to be sold—not at any price. He's convinced that Nina coached Amy into creating it as of publicly embarrassing him—payback for disagreements they've had it the past. I understand how he feels, but I couldn't bring myself to dash Amy's hopes when she told me about the offers. Instead, I told her I was proud of her and thrilled that her work was being so well received. To my surprise, what followed was the best conversation we've had in years. She talked about her hopes for the future and her dreams of going to art school next year. And she begged me to talk to her father because he's insisting that she pursue a more practical field of study."

Madeleine understood Rupert March's concerns. She'd watched plenty of talented young artists invest a fortune in their educations only to set aside their training in favor of more stable careers. But given her father's wealth, it was unlikely that Amy would struggle to earn a living, no matter what field she chose.

"I can relate to what Amy's going through," Fern said sadly. "Believe it or not, I was a lot like her when I was young—always drawing and painting and dreaming of being an artist. My parents insisted I study something 'practical,' so I set my dreams aside and became a teacher instead. I liked teaching, but my favorite part of the job wasn't the children or the subject matter—it was the hours spent making illustrations for the bulletin boards in my second-grade classroom and creating sets for our school productions.

"But this isn't about me," she was quick to add. "It's about Amy. She'd love to sell her work and see it go to someone who appreciates it."

"I'm sure that could be arranged. All I need is the go-ahead."

Storm clouds moved in again, threatening to unleash another round of tears. "It's not that simple. Just this morning my husband spoke about having it hauled out of here and burned."

Madeleine pictured Rupert March storming into her office, wresting the keys to the storage room from her hands and dragging the piece out the door to a waiting truck. Could that happen? Not if she had anything to say about it.

"Tell him from me," she said sternly, "that the artists in my gallery sign a contract guaranteeing that work will be released only to the person who created it or to a buyer who pays in full."

"I don't doubt that, but Rupert's lawyers will find a loophole. They always do."

"Let them try. And if your husband dares to show up and

make a scene, I'll call the police."

Fern dabbed at her eyes and looked away. "It's hard to believe that our lives have come to this. Rupert doted on Amy when she was little. Everything she said or did brought a smile to his face. But now? Now they can't say a nice word to each other. But that doesn't mean he doesn't still adore her. In fact, he worries about her to the point of obsession."

The words tugged at Madeleine's heart. Being a parent wasn't easy, and it seemed to get more difficult as each new generation pushed the boundaries that reined in the prior generation. Lately it seemed to her that there were precious few boundaries left to push.

"I have two grown sons," she said gently, "and there were plenty of sleepless nights as they navigated their teen years. Raising kids is a risky business, a fact we don't realize until we're in over our heads. Sometimes we need a bit of outside help, and if you'll give me a moment…"

She opened a desk drawer and rooted through odds and ends of paper clips, rubber bands, and memos. "A friend of mine is an art therapist. She's been quite successful at guiding creative individuals through rough spots in their lives. Who knows—a few sessions and the two of you might even come up with a way for you to fulfill your childhood ambitions."

Fern laughed at the suggestion. "I doubt that. I don't actually have talent. It was just a silly dream I had when I was young."

"It's not silly at all," Madeleine argued. "The dreams we have when we're young are road maps pointing us toward the adults we're meant to be." She found the art therapist's card and handed it to Fern. "If you call, be sure to tell her I sent you."

Fern took the card and got to her feet. "I can't thank you enough for taking the time to listen. And be sure to keep Amy up-to-date on the interest in her work."

Madeleine showed Fern to the door and watched her walk down the block. Over the years she'd known plenty of women in Fern's situation. Creative types who, instead of developing their talents, devoted their energy to meeting other people's expectations while ignoring their own. The results were always the same. A perplexing sadness and an anxiety that never seemed to go away.

Back in her office she thought again of Reverend Ray. Like Madeleine, Reggie had witnessed firsthand the explosive confrontation between Nina Powell and Rupert March. Perhaps that could be the springboard for conversation, and if the dialogue went well, Madeleine might feel free to open up in a way she couldn't with her peers.

She stared long and hard at the card on her desk. Should she do this? Should she call a relative stranger and invite her into her world? What was she so afraid of?

She knew the answer. She was afraid of being exposed. Over the years she'd sculpted an image of herself and placed it on a pedestal for the world to see. She was an artist. A scholar. A woman in full control of her life. But the pedestal was crumbling beneath her feet, and she felt herself groping wildly for something—anything—to slow the collapse.

Tears welled up in her eyes, threatening to break free. Ridiculous, she told herself. Crying was an escape mechanism for children and neurotic women like Fern March. Madeleine was above all that. Or was she?

A tear splashed onto the desk and then another. A torrent was building, a river threatening to breach its banks. Seeing only one way to hold it back, she picked up Reggie's card and reached for her phone.

Twenty-five

"Good news," Amy shouted when Brooke entered the auditorium on Monday evening. "Your coffin's here!"

The words were jarring. "Could you rephrase that please?"

"Ha! Dracula's coffin. The undertaker dropped it off this afternoon. It's in the prop room."

Brooke glanced at the kids sprawled across the stage, their eyes fixed on their phones. They'd never notice if rehearsal started a few minutes late.

The backstage area was dark except for a light escaping from beneath the prop room door. She opened it and found Erik Rimmer standing in front of two tech kids seated on the closed coffin. They appeared to be studying a document of some kind, and when Erik noticed Brooke, he grabbed the papers from one of the kids and stuck them behind his back.

"What'cha got there?" she asked.

"Nothing."

"If it's nothing, why are you hiding it?"

"Because I feel like it."

Personally, Brooke could have cared less what kind of garbage Erik and his friends were looking at, but she was sick and tired of Erik's attitude. "Hand it over. Now."

"Make me."

"Listen, Dracula. What you do outside of school is your business, but at the moment you're on my turf, and I get to call the shots."

"Is that so? Well, try this on for size. My mom gave a lot of money toward building this auditorium. Seems to me you're on my turf."

One of the tech kids spoke up. "Knock it off, Erik. Just give it to her."

He turned around to glare at the boy, and that gave Brooke the opportunity she needed. A quick lunge, and the papers were in her hands. Erik reached out to retrieve them, but she pivoted and left him clutching at the air. She expected a bunch of nasty photos downloaded from an internet porn site, but what she saw was even more disturbing. Swastikas, dozens of them, surrounding the front-page of a makeshift newsletter.

"What is this?" she asked, her voice shaky.

The boys didn't answer.

"The swastikas? What's this all about?"

"Nothing," one of the kids answered. "It's been floating around the school all day."

"That's right," Erik agreed. "We have no idea where it came from, do we?"

Instead of answering, the boys shrugged and looked away.

"Dr. Pierce needs to see this," Brooke said. "And the police as well."

Erik retained his defiant posture, but the two tech kids looked like they were about to puke. None of them said a word as Brooke headed out the door and hurried across the stage. "Run the Act Two lines," she shouted at Amy. "I'll be right back."

Jocelyn Fisher was packing up for the day when Brooke arrived in the main office.

"Is Dr. Pierce in?"

"Yes, but he's in a meeting with…"

She didn't wait for Jocelyn to finish. Instead, she rushed over to the headmaster's door and barged into his office without knocking. He looked up in surprise, and so did Schoolboard President Don Petrakis, Guidance Counselor Gretchen Coates and School Psychologist Ron Webster.

"We're in the middle of a meeting," Pierce said, his voice testy. "I'll be with you as soon as we're finished."

She held out the papers she'd confiscated. "You need to see this."

"Can't it wait?"

When she shook her head, he let out a sigh and fished his reading glasses from his pocket. "Really, I can't imagine what's so important that…" His jaw dropped as he looked at the front page. After rifling through the newsletter, he handed it to Don Petrakis who leafed through the document and handed it to Gretchen Coates. When she showed it to Ron Webster, he took one look and grabbed it from her hands.

"This is terrible!" he exclaimed. "Swastikas? Skinhead rock bands? Aryan youth rallies? Directions for recruiting other kids into the movement?" He pointed to a series of staples running down the lefthand side. "Someone threw this garbage together and ran it off on an inkjet printer. Assuming it was printed here in the building, the police IT experts should be able to comb through the network and find out who's responsible."

The headmaster shook his head. "There's no reason to assume it was printed here at school. Not when a student could just have easily run it off at home. We'll conduct our own investigation, and if we come up empty-handed, we'll ask the police to take a look."

"But sir," Webster persisted. "If there's a…"

Pierce held up a hand to silence him. "Once the police are involved, it's only a matter of time until the story leaks to the press. Can you imagine the uproar if word gets out about Neo-Nazi literature circulating through the building?" He looked to the schoolboard president for support, but Petrakis averted his eyes and said nothing.

"With all due respect," Webster continued after a lengthy pause, "there's a strong possibility that Nina Powell was the victim of a hate crime. This document…" he held it up and pointed to the swastikas, "…could be the evidence that leads to her killer."

The headmaster said nothing. Instead, he stared at his desk and fidgeted with a paperclip. The others exchanged glances, seemingly perplexed as to why their leader seemed unwilling to initiate a completely appropriate forensic audit of the school's computer network.

Finally, Pierce glanced up at Brooke. "What students were involved in this incident?"

"Two kids from the tech crew. And Erik Rimmer."

Pierce threw the paper clip on the desk and swiveled his chair toward the window. Brooke could appreciate his dismay. He'd soon be calling one of his most generous donors to inform her that, not only was her son an obnoxious jerk, he was also a Nazi.

"Thank you for bringing this to my attention," he said without turning around. "I'll report the incident to the police and to the parents of the boys involved."

Brooke left the office, her thoughts roiling. Ted was right after all. There were neo-Nazis at Sussex Academy, and she'd just busted them. Other thoughts assailed her as well. Was this the nasty secret Jane Acker had referred to on Saturday? A secret so dark that it had to be kept from the police?

Back in the auditorium, Count Dracula's sullen mood cast

a damper over the rehearsal, and in spite of Brooke's attempts at motivating the rest of the cast, they kept bungling the few lines they'd managed to memorize. Every now and then, she caught Erik glaring at her, his eyes filled with vengeance, but she ignored the unspoken threat. If she turned up dead, he'd be at the top of the suspect list. He was smart enough to have figured that out.

Tom-the-Rent-a-Cop showed up at nine, but when he called out a greeting, Brooke pretended not to hear. She was still annoyed that he'd told the information specialist about her moonlit meeting with Chris Van Auken, and while she knew it was childish to ignore him, she was sick and tired of having to act like a professional in every situation that presented itself.

Tom left to escort the kids to their cars, and after closing things up, Brooke headed to the prop room to inspect the coffin, a water-damaged demo model that had languished for years in the basement of a local funeral home. She opened the lid and pictured Erik Rimmer on the red satin lining, his eyes closed and a stake through his heart. If that didn't elicit a standing ovation from the faculty of Sussex Academy, she didn't know what would.

"Fine looking coffin," a voice said from behind her.

Turning, she saw Tom in the open doorway. "Not bad as coffin's go."

"You ready to head out now, or would you like me to wait around?"

"No need to wait. I'll see myself out."

He raised an eyebrow. "It's my job to keep you safe."

"I'll be fine. Don't give it a thought."

"Okay then." He said goodnight with a nod and left to continue his rounds.

Once he was gone, Brooke locked the prop room door and left the building. A chilly breeze rippled through her hair, and up above, thin wisps of clouds skittered across the moon. No doubt about it—fall was in the air. She stood on the stoop and glanced at the vehicles that remained in the faculty lot. Van Auken's Harley wasn't among them. When he'd told her the party was over, he'd meant exactly what he said.

A noise in the distance sent her thoughts racing back to the night at Peggy's Tavern. According to Detective Radley, the person who'd slashed her tires had done so as a way of telling her to mind her own business. She'd tried to do just that, but things kept happening to drag her back into the investigation. Like tonight's incident with Erik and his friends. Did those swastikas implicate the boys in Nina's murder?

She recalled the folders in the guidance counselor's office—the ones crammed with reports of Erik's noncompliance over the years. Was there more to his story than a list of personality and learning disorders? Was Erik dangerous when provoked? Did he kill Nina as an act of vengeance? Had Brooke handed him another reason to seek vengeance?

She thought of Tom-the-Rent-a-Cop and the gun at his waist, and then she thought of the look of vengeance in Erik's eyes. Should she go back in the building and tell Tom she'd changed her mind—that she'd welcome an escort after all? She pictured his reaction. A warm-hearted smile that showed he was happy to be of service.

The idea seemed sensible, but when she tried the door, it didn't budge. No problem—she had a key. She dug around in her bag, trying to find it in the clutter, and then froze at the sound of a car door opening and closing in the student parking lot, just around the corner from where she stood.

Had Erik lingered after rehearsal to have a word with her? Were his friends with him? Had one of them been keeping watch to let Erik know when she left the building? Would they gang up on her before she made it to her car?

She took off at a run, her heart in her throat—the worst place for hearts to be when vampires roamed the night. At the sound of approaching footsteps, her fingers groped wildly in her bag. The keys were there somewhere—they had to be.

Yes! She yanked them free and pushed the button on the key fob. The car lit up, but as she reached for the door, the footsteps drew closer and powerful hands grabbed her from behind.

Twenty-six

She screamed and drove an elbow into her assailant's gut. To her surprise, he let out an oomph and released her, but the fight wasn't over—not when he was free to strike again. She spun around, ready to slam a knee in his crotch but stopped when she caught a glimpse of his face. It wasn't Erik Rimmer. It was Ted Roslyn.

"Ted, you idiot! You scared me out of my wits!"

"I sent a text. I said I'd be waiting in the parking lot."

"Oh, really? Did it ever occur to you that I was running a rehearsal? That I turned off my phone so we wouldn't be interrupted?"

He shrugged his shoulders, his expression sheepish. "Oops."

"Oops? Is that all you can say? Do you have any idea…" Brooke's voice trailed off as she struggled to catch her breath. "Would you mind explaining what you're doing here?"

"Not at all. My friend got back to me about the location of the Nazi compound. They hold a powwow every Monday night, and I'm headed there to check it out. I thought you'd like to join me."

She stared at him in disbelief. "You thought I'd like to join you for a powwow at a Nazi compound? Are you out of your mind?"

He seemed surprised by her reaction. "I thought you wanted to know which kids were mixed up in this stuff. I don't know one from the other, so I figured you'd tag along and see who you could identify. Looks like I was wrong."

He left it at that and walked away.

Brooke watched his departure, her mind filled with images of the swastikas she'd confiscated. Another image rose to the surface as well. Thor's hammer on Van Auken's Harley. Was Van Auken mixed up in this stuff? If so, would he be at the compound tonight? And what about Erik? Would he be there as well? The idea would have seemed ridiculous a few days ago, but after seeing that newsletter…

"Wait for me," she shouted. "I'm coming with you."

▾ ▾ ▾

They left Brooke's car at an all-night diner and drove off together in Ted's Jeep. The journey took them in a northerly direction with the roads growing increasingly narrow as they left strip malls and tract houses behind. Before long, the paved surfaces gave way to rutted dirt lanes that wove through acres of forest. They passed an occasional house or run-down farm, but mostly there were trees and lots of them.

After a dozen axle-breaking miles, Ted pulled over to the shoulder and killed the engine. Reaching into the back seat, he pulled out a camouflage jacket similar to the one he was wearing and handed to her. As she put it on, he reached across and fished a pair of binoculars from the glove compartment. "Night-vision," he explained. "Not the latest military tech, but adequate for our purposes." He reached into the glove compartment a second time and brought out an aerosol can. "Pepper spray. Stick it in your pocket, and while you're at it…" He reached into the back seat and held up a black ski mask.

Brooke eyed it skeptically. "We're robbing a Seven-Eleven?"

"That would be child's play compared to this."

Ted's grin did little to assure her that he hadn't meant exactly what he said. By now the clouds had thickened, blotting out the moonlight, the silent woods lay thick and impenetrable on all sides, and Brooke was beginning to have second thoughts about this venture. She wondered if Ted would mind if she waited in the Jeep while he checked things out, but then she thought of Chris Van Auken. If he was a Nazi recruiter, she wanted to know about it. And if Count Dracula was part of this operation, she wanted to know that as well.

"So, what's our mission?" she asked, tucking her hair beneath the ski mask and trying to sound braver than she felt.

Ted pointed into the trees. "The compound's about a quarter mile in that direction. We'll head closer and study it through the binoculars to see if we recognize anyone."

"And then?"

"And then we'll leave."

Okay, so that didn't sound so bad. They fell silent as they headed into the forest, but even so, the night was alive with sounds. Crickets chirping. Small woodland creatures scurrying about. The breeze moaning a dirge. An owl hooting terrifyingly in the distance. And the shuffling sounds she and Ted were making—did the Nazis hear them trudging through the undergrowth?

"Lift your feet up high," Ted instructed.

"What for?"

"To avoid trip flares."

She had no idea what that meant. "Explain."

"They alert folks to trespassers. Snag one with your foot

and it shoots up in the sky like a rocket. At best, they're flares. At worst, they're explosives. So, be careful, okay?"

Great. She should have listened to the voice of reason back there in the Sussex Academy parking lot. Instead, she'd heeded the call of the wild, and now, rather than being at home with the doors and windows locked, she was trudging through an Aryan mine field, deep in the bowels of redneck hell. And she had no one to blame but herself.

She and Ted high-stepped it along the trail until they came to a clearing among the evergreens. In the distance an A-frame thrust its peaked roof into the starless sky.

Ted raised his binoculars. "I've got a great view through the front window."

"Recognize anyone?"

"Nope. There's a bunch of deer heads on the wall, but the room looks deserted. The meeting must be around back. Let's go closer."

Brooke wasn't sure about that, but since they'd come this far, she decided to see the mission through to its conclusion. They made their way through the trees, high-stepping all the way, until they were about 100 yards from the house. To their right, a parking lot overflowed with pickups, SUVs and an occasional Hummer.

Ted reached into his pocket and pulled out a couple of cell-phone-looking things. "Walkie-talkies," he whispered. He gave her one and handed her the night-vision binoculars. "I'm going around back. Keep an eye on the place and contact me if there's trouble."

She kept the binoculars trained on Ted as he crept beneath the lower edge of the A-frame roof and disappeared from sight, leaving her alone behind enemy lines. She shifted her focus from the rear of the property to the deer gazing at her through the wide front window. What kind of ammo were they guarding? Hunting knives? Rifles? Assault weapons? Grenades and exotic ammo obtained on the internet? She reached into her pocket and ran her fingers over the can of pepper spray. She was glad to have it, but she would have preferred something more powerful—like a surface-to-air missile.

Hearing a noise, she pivoted toward the parking lot as a white sedan eased into a space, looking oddly out of place among the pick-ups and SUVs. She trained the binoculars on the driver's side door, and to her surprise, Detective James Burleigh got out and headed toward the A-frame. What was he doing here, she wondered, and why was he wearing jeans and a flannel jacket instead of his usual gray suit? And why was he here alone? Where was his sidekick?

The detective sauntered over to the building and glanced around as though enchanted by the sights and sounds of the night. At least that's what Brooke hoped. The other possibility was that he'd heard Ted playing peek-a-boo at the back of the compound and was about to investigate.

She pulled the walkie-talkie from her pocket, ready to alert Ted, and then she put it back again. A lot of good these spy toys were doing her. If she tried to contact Ted, Burleigh would hear and be after her in a flash. Under the circumstances, the best she could do was hunker down in the darkness and watch through the binoculars as the detective sniffed like a Rottweiler at the frosty air. Things must have seemed okay in Nazi Land, because he stopped sniffing, and with the ease of a regular visitor, he climbed the steps to the deck, opened the front door and strolled inside.

A restful silence settled over the compound, but before Brooke could say, "All quiet on the Western Front," she heard a loud crackle followed by a thud. The sound came from behind the A-frame, and when she shifted the binoculars, she saw Ted sprinting toward her.

"I climbed a tree and looked inside," he shouted. "The limb broke!"

Brooke didn't wait to see if he was all right. Instead, she took off at a run in the direction of the Jeep. Ted was right behind her, and so, apparently were the Nazis—she could hear them shouting and cursing as they thundered across the deck and down the steps. It wasn't hard to imagine what would happen if they got hold of her. Torture. Rape. Murder. Her body burned, her ashes tossed aside and her existence erased forever. Saddest of all—Uncle Nelson—alone and grieving her inexplicable disappearance.

And then, as if confirming her fears, Ted let out a whoop. "He's got me!"

She whipped around, and there in front of her was Detective Burleigh. The older man was no match for Ted, but even so, he'd slowed things down, and at any second the Nazis would descend on Ted and rip him limb from limb. There was no way she could let that happen.

Reaching into her pocket, she pulled out the pepper spray and blasted it in Burleigh's face. The detective let out a howl and doubled over, his fists in his eyes. He'd been a breeze to take down, but his Nazi comrades ate raw steak for breakfast and twisted steel with their bare hands, and there was no way Brooke wanted to tangle with them.

She took off again, but Ted seemed to be lagging farther and farther behind. Was it any wonder? He'd just fallen out of a tree and was lucky both legs weren't broken. "Run!" she shouted over her shoulder. "I know it hurts, but run!"

They plodded along, their breath escaping in misty clouds, and then Ted let loose with another yell. Brooke wondered how many Nazis she could level with a can of pepper spray, but to her relief, Ted hadn't been captured. He'd stumbled over a trip flare and sent it soaring like a Roman candle into the sky. There was momentary confusion in enemy ranks as the Nazis stopped to yell and curse at the pyrotechnics playing out above their heads.

Brooke resumed her run, but by this time she was panting for air and her lungs felt like they'd burst. Just as she thought she couldn't take another step, she rounded a bend and saw the Jeep directly ahead of her. "Faster," she called over her shoulder. "We're almost…"

She let out a scream as a tall, bearded madman burst out of the trees and came at her, his eyes blazing hellfire and his large meaty hands reaching for her throat.

A single squirt of pepper spray brought the monster to his knees.

She and Ted raced for the Jeep and sped off in a spray of stones and dirt. As they gained speed, she kept her eyes on the side mirror and the Nazis chasing after them. There was a lot of profanity and a lot of rock throwing, but before long, their pursuers were reduced to hyperactive specks in the distance.

"That was a close call back there with Detective Burleigh," Brooke said once her vocal cords were up to the task.

"You're not kidding," Ted agreed breathlessly. "But I'm glad the old geezer showed up. Without him, we'd be dead by now."

Brooke found the remark puzzling. "Burleigh didn't save us. I did. Pepper spray—remember?"

"No doubt about it—you were terrific," Ted acknowledged. "But you can bet those Nazis thugs were toting tons of fire-power—more than you could have handled with a measly can of pepper spray. Why didn't they use it, you ask? Because no one in his right mind commits double homicide in front of a cop—even if the cop happens to be a Nazi comrade in arms. It's too big a risk.

"Having said that," he continued, "allow me to give credit where credit's due. You're a sharp shooter with that pepper spray. I'll have to call you Annie Oakley from now on."

"And what about you climbing that tree?" Brooke added. "That was a brave move. See anything interesting before the limb broke?"

"Burleigh's the only one I recognized. But here's a question for you. Was he following up on a lead, or is this how he spends every Monday night when he's not working a case?"

The question was a good one, but Brooke had no answer. "I'd love to find out," she said.

"Me too. But you're going to have to get someone else to do the reconnaissance for you. Once was enough for me."

Twenty-seven

The phone jolted Brooke out of a deep sleep. She reached for her cell and glanced at the time. It wasn't even seven a.m. Why was Jocelyn Fisher calling so early?

"Dr. Pierce needs to speak to you in his office half-an-hour before rehearsal," Jocelyn announced, her voice way too shrill for this hour of the morning. "He says its urgent."

Brooke yawned and waited for the day to come into focus. "Did he tell you what it's about?"

"Nobody tells me anything."

Dr. Pierce was waiting when Brooke knocked on his door late that afternoon. And so was Detective Burleigh, his eyes still bloodshot from last night's jolt of pepper spray. For a panicked moment, Brooke wondered if he'd recognized her at the Nazi compound. Was that the purpose of this meeting—to confront her and demand an explanation? Was she about to be fired? Could she be that lucky?

Neither of them said a word about firing her, and they didn't mention the Nazi compound. Instead, Burleigh asked for a play-by-play description of yesterday's incident with Erik and his buddies. Brooke told her story, but the detective said little in response, and she wondered if this interview was a mere formality to corroborate details he'd already heard. Or maybe he was hoping to minimize the Nazi issue lest his involvement come to light. Whatever the case, Brooke would never be able to trust him. A shame, because a year ago, she'd held him in high regard.

The topic shifted from the newsletter to Chris Van Auken and the mentoring sessions he led with various students, including Erik Rimmer. Brooke acknowledged that while she knew these sessions existed, she had no idea what they were about. From there, Burleigh hit her with questions about Van Auken being too familiar with his female students. She admitted she'd heard the rumors but had no idea if they were true.

After that, Burleigh announced that she was free to go, but as she rose to leave, Dr. Pierce called her back.

"I assigned Erik and his friends to in-school suspension for the day. That means no afterschool activities. You'll have to ask someone else to read Erik's lines."

Brooke tried not to show her elation at the thought of a rehearsal without Erik. Three hours with no sneering, no smirking and no breaking character to play chords on an air guitar. Things might actually go well for a change.

"And just so you know," Pierce continued, "I had a long talk with the boys. They've given their word of honor that they'll be more cooperative going forward."

Hah! There might be honor among thieves, but there was no honor among teenage boys with a grudge against a teacher who'd exposed them as Nazis. Even so, Brooke left the meeting with a song in her heart. For at least one night, Erik wouldn't be making her life miserable.

The song faded when Brooke stepped out of Pierce's office and saw her nemesis, Rupert March, conferring with School

Board President Don Petrakis. She tried to slip by without being noticed, but alas—it was not to be. March glanced her way and frowned, but Don Petrakis's greeting was far more cordial.

"To think we hired you to direct a play—a play and nothing more." Petrakis shook his head ruefully. "Let me say on behalf of the schoolboard that we appreciate your willingness to tackle the enormous challenges fate has thrown your way."

"Fate has nothing to do with it," March scoffed. "Everything that's happened in the last few weeks is related in one way or another to that vampire play." His gaze shifted from Petrakis to Brooke. "Under these trying circumstances, no one would fault you for resigning. In fact, doing so would force us to make the decision we've been too cowardly to make all along. We could cancel this show and put the nightmares behind us."

Petrakis placed a hand on the taller man's arm. "Now Rupert, we've been over this a thousand times. The play's the kick-off event for our bicentennial celebration. We've got a sold-out crowd both nights, and as per the saying, the show must go on."

"Bah! No good will come of it. Mark my words."

Petrakis turned apologetically to Brooke. "Hang in there, my dear. You're doing a spectacular job under very trying circumstances. And don't forget the gift certificate I gave you. You deserve a night out, so make a reservation and invite someone special to join you."

Someone special? The only someone special Brooke could think of was Uncle Nelson.

She continued on her way and found Amy waiting at the auditorium door. "Something terrible's going on" the girl whispered. "Mr. Van Auken didn't show up this morning, and Ms. Fisher was going crazy trying to find teachers to cover his classes. Dr. Pierce kept Erik and his friends locked in the office all day and wouldn't let anyone talk to them—not even at lunchtime. And the detectives were here, roaming the halls and dragging kids to the office to answer questions." She seized

Brooke's arm. "I'm scared, and so is everybody else."

Brooke let out a sigh. So much for the upbeat rehearsal she'd been anticipating. She called the cast to order, but with each bungled line and each missed cue, she felt herself longing for a return to normalcy. The thought was intoxicating. No murders. No vampires. No detectives. No Nazis. Just normalcy. Was that too much to ask?

And then she remembered what normalcy looked like. Normalcy meant missing Karl every minute of every day.

Twenty-eight

Ted congratulated himself for completing his early morning run. He'd taken a break yesterday after his fall from that Nazi tree on Monday night, but here it was—Wednesday—and already he was back in the game. He skipped the weightlifting, and after a shower, got down to business with a cup of coffee. He had a video to edit and upload, but that could wait until he'd scanned the headlines.

Breaking News! the first one read. *Suspect Named in Nina Powell's Murder!*

Wow! How about that. Action at last. He clicked on the link and brought up a local news website.

"Police have uncovered new evidence that links popular Sussex Academy history teacher Chris Van Auken to the murder of Nina Powell. Some of this evidence includes hate literature and inappropriate photos of teenage girls found under his log-in in the school's server. The suspect remains at large and should be considered armed and dangerous."

A photo appeared on the screen of a bare-chested, muscular guy in a Viking helmet, a shield in one hand and a battle axe in the other. Armed and dangerous to be sure.

Ted wondered how Brooke was handling the news. Should he call her? Of course, he should; it was only right.

"I heard about your colleague," he said when she picked up. "Are you okay?"

There was no answer.

"Wanna grab some coffee and talk?" He braced himself for excuses. She was too upset. Too overwhelmed. Too busy. Too this or that.

"I was awake most of the night," she said after a long pause. "Bad nerves, I suppose. But coffee? No thanks. It will make me even jumpier than I already am."

"Decaf then."

"Decaf won't wake me up."

Okay, so it sounded like coffee—decaf or otherwise— wasn't exactly a winning ticket. But he suspected that coffee wasn't the real issue. Brooke was blaming him for her near-death experience at the Nazi compound. And with good reason. He'd promised a quick look at the place followed by a silent retreat. Thanks to the tree limb breaking when it did, things had turned out otherwise.

He was about to say he'd catch up with her later—meaning probably never—when she surprised him with an alternative suggestion.

"I have a gift certificate for dinner at Don Giovanni's. If you're free Friday night, we could meet there after rehearsal. I realize 9:30's kind of late, so I totally understand if you can't make it."

Ted was stunned. Don Giovanni's was a five-star establishment with the price tags to match. Definitely not the sort of place he was known to frequent. "Sure," he said casually, as though he got invitations like this every day. "That sounds great."

"I'll make a reservation. There's a lot to talk about."

They hung up, and he stood in silence, staring at his phone. A reservation? Did that make this a date? It had been a long time since he'd been on one of those.

▾ ▾ ▾

Brooke tossed her phone aside. What was she thinking, asking Ted to meet her for dinner? The words had slipped out, probably because she was desperate to talk to someone who wasn't part of life at Sussex Academy. Someone who, while interested, had no skin in the game. Ted fit the part perfectly.

The phone rang again. "Can you believe it?" receptionist Jocelyn Fisher shrieked. "Chris—a murderer and a white supremacist? We're all traumatized, Dr. Pierce, most of all. And that's why I'm calling. He cancelled afterschool activities. Rehearsal will resume tomorrow at the usual time."

"But we can't afford to miss a rehearsal," Brooke argued. "We're already behind schedule."

"Any rehearsal tonight would be a complete waste of time. The students are hysterical, the media's circling like sharks, and we had to call in extra security to keep reporters from storming the building. Trust me, you don't want to be here."

Okay, so maybe cancelling the rehearsal made sense. What didn't make sense was trying to direct a play under these conditions.

Brooke wrapped up the call and sank into the sofa cushions. Her fears and suspicions about Van Auken had come true—all of them. She closed her eyes and tried to calm herself, but when she opened them again, it seemed like the walls were closing in. She needed to escape this tiny, miserable, apartment and breathe fresh air. It hardly mattered where she went—she just needed to get away.

In a matter of minutes, she was out the door and riding the elevator to the ground floor. As she fled the building, a reporter appeared out of nowhere.

"You and Mr. Van Auken have been seen together," the woman shouted. "Any idea where he is?"

A youngish guy emerged from a row of parked cars. "How would you describe your relationship with Chris Van Auken? Friendship, or something more?"

"Has he been in touch?" yelled a third. "Did he reveal his motive for killing Nina Powell?"

Brooke raced for her car and sped out of the lot, her eyes shifting from the road to the rearview mirror and back again. She finally relaxed when it became clear that no one was following her, but by then, she was miles from home. It didn't matter where she ended up, she decided, as long as there was open space and no reporters. But as she drove, a destination came to mind.

Thirty minutes later, she walked through the Infinity Gate at Columcille Megalith Park. Sometimes referred to as Pennsylvania's Stonehenge, the sprawling retreat was a tribute to the Scottish island of Iona, a place once marked with "giants' circles"—rings of enormous standing stones. Similar giants' circles now dotted the hills of Columcille.

She crossed the wide grassy lawn, past Oran's Bell Tower and on to St. Columba's Chapel, an octagonal stone building at the edge of a patch of forest. Turning left, she climbed a hill to a dolmen, a towering Pi-shaped structure called Thor's Gate. She thought back to the first time she'd caught sight of Thor's hammer on Van Auken's Harley. That's why she'd come to this spot—to say goodbye to the person she thought she knew and come to terms with a reality she'd suspected but had been unable to accept.

Feeling drained, she sank down in the grass and leaned against one of the two boulders supporting the overhead lintel. The autumn sun was warm on her face, the breeze cool as it played with her hair. It was quiet here. There was space to think—or better yet, not to think, but to allow her thoughts to unravel and slip away. She breathed in the afternoon warmth and as she closed her eyes, the tension seemed to melt from her shoulders.

She woke with a start, uncertain as to how long she'd been asleep. It seemed that an unseen presence was with her in that vast lonely space, and for a moment she expected to see Van Auken striding up the hill, a grin on his face as he announced that—ha, ha—it was all a joke. He wasn't a white supremacist, and he wasn't too familiar with his female students, and he hadn't killed Nina Powell.

But there was no Van Auken. Only silence.

She rose to her feet and descended the hill to St. Columba's Chapel. Finding the door unlocked, she slipped inside. The surrounding walls breathed out a mossy dampness while on the stone altar, a solitary candle cast its glow into the shadows. She would have prayed if she were so inclined—it was that kind of place and that kind of moment. But she wasn't so inclined. Instead, she lingered to soak in the presence of something ancient, and then she ventured back to the world she'd left behind.

Twenty-nine

Thursday arrived and with it, Brooke's appointment with the Vampire Expert Extraordinaire. She'd been tempted to cancel—she was in no mood to listen to some self-proclaimed expert lecture her about things she could just as easily look up on the internet. But since her uncle was keen on having her meet this guy, she decided to get it over with. At the worst it would be a waste of time. At best it would be a distraction from the horrors of life at Sussex Academy.

At a little before two she arrived at the campus where Dr. Rodney Cavendish served as chair of the music department. She found his office, and when she knocked on the door, a tall muscular man opened it and greeted her with a broad smile. "Von't you come in?" he began in a cheesy imitation of Count Dracula.

She was surprised by the professor's appearance. She'd expected someone older, a contemporary of Uncle Nelson who hadn't yet retired. But the man who greeted her was a youthful fifty-something with shoulder-length salt-and-pepper hair pulled back in a ponytail. He had broad shoulders and barrel-shaped chest tapered down to slender hips and legs, making him appear top-heavy, like a genie escaping a bottle. His attire was casual—jeans and a corduroy jacket with patches on the elbows—a complete contrast to her uncle's conservative dark suits and ties.

The only source of illumination in the professor's office was a solitary candle and the weak glow filtered through stained-glass panels covering the windows. In the dusky half-light, Brooke could make out figurines of vampires, gargoyles and ravens scattered among piles of books, papers and music scores. As her eyes adjusted, she saw a quivering line of incense smoke escaping from a burner on the professor's desk. That explained the strange fragrance that assailed her nose.

She took a seat on the wine velvet chair her host offered, and although it was hard to tell in the semi-darkness, he looked familiar. Where had she seen him before?

"Your uncle tells me you've been bitten by the vampire bug." He paused for her to appreciate his pun—ha ha—and then proceeded to describe a vampire tour scheduled for semester break. Whitby, England—the setting of Bram Stoker's famous novel.

She studied his face as he spoke. She'd seen him before; she was sure of it, but she couldn't remember where. A choir concert she'd attended with her uncle? A reception afterward where they'd rubbed elbows? No—that didn't seem quite right. And then it hit her. The Celtic festival. He'd been wearing a green and black plaid kilt that day, and he'd smiled at Amy March when she handed him an envelope sealed with red wax.

In that instant Brooke's entire mission changed. She was no longer here to humor Uncle Nelson by chatting up his friend. No, she was here to figure out Dr. Rodney Cavendish's connection to Amy. She quickly formulated a strategy. She didn't want to put Cavendish on the defensive, and that meant keeping silent on everything related to Amy, Nina, and Sussex

Academy. It also meant coming up with a story to explain why her uncle encouraged this visit.

She blurted out the first thing that came to mind. "I'm editing a book about modern day vampires. I'm clueless about the subject, and Uncle Nelson thought you'd be able to provide some background."

Cavendish leaned back in his chair, his fingers laced across his broad chest. "Your uncle sent you to the right place. Where would you like to begin?"

Amy's vampire obsession seemed as good a place to start as any, as long as Brooke kept Amy's name out of it. "I've heard that people sometimes become fixated on vampires. Is that just a fad or does it go deeper than that?"

"An excellent question. For most, the fascination is a passing fad that has its origin in the latest vampire movie or television series. But for others…" His eyes narrowed as he contemplated these "others." "For others the allure goes much deeper. There are groups—cults, if you will—who pursue a vampire lifestyle, as strange as that may sound to the uninitiated."

Brooke pictured Amy's black clothes, black eyeliner, pale face makeup and creepy jewelry. Was she part of a vampire cult?

"Academics hold varying opinions on the subject," Cavendish continued. "Most regard vampires as pop culture icons and hence not suitable subjects for serious study. But I would argue otherwise."

Brooke wasn't interested in what academics thought about vampires. She wanted to know what went on with these vampire cults. "These cults you mentioned. What can you tell me about the people who participate?"

"The answer varies from person to person," the professor explained. "Some are drawn to the vampire lifestyle as a way of compensating for a sense of personal inadequacy. By donning black clothes and fangs, a person of low self-esteem is instantly transformed into a sinister creature possessed of mysterious and deadly powers. For such individuals, this transformation can be as addictive as any drug."

"But it's all pretend—right?" Brooke asked, thinking again of Amy. "These people you're referring to don't really bite people's necks and drink their blood." She hesitated, noticing the expression on the professor's face. "Or do they?"

"Another excellent question. As you might surmise, consuming human blood is the medical equivalent of playing Russian roulette. To lessen the risks, feeders must take extreme precaution to assure that the person on whom they feed is a pureblood—an individual free of bloodborne pathogens. That, of course, requires a thorough knowledge of the person's history. When that isn't possible, it's generally safe to say that the younger the subject, the less likely it is that they've been exposed to deadly diseases."

Purebloods? Young subjects? Again Brooke thought of Amy.

"There are some," Cavendish continued, "who describe the act of drinking blood as a euphoric sensual experience. Others claim it sharpens their mental perception and increases their strength. Some insist that it restores their youthful vigor. The latter concept might not be as outlandish as it sounds. Studies have shown that aging lab mice regain strength and vitality when transfused with the blood of younger specimens. And interestingly, a handful of start-up companies have developed products derived from human blood that are reputed to increase longevity. So who knows? Maybe there's a clinical basis for the vampire's craving."

Brooke was having trouble wrapping her head around all this. "So, you're telling me there are actually vampire wannabes who drink human blood?"

"Some do; some don't. There's a sub-group of vampires we call psi or psychic vampires. Finding their lives in turmoil, they turn to well-intentioned mentors and feed off their energy. Once they've taken all their mentors have to offer, they move on to other victims."

Brook thought of Amy and her need for adult mentors. Suddenly boundaries seemed more important than ever.

"There are, however," Cavendish continued, "those who claim to be both psy-vampires and blood feeders. We call them psy-blood feeders."

Okay, so this was creepy. Brooke glanced around the room at the gargoyles and the stained glass and the flickering candles and the fake human skulls that served as bookends. She wanted to wrap this up and exit this chamber of horrors, but she couldn't until she'd figured out Cavendish's connection to Amy March.

"Do you actually know any of these blood-feeding vampires?"

The professor smiled at the question. "As you can imagine, vampires aren't likely to discuss their proclivities with outsiders—for obvious reasons. But to answer your question, yes, I've met a few in my time."

He pointed to something on the wall behind Brooke. "What do you think of that painting?"

She turned, but in the dim light, the details were unclear.

"Go ahead," he urged. "Take a look."

She rose from the chair and walked over to the canvas to study it at close range. Masterfully rendered in oils, it depicted a female vampire with blood dripping from her fangs. In her arms she held a seemingly lifeless child.

"Do you like it?" Cavendish asked from directly behind her. She started at the sound of his voice. She hadn't heard him get up from his desk and slip across the room.

"Like it? I don't know what to think. It's beautiful and yet..." she hesitated, her eyes studying the vampire's face. "It's beautiful but disturbing."

"Beautiful but disturbing. That's exactly the effect I wanted."

He touched Brooke's shoulder and sent an icy shiver down her spine. She turned around to face him, but drew back at the sight of fangs protruding from his mouth.

He laughed at her distress. "Did I scare you?"

She nodded but said nothing. All this talk of blood feeders was making her skittish.

"There are people," Cavendish continued, "dentists in most instances, who manufacture and install vampire fangs—if install's the word I want. Mine, however, aren't glued down." To demonstrate the point, he popped the fangs out and placed them in his jacket pocket.

"But back to the painting. I'm sure you've heard of Nina Powell. It's one of her last masterpieces."

It took a moment for Brooke to process the statement. Nina did this painting? The circle of connections linking Cavendish to Sussex Academy was drawing tighter. But what did it mean?

"Nina designed much of our music department's publicity materials over the last few years," he remarked. "I was well acquainted with her work, and that's why I commissioned her to create this painting. My directions were clear. Find the spirit of the vampire, a creature completely consumed by its thirst for human blood. At first Nina considered the stereotypical male seducteur, but came to believe that an image of a mother draining the life from her own child most perfectly caught the vampire's obsession."

A mother draining the life from her child? Brooke stared at the painting and thought, metaphorically, of Fern March. But that wasn't fair. She knew very little about Fern—only what she'd observed on a few occasions.

"I was in a jazz band years ago with Nina's father," Cavendish said, his voice subdued. "We were close friends, and when he died, I looked out for the family. Nina was a talented artist and a remarkable human being. Her father would have been proud of her."

Suddenly overcome, he turned his face away. "I'm glad the police have a suspect. That won't bring her back, but at least there's hope that justice will be served."

Brooke was spared a response by a knock at the door. "Sorry to bother you, Jack" said a young, clean-cut guy. "A student needs to reschedule a voice lesson. Can you take a moment to help her out."

The young guy vanished, and Brooke looked at Cavendish, confused. "Jack? I thought your name was Rodney."

"Rodney Jackson Cavendish," he clarified. My friends call me Jack. Or Jay."

Jay! Brooke had nearly forgotten about the third message on Nina Powell's answering machine.

"Excuse me while I take care of this," Cavendish said. "If the phone rings, would you mind taking a message? I'm expecting a call."

He left her alone with the vampire painting and the vampire figurines and the gothic reds, blues and golds of the stained-glass panels and the scent of incense that somehow linked them all together. But the surroundings no longer seemed significant. All Brooke could think of was the message on Nina's answering machine. *Listen to me, Nina. This is my last offer.*

She tried to recall the tone of the message. At the time the words sounded threatening, but maybe they weren't meant to be. Maybe the offer he'd referred to had to do—not with sinister threats—but with the price of artwork.

But what about the note Amy gave Cavendish at the Celtic festival? What had she told him and how was it all connected?

The phone rang, and Brooke answered it. "Is Dr. Cavendish in?" A female voice asked.

"He stepped out for a moment. Can I take a message?"

The voice on the other end hesitated. "I guess that'll be all right. Tell him everyone's meeting at eleven-fifteen tonight at the pit."

"Of course. And who should I say called?"

Again a hesitation. "Mordonna. Just tell him Mordonna called."

Mordonna? What kind of name was that?

The caller hung up.

Wait a minute.

Brooke knew that voice. It didn't belong to someone named Mordonna. It belonged to Amy March.

▼ ▼ ▼

Cavendish returned and announced that their meeting was regrettably at an end—he had a class in fifteen minutes. Brooke gave him the slip of paper on which she'd scrawled the message and as she drove home, she thought about the things she'd just learned.

Vampires.

Psychic vampires.

Psychic blood-feeding vampires.

No wonder Rupert and Fern March were worried about their daughter. Who wouldn't be?

And seriously—Mordonna? Where'd Amy dig up a name like that? And the message she'd left for Dr. Cavendish: *Eleven-fifteen tonight at the pit.* What was that all about?

Brooke wracked her brain for pits.

Pit stop.

Barbecue pit.

It's the pits.

Armpit.

Peach pit.

She picked up her cell and called her neighbor from the Beacon Arms. "Maggie," she said breathlessly. "Do you know any place called The Pit?"

Maggie was silent for a moment. "There's a bar by that name in Jersey, about twenty miles from the river. It's called The P and P—short for The Pit and the Pendulum. Some people call it The Pit. It's kind of a dump. Old-school goth bands. Weird clientele. Lots of bikers."

"You doing anything tonight?"

"Yeah—watching a movie with Bernie. Why do you ask?"

"I need to check out the Pit and the Pendulum. I'd rather not go alone."

Again there was silence. "You sure about that? I can't picture you liking the place."

When Brooke explained her interest, Maggie let out a laugh. "Rupert March's daughter at The P and P! That's hilarious. Sure we'll go, but we'll let Bernie drive. If Amy March sees your car, she'll know you're on to her."

Thirty

Rehearsal that night was a complete waste of time. The students were devastated by the news about Chris Van Auken, and as a result, they kept missing cues, fumbling lines and acting peevish when Brooke interrupted to give directions. Amy was just as downcast, but she'd found a silver lining in this latest dark cloud to settle over Sussex Academy. Now that Van Auken was the chief suspect in Nina's murder, Rupert March's anonymous death threats had ceased. He'd decided to resume his business trips and would soon be departing for Miami.

That, of course, explained Amy's phone call to Rodney Cavendish. She was letting him know that with her dad out of town, she was free to sneak out at night and indulge in whatever fun and games were about to unfold at the Pit and the Pendulum.

Tom-the-Rent-a-Cop showed up at nine to escort the students to their cars. He returned a few minutes later to do the same for Brooke, and as she slid behind the wheel, he wished her a safe evening. She thanked him, but as she drove off, she wondered just how safe the evening would prove to be. Back in her apartment, she grabbed something to eat and thirty minutes later, joined Maggie and Bernie outside the building. At eleven, they pulled into a parking lot packed with SUVs, pick-ups and motorcycles.

"This is it," Maggie announced as they got out of Bernie's truck. "The Pit and the Pendulum."

From the outside, the P and P was just another boxy, run-down bar—the kind of place where aging losers congregate to drink beer, watch football and swap stories about the good old days. But the interior told a different story. There wasn't a geezer anywhere in sight. Instead, the bar and adjacent pool room were crammed to the rafters with Goths, bikers and a colorful array of misfits.

A multiply-pierced, tattooed creature of undiscernible gender showed up to escort them to a booth. Brooke opted to avoid recognition by sitting with her back to the door while Maggie and Bernie sat across from her, keeping watch on those who entered and exited. Shortly after eleven Amy arrived with a guy Maggie described as tall and gangly with shoulder-length brownish hair and a pale, narrow face. Ten minutes later the door jerked open, and Maggie provided a brief description of the newcomer. Tall. Fifty years old or so. Broad-shouldered. Longish salt and pepper hair. Black shirt. Tight black jeans. Black boots.

"That's him," Brooke whispered. "Rodney Cavendish."

"He's glancing around and nodding at people," Maggie said, her eyes flitting to those seated nearby. "They're getting up and following him out the door."

"This is the rendezvous point," Bernie chimed in. "The real party's elsewhere." He drained his beer and clunked the empty mug on the table. "Whad'ya say we follow them?"

Once Cavendish and his followers were gone, Brooke slid out of the booth, crossed the room and peeked out the window from behind a neon Coors sign. Out in the parking lot, Amy tucked her pink and purple hair beneath a helmet and climbed on the back of a motorcycle behind the tall, skinny guy Maggie'd described earlier. He revved the engine and eased the bike onto the road behind a line of vehicles heading in a northeasterly direction.

When Brooke beckoned from the window, Bernie tossed a few bills on the table and the three of them raced out the door and climbed into the cab of his pick-up truck.

"Faster," Maggie urged as they set out. "We'll lose them."

"Cool your heels," Bernie told her. "We don't want them seeing us, do we?"

"No, but we don't want them getting away from us either."

"Don't worry, babe. They won't get away. Not with me driving."

After a few miles, the road veered sharply to the north. Bernie stayed well behind the red taillights weaving through forests and farmland, and before long the convoy make a left-hand turn onto a dirt lane. Bernie approached the turn and switched off his headlights. "That way we can see them, but they can't see us," he explained.

Five minutes later the caravan turned up a long driveway, bordered on either side by rows of corn running parallel to the unpaved surface. Instead of following the cars, Bernie pulled onto the side of the road, killed the engine and studied the lonely setting. "So here's the plan. We'll leave the truck here and take it the rest of the way on foot—up through the cornstalks."

It would have been nice to have a getaway vehicle near at hand, but other than that, Bernie's plan sounded like a good one. Soon the three of them were brushing aside the corn leaves that grazed their faces as they trudged over the rough, uneven terrain. At the sound of car doors opening and closing, they halted their forward momentum and parted the stalks for a better view of what turned out to be a ramshackle farmhouse. As Brooke scanned the people getting out of their vehicles, it occurred to her that they appeared to be a good deal older than Amy. She recalled Dr. Cavendish's words about vampire wannabes feeding off of pure-blood subjects. Is that why Amy was here? Was she about to become the evening's main course?

Once the last person passed through the front door, Brooke and her friends resumed their trek and emerged from the cornfield at a distance from the house. From there they raced across the overgrown lawn and huddled together in the shadows of a dilapidated back porch.

Maggie glanced around and shivered. "What are we doing here?" she asked. "We were supposed to go to the P and P, not to some dilapidated farmhouse in the middle of nowhere. Let's beat it before someone sees us."

"We're here for Amy," Brooke reminded her.

"That's right," Bernie agreed. "I rescued that poor kid once before, and if I have to, I'll rescue her all over again."

"Oh really?" Maggie shot back. "As I recall, your yelling didn't do a thing to stop Rupert March from dragging Amy out the window and down the fire escape. I don't call that being rescued."

Bernie's mouth dropped open. "Just last night you said I was your hero for the way I pulled that off. And now...? He threw his hands in the air. "I don't believe it."

"So, that's your plan?" Maggie continued. "You're going to barge into a room of strangers and start yelling insults? Gee, I wonder how that will turn out."

"Pipe down," Bernie hissed. "We've got a job to do and the sooner you shut up, the sooner we'll be out of here."

He didn't say what that job was, but even so, his words seemed to settle the matter. Together they tiptoed along the edge of the back porch and peered around the side of the house.

In the distance a faint ribbon of light spilled through a window and drew a line across the grass.

"That's where the action is," Bernie whispered. "Keep your mouths shut, both of you."

They inched forward, the long grass bending and swaying against their legs. Up ahead, the sound of chanting filtered into the night, the Latin words growing louder as Brooke and her friends approached the wide-open window. There was no screen covering it—only thick drapes cracked just enough to allow a beam of light to escape.

"Not much to see with that curtain in our way," Maggie whispered. "I guess we'll have to call it a night."

"I'm not giving up that easily," Brooke whispered back. Creeping forward, she reached out and parted the velvet curtain just a couple of inches. And then, fearful of being seen, she ducked down. She expected to hear angry shouts and people stampeding over the window, but the chanting continued. Rhythmic. Repetitive. Hypnotic.

She inched up to the sill, just enough to gaze into a large, unfurnished space lit by candles set in Gothic candelabras. Hooded figures huddled together in the center of the room, and when a bell sounded, the figures glided slowly back, widening the circle and revealing a coffin resting on a wrought iron stand. The circle widened further and that's when Brooke saw who lay inside. It was Amy, her eyes closed.

Brooke gasped—she couldn't help herself. And then she drew back. Had anyone heard her?

Maggie slid into the space Brooke vacated. "She's dead," she whispered. "We're too late."

Bernie elbowed Maggie out of her spot and peered over the edge of the sill. There was silence for a moment and then he grinned. "False alarm. A bunch of people just lifted her out of the coffin and set her on the floor. She's walking around the circle. Not to worry."

Brooke resumed her spot. Amy wasn't dead, but her motions seemed trancelike as she drifted from person to person in the circle. She stopped suddenly in front of someone and lowered his hood, revealing the tall, gangly guy she'd ridden with from The P and P. The chanting grew louder as she steered him over to the coffin, gazed up into his eyes and buried her teeth in his neck.

Six figures emerged from the circle and placed Amy and her friend next to each other in the coffin. The figures returned to the spaces they'd vacated, and at the sound of a bell, everyone in the circle dropped to their knees. With one exception. A tall hooded figure stepped forward, a jeweled chalice raised above his head. After breathing an incantation, he brought the chalice to his lips and drank. He repeated the incantation as he made way around the circle, offering the cup to each person. It was then that Brooke saw his face—Professor Rodney Cavendish.

"It's like communion," she whispered. "But with human blood."

"Human blood?" Maggie echoed. "These people are real vampires? She didn't wait for an answer. Instead, she tugged at Bernie's arm. "That does it. Let's get out of here."

"I'm with Maggie." Bernie said. "It's time to go."

"But we can't leave Amy," Brooke told them. "I need to make sure she's all right."

"What do you mean, all right?" Maggie argued. "The girl's a friggin' vampire. Let her take care of herself."

"Come on," Bernie urged. "We're getting out of here before the blood suckers come after us."

He and Maggie took off, leaving Brooke alone at the side of the house. A chilly wind rustled through the trees as the chanting grew louder. She glanced at the cornfields and the vast loneliness surrounding her. The last thing she wanted was to be stranded there, forced to hitch a ride home while vampires roamed the night, thirsty and wondering where their next drink was coming from.

She turned away from the window. "Wait for me," she whispered into the darkness, and then she started running.

Thirty-one

The sun was low in the Western sky when Brooke arrived at Sussex Academy for Friday's rehearsal. She wanted to be anywhere but here. With the exception, of course, of the vampire house. And the Nazi compound. She didn't want to be there either.

"Amy stayed home today," a girl announced when Brooke entered the auditorium. "Somebody said she's sick."

She's sick all right, Brooke thought to herself. *Sick in the head.*

She called the cast to order, but Count Dracula was nowhere to be seen. "Where's Erik?" she shouted.

"In the office," a kid shouted back.

"With the cops," another chimed in. "And his mom. Dr. Pierce is pretty upset."

By now, Brooke was sick and tired of kids and vampires, and she had no heart for the play or anything else for that matter. "I'll be right back," she shouted to whomever cared to listen. "If there's a problem, call Tom-the Rent-a-Cop and let him solve it. And don't destroy anything while I'm gone."

This was the last straw, she fumed as she strode toward the office. She'd tell Dr. Pierce and Erik's mom and the cops and whoever else cared to listen that if Erik didn't report to the stage immediately, she'd find another Count Dracula. There was still time to put an understudy in the role, and she didn't care if Erik's mom threw a hissy fit and withheld every penny of the precious money she donated. The success or failure of this play was at stake, and Brooke was tired of being sabotaged by the very people who expected her to produce a hit so they could boast about it in their publicity literature.

She entered the main office, but instead of marching to Pierce's door, she stopped and stared at the scene in front of her. The normally quiet reception area was packed with reporters, their cameras and microphones aimed at School Psychologist Ron Webster.

"What's going on?" Brooke whispered to the receptionist.

Jocelyn snorted and rolled her eyes. "Dr. Pierce asked Ron to hold the media at bay until his meeting's over. He should have known that Ron would turn our latest fiasco into a campaign event."

"Our latest fiasco? I'm sorry but…"

"You mean you haven't heard about our hacker?"

"You mean Chris Van Auken?"

Jocelyn shook her head and made a tsk-tsk sound. "You, my dear, are sadly behind the times. Apparently, Chris wasn't the only one taking advantage of our lax security system. No, someone broke into our sever, changed student transcripts, posted salacious lies about our most generous donors, and filled our human resource files with even worse lies—most of which are too vile to repeat. And in addition…" She pointed to a mountain of cardboard boxes stacked along one wall. "Those packages arrived this morning. Ordered online and charged to our account."

"And they are…?"

"Condoms—250,000 of them."

Brooke tried not to laugh. She wanted to learn more, but she had to get back to rehearsal, so she asked Jocelyn to send Erik to the auditorium as soon as the meeting was over.

The receptionist let out a laugh. "Don't hold your breath. As it turns out, Erik's our hacker. If it were any other kid, he'd have been expelled by now. But not Erik. Not with his mother's money hanging in the balance. No, I'm afraid the board will find a way to sweep the whole mess under the rug like it never happened."

Brooke glanced at the stack of boxes. "Hacking's a pretty serious issue."

"So is money. Try running a school without it."

She returned to the auditorium and asked another student to read Dracula's lines. He did a decent job, but it hardly mattered. The kids couldn't concentrate, and after last night's foray into the world of the undead, she couldn't either. The minutes dragged by, and when nine o'clock rolled around, a sense of elation—a joy beyond words—took hold of her as she watched the students depart.

▾ ▾ ▾

The vestibule was empty when Ted arrived at Don Giovanni's, but a glance into the dining room revealed a sizable crowd still noshing away. Most of them appeared to be in good spirits in spite of the ear-shattering racket erupting from the lips of a young woman in a purple gown. Ted wasn't a fan of opera, and if that was a taste of what lay in store, he doubted that an evening at Don Giovanni's would change his mind.

He turned back to the vestibule and met the silent gaze of a statue standing on a pedestal with a bunch of angels hobnobbing at his feet. Having nothing else to do, he went closer to check out the information posted on the wall next to the sculpture. It turned out to be a description of the original—a huge marble statue of Wolfgang Amadeus Mozart located somewhere in Vienna. Photos showed off the details not provided in this faux-marble model, namely carvings of two scenes from Don Giovanni and another carving of the child Mozart strutting his stuff while his father accompanied him on violin.

From there, Ted wandered off to take a look at framed portraits of famous opera stars. Some of these portraits included summaries of the singers' lives, and as he made his way from portrait to portrait, he paused to read the details. Enrico Caruso, for instance, was born in 1873 in Naples, started out as a street singer and made his professional debut at age 22. After that, he did this and that, and this and that, and finally performed at la Scala and later at the Met and then...

Ted gave up with a sigh. He wasn't interested in Caruso or any of the opera greats whose portraits graced the vestibule. Instead, he thought about Brooke, and for the thousandth time that day, he reminded himself that this wasn't a date. He and Brooke were friends, and in a sense, colleagues. There was no possibility of anything more than that.

He glanced at the time. She was fifteen minutes late. Had she run into trouble? The rioting following Nina Powell's murder was supposed to have abated once the police identified a suspect, but that all changed when Chris Van Auken went on the lam. Instead, an angry public was foaming at the mouth over police incompetence, and for the third weekend in a row, authorities were wringing their hands and predicting pandemonium and violence.

Ted was relieved when Brooke came through the door, but to be honest, he was a tad disappointed as well. In the last few days, he'd built her up in his mind as a paragon of female vitality—a sort of Wonder Woman on steroids. But the person who greeted him was a frazzled, sad-eyed reiteration of last year's Brooke, not the updated version who'd joined him Monday night to storm the gates of Nazi hell. To be fair, she'd been through a lot since signing on for the gig at Sussex Academy, and a touch of burn-out was to be expected.

As they made their way through the hellos and how-are-yous, the hostess, an older woman in a Renaissance-style gown, showed up and led them to a table next to a window at the front of the restaurant. The menu she handed them was a large, complicated affair with the choices written in Italian and Greek. Subtitles explained what was what, but it took a bit of work to dig through it.

Once they'd placed their orders, a heavy-set, gray-haired guy in tights and a jeweled tunic approached the table. He set a plate of Greek and Italian appetizers in front of them and then took Brooke's hand and kissed it in an overstated gesture of hospitality. "My compliments signora," he said with a nod toward the appetizers. Once that was done, he turned to Ted and bowed. "Welcome to Don Giovanni's, where opera is always on the menu. We're honored to serve you, signor."

Ted was impressed. Other than the music, this was turning out to be a terrific night on the town. And it wasn't costing him a dime.

Brooke introduced the man as Donatello Petrakis, school board president at Sussex Academy and owner of the restaurant. There was some small talk back and forth, but instead of wrapping it up and making an exit, Petrakis pulled up a chair, sat down and gave Ted the once over. "You look like a smart fellow," he said once he'd concluded his appraisal. "Perhaps you can tell me why the world and everything in it is falling apart."

Ted had some definite thoughts on the subject, but before he could respond, the man launched into an explanation of his own.

"Take a look around," Petrakis said, his gaze shifting from Ted to the well-groomed patrons sucking down forkfuls of expensive food. "They're everywhere these days. In our schools.

In our universities. In our media and in our government. Wolves in sheep's clothing, stalking the halls of power and destroying everything they touch."

Before Ted could comment, Petrakis was off again with more of the same. "They've poisoned our airwaves with their lies. Infiltrated our schools with their propaganda. Flooded our sacred institutions with their corruption and filth." He went on in that vein with only a brief lull when the server returned to the table with entrees and an aria—something mournful Ted had never heard before and hoped never to hear again. Once it ended, Petrakis got back down to business.

"Imagine life without Shakespeare or Milton," he continued. "Without Bach or Mozart or the glories of Italian opera. Imagine, if you can, a world stripped bare of the monumental achievements that characterize our great civilization. That, my friend, is the world these madmen offer us." He leaned closer, his eyes level with Ted's. "The devil's at our doorstep, wrapped in ribbons and bows. Once the package is opened…" He snapped his fingers. "It will be too late."

This went on for some time, and while Ted agreed with much of what the man said, he hadn't come here to listen to a fat guy in a costume shout gloom and doom in his ear. He'd come here to enjoy a quiet conversation with Brooke and to process the adventure they'd shared. He glanced in her direction and saw her staring out the window, her mind seemingly elsewhere. Nice. She'd left him on his own to hold back the fall of Western Civilization. This was so not the evening he'd had in mind.

▼ ▼ ▼

Brooke's attention had begun wandering when Don Petrakis started shouting about wolves in sheep's clothing. She'd caught Ted trying to interject a remark about the collapse of civility in post-Christian culture, but Petrakis kept cutting him off with lamentations about the glory that was Greece and the grandeur that was Rome.

It wasn't that Brooke wasn't interested in the topics being discussed, but rather that she'd heard a motorcycle roaring through the shopping center and it made her think of Van Auken. Where was he tonight? Was he safe? Was he thinking of her as he dodged the cops and lived the life of a fugitive? Probably not. At the moment, survival was his most pressing concern.

She tried to tune back into the conversation, but Ted seemed to have it covered. Sort of. Basically, he was tolerating Petrakis's rantings while seeking opportunities to score a point or two of his own.

She heard another motorcycle somewhere nearby, and this time her thoughts drifted to the tall, skinny vampire who'd ended up in the coffin with Amy March. Was he back at the Pit and the Pendulum tonight? If so, she'd love to have a word with him. Was there a way to make that happen? She glanced over at Ted. Would he be up for the challenge? Of course, he would. A man who'd fallen out of a tree in a Nazi compound wouldn't be fazed by a few vampires.

She turned her gaze back to the parking lot and sat up a bit straighter at the sight of a crowd of people off in the dis-tance. She'd heard warnings about protestors moving out of downtown business districts and into the surrounding shopping centers. Were the predictions coming true?

She touched Don Petrakis's arm. "Excuse me," she said, but he waved her off, intent on making sure that Ted under-stood that a cabal of global elites was about to usher in a one-world government. Apparently, Ted shared his concerns, because by now he was deeply engaged in the conversation and seemed oblivious to everything else.

She looked out again at the parking lot. The crowd was

closer now, some of them wearing ski masks and wielding bats. "Don," she said, "There are people out there with…"

A masked figure charged at the window and blasted it with red paint. Screaming, Brooke sprang to her feet, while all around her, startled restaurant patrons looked up in horror, their forks poised in midair and their mouths open.

In a flash, the mob was inside, tipping over tables and sending expensive entrées splattering onto the rug. Frantic customers lurched out of their seats, shrieking and swearing as they wiped food from their clothes. Some rushed about as though deranged while others stabbed at the marauders with forks and still others retreated to the walls to tape the melee with their phones.

By now Petrakis was on his feet, fists flying, but his blows failed to connect with his younger, more agile targets. Ted moved in to offer backup, and in the process, took a hit to the jaw. He recovered quickly and sent his assailant hurtling against a wall.

Out in the vestibule, rioters ripped down the portraits of opera greats, stomped on the glass and tore at the famous faces until Caruso, Pavarotti, Maria Callas and others lay shredded on the floor. A masked figure with a baseball bat emerged from their midst and lunged at Mozart, causing the composer to teeter back and forth on his pedestal. Subsequent blows sent him tumbling to the floor, at which point, a jubilant rioter let out a howl and sprang forward, a knife in his hand. After some slashing and hacking, he held up Mozart's head to the thunderous applause of his compatriots.

The applause faded when the hostess emerged from the kitchen, an iron skillet in her hand. She took a swing at Mozart's assassin, but missed her mark, and instead, sent the severed head crashing into the opposite wall. Her second attempt was more successful, and once it became apparent that baseball bats were no match for an old lady with a skillet, the rioters beat a hasty retreat just as police in riot gear stormed inside.

To Brooke's amazement, the cops ignored the departing rioters and instead, cuffed the hostess and confiscated her weapon. In spite of protests from Don Petrakis and his guests, the officers hustled the hostess to a waiting car and sped off, leaving Petrakis standing dazed and bewildered among shredded images of operatic icons and the crushed, headless body of Wolfgang Amadeus Mozart.

Defeated but not broken, Don Petrakis drew himself to his full height and faced his guests. "The restaurant is closed until further notice. You will not be charged for your meal. Pray for me—I beg of you—as I set off to rescue my wife."

▾ ▾ ▾

Outside, the smell of smoke hung in the air, and in the distance, flames licked the sky. Closer at hand, the damage manifested itself in broken windows, looted stores and overturned vehicles.

Brooke felt Ted's hand on her back as he hurried her to her car. "Thanks for dinner," he said as she slid behind the steering wheel. He gazed back at the darkened restaurant and heaved a sigh. "This was certainly an evening to remember."

It was, but so was each one of the few evenings Brooke had spent with Ted. There was something about him that made all hell break loose.

Her thoughts wandered to the Pit and the Pendulum and the questions she longed to ask Amy's tall, gangly vampire friend. A scheme formed in her mind, and she decided to give it a go. "It seems a shame to have it end so abruptly," she said, gazing into Ted's eyes. "I can't believe we didn't get to finish our meal."

He nodded in agreement. "I had my heart set on dessert—chocolate chip cannolis, to be exact. I guess that won't be happening now."

"And I had my heart set on a nice, relaxing conversation about everything that's happened over the last few weeks. But now, instead of feeling better, my adrenalin's pumping, my heart's racing and I'm totally frazzled. I'll probably lie awake all night, too keyed up to sleep."

Ted fell silent as though weighing the options. "I suppose we could grab decaf and dessert somewhere, assuming we can find a place that's not under assault."

She smiled inwardly—he'd taken the bait. "There's a place over in New Jersey you might like. I don't think anyone's rioting there, but I can't guarantee cannoli."

He brightened at the suggestion. "Lead the way, and I'll follow."

Forty minutes later, Brooke squeezed into a tight space between a Harley and a beat-up pick-up truck. She watched Ted emerge from his Jeep some distance away, and as he approached, he cast a wary eye over the P and P.

"This place is a dump," he announced.

"True. But no riots."

"No, but I'll bet there are fights. Head bangers. Beer bottles crashing against the wall. Knives pulled. That sort of thing. But you're right. No riots."

As they entered, it dawned on Brooke that they were walking into this den of weirdness at 11:45 on a Friday night, just as the insanity was about to reach critical mass. She glanced at her surroundings. There were no empty tables, and every seat at the bar was taken by beefy, leather-clad bikers, their shoulders hunched over glasses of beer and shots of whiskey. She was hoping to see Amy's scrawny vampire biker in the crowd, but these bikers seemed to be the large, bone-crushing variety.

"So," Ted began, "Is this a favorite spot of yours?"

"I've only been here once. It's kind of interesting, don't you think?"

"Oh, it's that, all right. But I don't think dessert's their specialty."

Brooke scanned the faces in the crowd, and to her surprise, Maggie and Bernie waved at her from a booth across the way.

"Last night wasn't enough for you?" Maggie asked when they joined them. "You're hungry for more?"

"Not exactly." Brooke glanced around and lowered her voice. "I'm looking for Amy's vampire friend. Lay low and act inconspicuous."

They were barely through the introductions when a wait person came to the booth for their orders. No cannoli, but Ted seemed pleased that cheesecake was an option. He ordered a slice for himself while Brooke and Maggie ordered a slice to share. While they waited, Ted launched into an animated description of the evening at Don Giovanni's.

Once again Brooke let him handle the conversation, but this time she shifted her attention to the patrons of the P and P. The booth offered limited visibility, so after making a comment about visiting the restroom, she slid out of her seat and circled the place until she had a clear view of the bar. Dr. Rodney Cavendish was there, chatting with some guys in Harley jackets. She didn't go any closer. The last thing she wanted was Cavendish figuring out that she was spying on him and his vampire cult.

She retreated to the other side of the crowded room, just beyond the pool table. She had to stand on tiptoe to see over peoples' heads, but even so, visibility was limited. And then she spotted him.

The tall, gangly vampire sat at a table with two other guys Brooke didn't recognize. The three of them appeared to be playing a game that involved pitching pennies into a saucer and howling with laughter whenever the coins missed their target and rolled onto the floor. Stoners to be sure—enjoying the simple pleasures of a night out.

She took a moment to ponder the situation. Now that she'd found Amy's vampire friend, what would she do about it? The best approach, she decided, was a direct confrontation, voice lowered to remain inconspicuous. She fought her way through the crowd, and when she tapped him on the shoulder, he looked up and scowled, clearly annoyed at having his fun interrupted.

"You don't know me," she began, "but I'm a friend of a girl named Amy March. You might know her as Mordonna."

The guy's eye's widened, and he rocketed out of his seat, knocking over beer bottles and sending pennies flying in all directions. In an instant, his friends were on their feet as well, shouting profanities and dabbing at the beer streaming down their leather jackets and onto the floor. So much for being inconspicuous.

A waitress rushed over to mop up the mess, and Brooke took advantage of the chaos to steer the tall, skinny vampire away from the table for a word in private. As private as a person could get in a place like this. She would have whispered, but with the music and background noise, she had to shout to be heard.

"My name's Brooke Roberts. And yours is…"

"Why should I tell you my name?"

"Because I know all about the vampire ceremony and the coffin."

A look of panic crossed his pale, narrow face. "Who told you about that?"

"It doesn't matter. Just tell me your name."

He frowned and refused to answer, but Brooke wasn't intimidated by his silence. Weeks of dealing with Erik Rimmer had toughened her up, and she wasn't about to let this guy push her around. "The police have been keeping an eye on Amy March," she told him. "I'm sure they'd enjoy speaking to you."

The guy's eyes darted back to his compatriots and then

around the bar as though searching for an ally. Apparently there were none, because he finally turned back to Brooke and spit out his name: Steve Haskins.

"Glad to meet you, Steve. Now tell me about last night."

Again he looked around the room. "We can't talk here."

"Why not?"

"Trust me. It's dangerous."

Brooke thought about the rundown farmhouse and the chalice full of blood. Yeah—it probably was dangerous. "Name a time and a place where we can meet," she said. "And it had better be soon, and it had better be nearby."

"Ten thirty tomorrow morning. I got business here to-night." He nodded toward his buddies who appeared to be en-tertaining the waitress with a reenactment of the beer-spilling fiasco. He gave Brooke the name of a truck stop off I-78 and they agreed to the plan.

"One last thing," Brooke said as Steve turned to leave. "Don't even think about not showing up. If that happens, I'll make sure the cops turn over every bar stool in this place until they find you."

That accomplished, she drifted back to the table. "What took so long?" Maggie asked.

"I stopped to chat. The people here are really friendly."

Ted gave her a suspicious look but said nothing. By now he'd eaten his cheesecake and Maggie had devoured the slice she and Brooke were supposed to share. The conversation seemed to be waning, so Brooke and Ted excused themselves. He followed her back to Easton, and while she thought about asking him up to her apartment to analyze the night's adven-tures, she decided against it. No point in sending the wrong message.

Her first item of business once she'd locked the door was the news. She watched a state cop inform the public that while Chris Van Auken was still at large, the authorities had the situation well in hand and an arrest was imminent. In other words, Brooke concluded, they had no idea where he was.

From there, she checked out footage of the evening's riots, beginning with the incident at Don Giovanni's. Cell phone videos showed rioters upsetting tables, destroying portraits, spraying graffiti and hacking off Mozart's head. The scene shifted to the restaurant owner emerging from the police station, grim-faced in his tights and tunic with his wife at his side, looking dazed and confused in her crumpled Renaissance gown. When asked what happened, Petrakis shook his fist at the camera and launched into an angry spiel about Goths and Visigoths and the impending fall of Western Civilization. The camera followed the couple as they trudged into the night, while in the background, the opening strains of Mozart's Requiem swelled to a crescendo and faded out.

Thirty-two

Amotorcycle glided up to the truck stop and the rider yanked off his helmet. It wasn't Steve Haskins. Either Amy's vampire friend was seriously late or he had no intention of showing up. Brooke decided to give him ten more minutes, and then…

And then what? She hadn't figured that out yet.

She took another sip of coffee and glanced at the time. Ten minutes came and went, and then another then ten minutes. There was no point in waiting any longer, so she signaled the waitress for her check and was just about to slide out of the booth when a motorcycle roared into the lot. The driver took off his helmet and shook out his longish brown hair. Steve Haskins. Better later than never.

In the light of day, he appeared to be in his late twenties or early thirties—young, but way too old to be snuggling in coffins with seventeen-year-old girls. His hair hung in greasy tangles against his collar, his nose seemed too long for his face, and while his jeans and flannel shirt suited his height, they were too big for his scrawny body. Brooke wondered what Amy saw in the guy, but perhaps he possessed charms that weren't immediately apparent.

Once inside, he brushed past the hostess, strode to the booth and sank down across from Brooke.

"Glad you could make it," she began.

He responded with a snort, but his attitude improved when she offered to treat him to breakfast. He opted for the all-you-can-eat buffet and returned to the table a few minutes later with his plate piled high.

"I'd like to know how you got wind of what was going down in that farmhouse," he growled as he dumped ketchup on a mountain of home fries. "Mordonna told me everyone was sworn to secrecy, so how did you find out? Did she tell you?"

Brooke shook her head.

He pointed his fork in her face. "If I find the person who opened his mouth, I'll be happy to close it for him. Or her. And if anybody asks, you can tell them I had no idea she was only seventeen. I didn't even know her real name until the other night. She said her friends called her Mordonna, and she'd been undead for centuries. She was like that, pretending to be a vampire one minute and a goddess the next. At first I thought it was cool. 'This chick is far out,' I said to myself. But I could tell she wasn't into me, if you know what I mean, and it didn't take long to figure out that she was using me."

"Using you—how?"

"She needed a gofer. Somebody to deliver messages. Any imbecile would do."

Brooke knew what Steve meant. She'd felt the same way that day at the Celtic Festival. Somebody to deliver Amy's messages. Any imbecile would do.

"These messages," she said, thinking of Rodney Cavendish. "Did you deliver them to the same person each time?"

Steve shrugged at the question. "Hard to tell. It could have been the same guy, but there was always a different weird-sound-

ing name written on the envelope. No surprise there—weird -
sounding names are part of this make-believe garbage she's into.
I had nothing better to do, so I went along with it. It was a
bunch of laughs until I ended up in a coffin in a room full of
vampires. Trust me—that was way more than I signed on for."

Brooke looked at him, surprised. "You mean you didn't
know about the vampire ceremony ahead of time?"

He smirked at the question. "Mordonna told me we were
meeting a bunch of people at the P and P and going from there
to a party. I was good with that until we walked through the
door and somebody handed me a robe with a hood. Once things
got going, I played along because I didn't want to be the only
clueless idiot in the room. I found out afterward that it was an
initiation. That she had to bite somebody's neck and turn him
into a vampire in front of all the other vampires if she wanted
to be part of their group. 'I hope you don't mind,' she said after
the whole thing was over, like being turned into a vampire is
something that happens all the time."

He scowled and shoved French toast in his mouth. "Once
it was over, I told her she was crazy and I was done with her.
'You are one scary chick,' I said, 'and this crap is way too weird
for me.' She laughed in my face and said I couldn't leave—
ever—because I was a newly created vampire, and my will was
no longer my own." He chomped down on a slice of bacon.
"We'll see about that."

He chased the bacon with a swig of coffee and signaled the
waitress for a refill. While that played out, Brooke leaned back
in her seat and eyed Steve curiously. Amy had given her so-
called love potion to two guys—Erik Rimmer and someone else.
Was Steve the someone else?

"Did Amy—I mean Mordonna—ever give you a love
potion?"

He laughed at the question. "No, but that's the sort of stuff
she was into. Like those envelopes sealed with different colors.

She told me the colors were part of some mystical code known only to the person receiving it."

"And the person who got the messages? What can you tell me about him?"

"Not much to tell. The guy wore a mask and once I handed him the envelope, he walked away without saying a word. To be honest, I wouldn't be able to identify him if he came up to me right now and shook my hand. Married, is the way I saw it and looking for some action on the side.

"Did he speak to you—would you recognize his voice?"

Steve shook his head. "We only said a few words on the phone. He'd tell me where and when to meet him, and then he'd hang up. Part of the make-believe is how I saw it."

"His height?"

"Shorter than me. Maybe six feet or a bit more. Not fat. Not thin."

That ruled out Rodney Cavendish. He was at least six-three. But the person Steve just described could have been Chris Van Auken. Or about 800 million other guys.

"What about his hair?

"I already said he wore a mask and a hoodie, so how was I supposed to see his hair? I'm telling you, it was all make-believe—like a role-playing video game where everybody pretends to be a character."

"And you never got his real name?"

"Never."

"How about a phone number?"

"I didn't notice."

"But his number would be in your phone—right?"

Steve hesitated, deep in thought. "Yeah—I guess it'd be there, along with about a thousand others. If I find it, I'll let you know."

▾ ▾ ▾

Brooke watched through the window as Steve got on his motorcycle and sped away. The information he'd shared with her was more than disturbing. Amy's parents needed to know about her late-night excursions so they could protect her from harm. But was it Brooke's responsibility to tell them? Things were already tense between her and Rupert March, and not much better where Fern was concerned. Maybe she should share the information with Guidance Counselor Gretchen Coates and let her break the news to the Marches. Or maybe not. The Owl Lady wasn't known for keeping secrets. Perhaps School Psychologist Ron Webster was better suited to the job.

That decided, Brooke fished around in her bag for Webster's card and placed the call.

"Sounds bad," he agreed after a brief rundown. "I've got a campaign event in two hours, but I can spare a few minutes beforehand. Can you meet me at the school?"

She agreed to the plan and arrived at Sussex Academy half-an-hour later. Webster met her at the front door and after a quick greeting, ushered her into his tiny office.

He began the meeting by glancing at his watch. "I'm seriously pressed for time. I've got a campaign rally this afternoon, a triathlon tomorrow morning, visits to businesses affected by the riots tomorrow afternoon, and sometime in the next few days I need to finalize the details of the computer games I've been developing." He let out a sigh. "My family's beginning to think I've deserted them."

Brooke got the message. Keep it short and get out of there. She got down to business with a brief synopsis of her visit to Dr. Rodney Cavendish's office followed by a description of the creepy vampire ceremony, and then she wrapped things up with a summary of her conversation with Steve Haskins. "If Amy's involved with an older man," she said, "the authorities need to be alerted immediately. And her parents as well."

Webster leaned back in his chair, his brow furrowed as he

processed the things he'd heard. "Has Amy ever mentioned being interested in an older man?"

"Not exactly, but..." Brooke recalled the conversation with Amy after the Celtic Festival. She told Webster about the love potion Amy had given to Erik Rimmer, and to someone else as well."

"Could Amy be meeting someone closer to her own age?" Webster probed. "Someone her parents don't approve of?"

"That's a possibility," Brooke acknowledged. "All I know is that she laughed when I asked if she'd given the potion to Dr. Cavendish, but she seemed upset when I asked the same thing about Chris Van Auken."

"Believe me," Webster said gently, "we all liked Chris, and while we're shocked by the things we've learned about him, is it a stretch to imagine him participating in something like you described? He has a pretty active fantasy life of his own. Vikings. Norse Gods. Battle reenactments. I can imagine him being intrigued by vampires and love potions."

Brooke said nothing. She could imagine it too.

"I tell you what," Webster continued. "This is a lot to deal with when you're trying to put a play together. How about if I discuss this with Amy's dad and encourage him to turn the matter over to the authorities? If he asks where I got the information, I'll keep your name out of it. Client confidentiality. Fair enough?"

Brooke felt a weight lift from her shoulders. Webster's offer was the perfect solution to her problem. A way for her to behave responsibly without complicating her life any further.

He rose to his feet. "I'm glad you brought this to my attention. Keep a close watch on Amy, and if she hints at anything that's even vaguely disturbing, let me know and we'll deal with it immediately."

▼ ▼ ▼

Back at home, Brooke headed straight for the steamer chest. In the upheavals of the past week, she hadn't had the presence of mind to insist that Amy find another hiding place for her art journal. The matter had slipped off her radar, but to be fair, Amy hadn't followed through on her end of the bargain. Did that make it okay to take a look? Brooke laughed at the question. Given what she'd learned in the last forty-eight hours, it was more than okay—it was her responsibility to find out what secrets Amy was hiding.

She opened the chest and stared at the ravens on the cover of the journal. Once again she was struck by the similarity to the ravens on Van Auken's wristband. So far, there'd been no mention of anything inappropriate going on between him and Amy, but Amy was a minor. Did that explain the silence?

Brooke reached for the journal and drew back again, torn between the need to know and the need to respect Amy's privacy. The need to know won out, and soon she was seated on the sofa with the journal open on her lap.

The first few pages featured well-rendered images of historic vampires such as Vlad the Impaler and Elizabeth Bathory. These were followed by an assortment of blood-sucking creatures culled from myth and legend. Particularly chilling were images of the child vampires of Glamis Castle where, according to Shakespeare, King Duncan met his fate at the hands of Macbeth. Next were illustrations of iconic movie vampires such as Nosferatu, Dracula and Lestat. These were followed by a double-page spread devoted to Amy's so-called love potion. Delicate images of rose petals, cinnamon sticks, vanilla beans, honey, pomegranate juice and rain water surrounded a "recipe," hand-written in Gothic script. The next page featured a watercolor of Erik Rimmer holding a vial in his hand and the one next to it showed him drinking the contents. The following two pages featured a prom picture of Amy and Erik in steampunk vampire outfits with an image of the Eiffel Tower in the background.

Subsequent illustrations offered a glimpse into their sizzling, summer romance. No wonder Amy didn't want her parents seeing these drawings—her mother would have freaked out, and her father would have ripped Erik limb from limb. The steamy drawings were followed by a depiction of Erik in a coffin, his eyes closed as a girl with pink and purple hair plunged a stake into his heart.

The last image was a self-portrait of Amy placing the love potion in someone's hand. There was no arm. No face. No body. Just anonymous fingers wrapped around a slender vial filled with pink liquid. Whose hand was it?

The journal stopped there. Sort of. The last few pages were ripped out, leaving only ragged edges to hint at the story's ending. Did Amy destroy the drawings because they didn't turn out as she'd hoped? Or—as seemed more likely—did she remove them to protect the identity of the unnamed person who'd brought the potion to his lips?

Thirty-three

The Sunday morning talk shows were all about Chris Van Auken. He was still at large. Still armed. Still dangerous. Still outsmarting the authorities with their technology, their dragnets and their dogs. And now, with the story gaining national attention, acquaintances from years ago were creeping out of the woodwork to tell their stories.

"Chris ran with a gang of hooligans," an old geezer from Van Auken's hometown told a reporter. "Fighting. Drinking. Drugs. A bad lot all the way around."

"Were they racists as well?" the reporter asked, seemingly eager to enhance the narrative.

"It wouldn't surprise me if they were," the geezer responded. "Those kids had a nose for trouble and they managed to find it wherever they went."

A high school friend offered further details. "Chris and I were in the same class," she said. "He was lots of fun, and a bunch of us girls had crushes on him. He was always getting into trouble, but that just made him seem wild and daring." Her smile faded as reality bore down on her. "We heard he settled down and became a decent person, but it just goes to show that people never really change, do they?"

A retired English teacher came forward as well. "Oh yes. I remember him. Rude. Arrogant. Unmanageable. Suspended from school more times than you can count. I predicted he'd come to no good, and I was right."

Shortly after eleven, Brooke shut down her laptop and headed to Uncle Nelson's apartment at a nearby senior-living facility. They met once a month for Sunday brunch, and while there were three restaurants they typically enjoyed, each one was boarded up to keep out the rioters. Not wanting to spend a bright autumn afternoon encased in plywood, Uncle Nelson had offered to play host.

He welcomed her at the door with a kiss on the cheek. "I hope you don't mind, but I've asked someone to join us."

She did mind. She'd been looking forward to a relaxing meal with candles on the table and Bach Cello Sonatas playing softly in the background. Afterward, she and her uncle would work together on the *New York Times* Crossword Puzzle, and the visit would end with a walk around the landscaped grounds. An intruder would spoil everything.

"Anyone I know?" she asked warily.

Something in her uncle's mischievous smile put her on guard. Yes—the glint in his eyes could mean only one thing— he was back to his matchmaking tricks. Her stomach clenched at the thought of making forced conversation with David Price, the man Uncle Nelson kept throwing in her path. To be fair, David had a lot going for him. He was handsome, intelligent and witty, but he wasn't Karl. Not even close.

But to her horror, the person who rose to greet her wasn't David Price. It was Dr. Rodney Cavendish. Brooke stumbled through an awkward greeting and was grateful when her uncle jumped in to take charge of the conversation. Grateful, that is, until she realized that in her absence, Uncle Nelson had laid bare the things she'd taken pains to keep hidden during the interview in Cavendish's office.

"Funny, isn't it?" the professor began. "We spoke for at least 45 minutes last Thursday, and yet you never breathed a word about directing *Dracula* at Sussex Academy."

Her uncle looked at her, perplexed. "I was surprised to hear that. The play was the whole reason I suggested the two of you meet, but Rodney tells me you never mentioned it. Instead, you told him you were editing a book about vampires. That was news to me, but I'm looking forward to hearing more about the project."

Brooke hated to lie to her uncle, but she was in over her head and could see no other way forward. She mumbled an apology for forgetting to tell him about the editing project and backed up the lie with excuses about being busy and overwhelmed. And yes—the book was proving to be an interesting challenge. Maybe by the end of the assignment, she too would be an expert on vampires, just like the professor.

Cavendish's eyes never left her as she rambled on, and the more he stared, the more disconcerted she felt. "I find it extremely odd," he said when she finished, "that you never once mentioned that you worked part time at Sussex Academy. You had a perfect opportunity to do so when I showed you Nina's masterpiece."

Brooke searched her brain for a response, but nothing came to her. Nothing other than flickering images of hooded figures drinking blood from a chalice in Cavendish's outstretched hand.

"I find it difficult to discuss painful subjects," she blurted out. "Especially with a stranger."

The professor eyed her skeptically. "You mean to tell me that you stood there in my office—a space devoted to vampires—and you were too distraught to mention that you're directing *Dracula*? But that's not the only thing I find strange.

For some reason, you failed to mention that you were with the student who found Nina's body."

He kept staring at her, and her uncle stared as well until Brooke felt compelled to speak. "I didn't know what to say. I felt uncomfortable and awkward and tongue-tied. It's hard to explain."

Cavendish released her from his stare and turned to her uncle. "Your niece is a nervous Nellie, isn't she?"

Brooke was pretty sure Uncle Nelson didn't see her as a nervous Nellie. And why should he? While she'd kept him in the loop about Nina's murder and the riots at Don Giovanni's, she'd avoided mentioning the two slashed tires, the Nazi compound and the creepy, candlelit vampire ceremony.

To her relief, Uncle Nelson responded to his guest's comment with his usual tact and diplomacy. "My niece has many reasons to be unsettled at the moment. And now, if you'll excuse me, I'll get brunch on the table."

"Allow me," Brooke offered. "Stay here and visit with your friend."

She fled to the kitchen, her hands shaking as she opened the oven door. This was horrible. Cavendish kept backing her into corners, and if he persisted, she just might slip up and reveal what she knew about Amy and the ceremony in the deserted farmhouse. She needed to take control of the conversation and steer it away from anything that involved Amy, Nina, Sussex Academy or vampires. But what else was there to talk about?

Bach—that was the ticket. Her uncle knew Cavendish through the Bach Choir. If she could keep the focus on music, she might emerge from brunch unscathed.

She put a plate of pancakes on the table along with an egg and sausage casserole and stood back to admire the results. The table looked lovely with fresh flowers, special-occasion china and real silverware. Uncle Nelson had gone to great lengths to make this a nice occasion, and here she was, spoiling things with her awkward attempts at wriggling out of the mess she'd gotten herself into.

She called the men to the table, and as soon as they were seated, she launched into a series of questions about the Bach Choir's upcoming season. Soon Cavendish and Uncle Nelson were reminiscing about past performances—some stellar—some not so much. As they reminisced, Brooke felt the tension gradually dissipate. This wasn't so bad. She didn't need to be afraid of Dr. Cavendish. There was no way he'd figure out that she'd gone to the P and P and followed him to the vampire ceremony.

Things hummed along smoothly, and just as she was beginning to enjoy the conversation, Uncle Nelson mentioned a Mozart concert he'd recently attended.

"Speaking of Mozart," Cavendish said, pausing to wipe a bit of syrup from his lips, "did you hear about the ruckus at Don Giovanni's on Friday night?"

"Indeed, I did," Uncle Nelson responded. "As it so happens, Brooke was having dinner there and witnessed the whole thing."

Cavendish shifted his vampire eyes in Brooke's direction. "You have a way of showing up in the most interesting places."

She responded with a weak smile. If he only knew.

"I've referred a number of our vocal students to Don Giovanni's," Cavendish remarked, his eyes still glued to Brooke's. "The last time the owner and I spoke, we discussed the challenges of being school board president at Sussex Academy. Not easy keeping a school afloat during a murder investigation. Especially a high-profile murder like Nina's."

Terrific. Just like that Sussex Academy was back in the conversation.

"Interestingly," Cavendish continued. "He informed me that your stage manager is Amy March, Rupert March's daughter."

That did it. It was time to wrap things up and get out of

there. The dots were connecting in Cavendish's brain, and at any moment he'd realize Brooke was on to him.

"I can't imagine the Amy's grief at losing the woman who was her mentor and close friend," he added, his gaze never wavering. "Instead of struggling with heartbreak and loss, the girl should be having fun and enjoying life."

Brooke drew back in her seat. Having fun and enjoying life? Was that what he thought of those weird, blood-drinking rituals? Was he crazy? The answer was yes—the man was part of a vampire cult. What more did anyone need to know?

"I met Amy at a summer workshop at Nina's church," he explained. "The whole thing was a bit comical in retrospect. I told Nina I'd bring my cello and provide background music while the women worked on their projects. After I left, they told Nina they hated the music and made her promise she'd never subject them to it again. She and I had a good laugh about it afterward."

Brooke smiled politely at the remark. Cello music. Art projects. Vampires. It was all fun and games.

Once the meal ended, Cavendish and Uncle Nelson carried their coffee to the living room while Brooke cleaned up. She joined them a few minutes later and mumbled a made-up story about having promised to visit the feminist art exhibit at the Hewitt Gallery. Her uncle seemed disappointed by the announcement, but she didn't care—she had to get out of there— the sooner the better.

Out in the parking lot, she raced to her car and collapsed against the steering wheel. Was Cavendish onto her? Had he noticed her sneaking around the P and P on Friday night? What would he do if he found out she'd spied on the vampire ceremony and told Ron Webster all about it?

Calm down, she told herself. The encounter was over, and with any luck, she'd never see Cavendish again.

The thought did little to calm her nerves, and she was still jittery when she entered the boarded-up art gallery. There were no customers at the moment, and the place seemed lifeless and uninviting until Madeleine Hewitt poked her head out of her office and waved a greeting. She and Reverend Regina Ray were having tea, she said, and they'd be glad to pour another cup if Brooke cared to join them. Brooke declined the offer. The women were sharing a private tete-a-tete—something that happened often in Madeleine's office. Frustrated artists, friends in crisis, parents worried about their children—all of them found their way to Madeleine's door.

She left the women to their conversation and passed the time wandering among the feminist works in mixed media. While the messages were compelling, she paid only scant attention. Instead, she thought about her conversation with Dr. Cavendish and bemoaned the times she'd nearly given herself away.

The buzzer over the door sounded, and to her surprise, Ron Webster walked into the gallery. Before Brooke could ask about his conversation with Rupert March, Madeleine and Reggie emerged from the office and introduced themselves. When Webster asked how they were faring in light of the recent riots, Madeleine complained about boarded-up windows and graffiti, but the reverend spoke of more serious damage—a stained-glass window destroyed the night of Nina's funeral. Webster expressed outrage at the desecration of a place of worship, and followed up on his remarks by assuring the women that he'd rally the troops to come to their aid.

In the end they all knew his promises carried little weight. Ron Webster held no office as yet and had no power to rally any troops. But he'd made a good show, and Brooke could tell that Madeleine and Reggie appreciated the interest he'd shown.

Before leaving, he accepted Madeleine's offer of a guided tour of the current exhibit. He paused now and then to comment on specific works and to drop a few feminist buzzwords—

patriarchy, privilege, intersectionality—enough to suggest that if women wanted a supportive guy in the county courthouse, Ron Webster was their man. He earned further points when he described the therapeutic computer games he'd been developing. Madeleine and Reggie gushed with compliments, and by the time the love fest was over, it was clear that Ron Webster had earned their votes.

When he said goodbye, Brooke did as well and they left the gallery together. "So, tell me," she said eagerly, "how did Rupert March respond to the news about the vampire ceremony?"

Webster let out a sigh. "It's tough getting hold of that guy. I've left a couple of voicemails, but I'm still waiting for him to get back to me. But don't worry. I'll make sure he hears every detail."

He shook Brooke's hand and went into a boarded-up boutique to sweettalk the owner, just like he'd done with Madeleine and Reggie. Brooke turned to leave, but stopped at the sight of a Lexus SUV idling across the street. The driver had his back to her, but she had no trouble recognizing him. Why had Dr. Cavendish followed her from her uncle's apartment?

He turned and looked at her with that same dark-eyed gaze, and then he gunned the engine and pulled out of the space without saying a word. She watched the Lexus disappear down the block. Why had Cavendish followed her? Was that his way of telling her to back off? But why—what was he hiding? Had Nina learned something about his vampire ceremonies—something terrible involving Amy? Did he silence Nina because she intended to tell the police? Was he the murderer and not Van Auken?

Brooke darted into the boutique and found Webster schmoozing the owner. He glanced at her as though puzzled by the interruption, and once his spiel was over, he walked with her to the sidewalk outside the store.

"Cavendish followed me from my uncle's apartment," she gasped. "Maybe this isn't the first time he followed me. Maybe he's the person who slashed my tires, and maybe he'll…"

"Tires? Slowdown. I don't have a clue what you're talking about."

She took a deep breath and told him about the slashed tires several weeks earlier. And then she told him about brunch today and about Cavendish studying her with his vampire eyes.

"I'm on this," Webster said when she finished. "I'll speak to Rupert March this evening, and then we'll both have a word with the police. And who knows," he said with a shrug. "This might overturn their case against Chris Van Auken." He hesitated a moment. "Let me take that back. The evidence against Chris is pretty damning, but the things you've uncovered this week suggest that this business is a lot more complicated than anyone thought."

Brooke nodded in agreement, but her thoughts were far from Chris Van Auken. At the moment he wasn't nearly as terrifying as the man with the dark, vampire eyes.

Webster gave her a friendly pat on the back. "I gotta' hand it to you," he said with a smile. "It was pretty clever of you to follow Amy to that old farmhouse. Seems like you're a bit of a sleuth yourself. Maybe Detective Burleigh should consider putting you on the force."

Thirty-four

Monday morning brought a flurry of emails related to the Chris Van Auken debacle. The first was from Guidance Counselor Gretchen Coates offering suggestions for helping students navigate the disaster. Dr. Pierce sent out an agenda for a faculty meeting on the subject, and a notice from the schoolboard listed talking points to use when speaking to parents and the media. A particularly urgent email from the school's attorneys advised saying as little as possible to anyone—ever.

Given all this excitement, Sussex Academy seemed eerily quiet when Brooke entered early that evening. Quiet, at least, until Jane Acker came down the hall. When she saw Brooke, she rushed in her direction, her face flushed and her high heels clickety-clacking on the linoleum floor.

"I was right about Chris, wasn't I?" she exclaimed. "I told you he was up to no good, and I was right, right, right! Of course, I'm terribly sad it's come to this," she continued, her lips twitching as she struggled to contain her glee, "but at least we can breathe a sigh of relief now that the murder investigation's finally wrapped up. Assuming, of course, that those lame-brained cops find Chris and drag him back to face justice."

She grabbed Brooke's arm to keep her from walking away. "If you have a few minutes, we can go back to my office and talk. I'll put on a pot of tea."

"Sorry, I've got a rehearsal to run." That much was true, but there were other things on Brooke's mind as she left Jane and headed for the auditorium. She found Amy in the front row, oblivious to everything but her phone.

"You and I need to talk," Brooke announced.

Amy brushed aside a strand of pink and purple hair and looked up from the screen. "Okay. So, talk."

Brooke intended to do just that, and she wasted no time getting down to business. "Last week I met a man named Rodney Cavendish. He had a lot to say about vampires, psychic vampires and psi-blood feeding vampires. Does any of that ring a bell?"

A look of panic swept across the girl's face. She averted her eyes and didn't respond.

"Answer me, Amy. I'm not angry—just concerned."

But Amy didn't answer. Instead, she got out of her seat and started toward the door at the rear of the auditorium.

Brooke followed and stopped her midway up the aisle. "It's time to get things out in the open. Let's start with Dr. Cavendish."

The look of panic deepened. "I have no idea who you're talking about."

"Of course, you do. He's the guy in the kilt—you gave him a message at the Celtic Festival."

The words seemed to rattle her. Frowning, she jerked away and continued toward the door.

Brooke was right behind her. "You met him at one of Nina's workshops, didn't you?"

"How would you know about that?"

"He told me. What happened next? How did you come to be friends?"

"I told him I was the stage manager for *Dracula* and he said that sounded like fun. He's a nice man. That's all."

"A nice man who hosts vampire ceremonies in a deserted farmhouse?"

Amy's face went white. Whiter, if possible, than usual.

"How involved are you with this vampire cult?"

"Vampire cult? I have no idea what you're…" Amy's voice trailed off and she pointed toward the stage. "Can we talk about this later? You need to start rehearsal."

She was right. Dracula was trying to stuff a skinny tech kid into the coffin while cast members egged him on. If Brooke didn't get things under control, the evening would be a total loss.

"We'll talk afterward," Brooke told her.

"Fine. But first I'm going to the lav. I'll be right back."

Amy didn't return.

In fact, she didn't report for school or rehearsal for the rest of the week. Brooke repeatedly tried her cell, and when she didn't get an answer, she called Amy's mom who said Amy's diabetes was out of control. The doctors were adjusting her insulin, and she'd be staying home until the problems were resolved. In the meanwhile, her teachers were emailing assignments, and the Marches had hired a tutor. When Brooke called again, neither Amy nor her mother answered. The following day Dr. Pierce told Brooke to ask someone to take over Amy's responsibilities.

It might have been true about Amy's health. Or, as was more likely, Ron Webster had spoken to Rupert March about Amy's nocturnal activities and March had opted to pull her out of school in order to keep her under close surveillance. Or maybe the death threats had started up again, and the March family was hiding out in the well-stocked bunker Amy had spoken about. Brooke tried to get the details from Dr. Pierce, but he remained tight-lipped while Receptionist Jocelyn Fisher claimed to be totally clueless because, after all, no one ever tells her anything.

One rainy afternoon Brooke drove down the narrow lane leading to the March's house. She stopped in front of the wrought-iron gate and sat there with the engine idling and the headlights gleaming on the shiny, black metal. Lights glistened inside the massive dwelling, and a solitary SUV kept watch from the driveway. Were the Marches home, she wondered, or were the lights and the car merely stage pieces put in place to create the illusion that the house was occupied?

By now another student had stepped forward to take Amy's place, and as per the expression, the show went on, and so did the long dreary days leading up to opening night. The Chris Van Auken saga continued to take center stage, and each night the kids showed up with rumors about motorcycle-sightings on rural lanes, abandoned campsites in distant woodlands and solitary strangers appearing in out-of-the-way villages and disappearing without a trace.

The legends took on an increasingly disturbing tone with each story that surfaced. Van Auken attended survivalist camps as a kid. He possessed skills the average person didn't possess. He was a hunter and a gatherer. He knew which plants could nourish and which could kill. He could run and hide and outfox those less crafty than himself. He was dangerous. A menace. A feral creature who was nowhere and everywhere at the same time. He was Clyde Barrow. John Dillinger. Billy the Kid.

Brooke finally heard from the tall, gangly vampire, but the information Steve Haskins provided, while initially encouraging, led to a series of dead ends. He'd managed to track down a few numbers in his cell phone—each one a possible connection to Amy March's masked contact. Brooke checked them out, but they led to land lines in public places—one at a sports bar, one at a truck stop and one at a convenience store.

And Dr. Rodney Cavendish? Instead of haunting her steps as Brooke had feared, he was keeping to himself. There was no mention of him on the news, and even Uncle Nelson seemed to be avoiding the topic.

Meanwhile Ron Webster's political campaign was shifting into high gear as election day drew near. Billboards kept springing up across the region, featuring enormous photos of the candidate shaking hands with veterans, kibbitzing with senior citizens and schmoozing families at fall foliage festivals. One showed him in skintight black spandex, his arms raised in victory as his racing bike sped across the finish line. Another depicted him in Native American feathers and buckskins, whooping it up for wide-eyed Cub Scouts gathered around a campfire.

And now it was Friday, one week before the show's Halloween opening. Rain darkened the skies, and with sports practices canceled, the rehearsal got started right after school. Normally the energy would be building as opening night approached, but the dreary weather and even drearier circumstances dampened everyone's spirits.

The weather was no deterrent, however, to the individuals gathered outside the building. Descendants of the Lenni-Lenape tribe had assembled in the parking lot to protest Webster's misappropriation of their clothing, culture and customs. They wanted the offending billboards removed, and they wanted a public apology from the Webster campaign. The gathering was peaceful as they stood in the rain, waving signs and giving voice to their traditional chants, and as usual, the press was there to capture every detail.

Brooke found Dr. Pierce in the faculty lounge. "I've always been a quiet man," he said as he watched the protest from the window. "All I ever wanted was a well-stocked library and the hushed silence of minds engaged in learning. How is it that these things keep happening at my school?" Mystified, he shook his head and left the room.

Back in the auditorium Brooke tried to call the cast to order, but the kids were distracted by the protest rally. When not needed on stage, they left to stare out the windows or sneak out to the parking lot and return with water-soaked brochures about the Lenni-Lenape and their customs. With opening night only a week away, the rehearsal was a flop, and the evening ended with a sense of discouragement that bordered on hopelessness.

But it wasn't just the rehearsal. A tedium had settled over everything, a soul-sickening lethargy resulting from Rachel Leventhal's accident, Nina Powell's death and the dismal circumstances surrounding Chris Van Auken's disappearance. Halloween approached, brightening the Lehigh Valley with jack-o'-lanterns and strings of orange lights, but for Brooke, everything had become dull and lifeless. Hamlet once complained, *"how weary, stale, flat, and unprofitable seem to me all the uses of this world,* and she was inclined to agree with him.

Thirty-five

The week leading up to Halloween brought good news for a change. Rachel Leventhal was steadily improving, and unlike Brooke's cast members, she was responding to directions. Lift your index finger. Nod if you hear my voice. Wiggle your toes. She even opened her eyes and smiled at her husband.

These signs were taken as harbingers of better things to come. The possibility of full recovery was being bandied about, and reports indicated that the doctors were encouraged by her progress.

Brooke wished someone was encouraged by the progress of the play, but no one was. She straggled into the auditorium on Tuesday, three nights before the Halloween opening that would launch the school's Bicentennial celebrations. With opening night just around the corner, she did all she could to inject life into a performance that seemed pretty much dead-all-over, and amazingly, it seemed to work—with everyone except Count Dracula.

At home that evening, Brooke checked her messages and

was surprised by a text from Amy: *I'm coming back to school. See you at rehearsal tomorrow night.*

▾ ▾ ▾

Erik Rimmer was the first person Brooke encountered when she arrived for Wednesday night's tech rehearsal. He greeted her with a sneer and turned away without speaking. While his attitude was annoying, Brooke had no trouble understanding why he kept being a jerk. If she hadn't busted him for that newsletter, the police wouldn't have conducted the massive computer audit that exposed his hacking skills. He was in big trouble, and there was talk of expulsion as well as criminal charges once the investigation was complete. That explained why he was being difficult, but Brooke clung to the hope that at the last minute, his enormous ego would kick in and lead to a stellar performance. The other possibility was that he'd bring *Dracula* crashing down around him as a statement of his contempt for the school and everyone in it.

The auditorium door swung open, and Amy appeared in the opening. The new insulin regimen her mother mentioned must have been successful because she looked surprisingly healthy. The fact that she'd ditched the dark eyeliner, the pale makeup, the pink and purple hair color and the occult jewelry added to the appearance of well-being.

"You'll never guess what," she said to Brooke, her eyes bright. "On my way here I stopped by the rehab center to visit Rachel Leventhal. She opened her eyes and said my name. The nurse said she ate some Jell-O®—the first real food since the accident!"

The good news energized the students, and even Count Dracula gave the best performance of the rehearsal season. At the close of Act III, Brooke gathered the cast and crew together for a critique of their performance. She ended her remarks by reminding the tech crew to double-check the switch that released the plastic vampire bat—if the timing were off by even a second, a critical scene would be ruined. Once that was settled, she laid her clipboard aside and congratulated the kids for pulling things together in spite of unbelievable obstacles. "If you keep this up at dress rehearsal tomorrow night," she told them, "we'll have a hit show when the curtain…"

"Sorry to interrupt," a voice shouted from the rear of the auditorium. Turning, Brooke saw Dr. Pierce and Ron Webster hurrying down the center aisle. Something was up—you could see it in the headmaster's expression and in the way Webster seemed to be avoiding eye contact with the students seated along the edge of the stage. Brooke could only imagine what the kids were thinking. Had Van Auken been arrested?

"I'd prefer not to be the bearer of bad tidings," Pierce said, his eyes darting from one puzzled face to another. "But after discussing the matter, Mr. Webster and I agreed it would be better if you heard this from us rather than on the ride home tonight."

An ominous silence followed those words. "This isn't an easy announcement to make," he finally said. "I'll try to keep it brief—just the facts as they were told to me a few minutes ago."

It had to be Van Auken, Brooke decided. The police caught up to him. There was a shootout, and he was dead. What else could this be about?

"I regret to inform you…" The words seemed to catch in the headmaster's throat. He shifted his gaze to the floor, lips pursed, brow furrowed. Finally, he looked back at the students. "I regret to inform you that earlier this evening, Rachel Leventhal passed away."

Amy bolted to her feet. "That's not possible! I was with her until five o'clock. She smiled and said my name. The nurse said she was getting better."

Webster looked up for the first time. "Be careful what you say, Amy. Ms. Leventhal died from a lethal dose of insulin someone placed in her IV bag. It might have been an accident, or it might have been…"

"It wasn't me!" Amy shrieked, her eyes racing from face to face. "You believe me, don't you?"

The students' silence suggested otherwise.

"Very little is known at this point," Dr. Pierce said. "As the investigation unfolds, Mr. Webster and I will do our best to…"

The door nearest the stage flew open, and Detective Burleigh strode into the auditorium, followed by his younger sidekick. Burleigh scanned the faces lined up in front of him and then pointed to Amy. "A word with you, Ms. March,"

"Me?" She looked around, her eyes wild with fear. "Why do you need to talk to me? I went to see Rachel this afternoon. She was fine. I had nothing to do with…"

"Silence!" a voice roared from the back of the auditorium. It was Amy's dad, flanked on either side by his two bodyguards. "You'll speak to no one, Amy," March shouted as he made his way down the center aisle. "Not the detectives, not Dr. Pierce, not Mr. Webster, not the police—not anyone. Not without my attorneys being present."

Amy's eyes darted from her father, to Burleigh, to Jason Radley, to Dr. Pierce and finally to Ron Webster. And then, as had happened that day at Brooke's apartment, a look of resignation took hold. Her face went blank, her shoulders sagged, and she fell silent as her father approached the stage and escorted her up the aisle. The body guards followed and so did the detectives and Dr. Pierce, leaving Ron Webster to deal with the fallout.

"Did Amy kill Ms. Leventhal?" a student asked.

"She has insulin with her all the time," someone responded.

"Does that mean she killed Nina, too?"

"Mr. Van Auken killed Nina—remember? That's why he ran off."

"Maybe the police made a mistake and it was Amy all along."

"It wouldn't surprise me. She's a total whack job."

Instead of mentoring the kids through this crisis, Webster stood on the sidelines as the accusations escalated. Finally Brooke spoke up. "Amy's your friend," she shouted over the uproar.

"That's right," Webster chimed in. "We shouldn't jump to conclusions although…" He left the unspoken accusation hanging in the air.

There was no point in trying to turn the tide. The students continued to heap suspicion on Amy, their voices shrill as they gathered their things and straggled out of the auditorium. Brooke said a less than friendly goodnight to Webster, and without waiting for an escort, raced to her car and tuned the radio to a local news channel. An anxious reporter added a detail to the story—the killer had left a calling card at the scene of the crime—the mark of the vampire on Rachel Leventhal's neck.

"Has Chris Van Auken returned to the region?" the reporter asked. "Or—as is more troubling—has he been among us all this time, armed, dangerous and waiting to strike again?

The questions, while chilling, struck Brooke as absurd. Van Auken was a wanted fugitive. For weeks his face had been all over the news. How could he have slipped, undetected, into a rehab center to kill Rachel Leventhal? It didn't seem remotely possible.

And what about Rodney Cavendish? Did the police follow up on the information Ron Webster shared? So far, Brooke hadn't heard a word about Cavendish on the news. Did that mean he wasn't a suspect? And what about Van Auken—was he innocent of these murders? What if the police misinterpreted the evidence and the case was no closer to being solved than when it opened? That meant the killer was still out there and no one knew who he—or she—was.

Brooke glanced up at the rearview mirror. Headlights in the distance seemed to be moving too fast for this narrow road. Is that the explanation for Rachel Leventhal's accident? Did someone speed up behind her and force her off the road? Was the same thing about to happen again?

She felt her palms sweating as she gripped the steering wheel. By now a black SUV was on her tail and drawing closer. Should she speed up? No—she was already driving too fast. The car pulled closer, and then, with a blare of the horn, lurched out of the lane and sped past. Not a killer after all. Just some hotshot in too big of a hurry.

Other headlights came and went, and with each approaching vehicle, Brooke narrowed her eyes and squinted at the faces in the mirror. At this distance and in the dark, the features were indiscernible. Someone could be following her and she'd have no idea who it was. But maybe she wasn't being followed. Maybe the killer already knew where she lived.

She pictured that person hiding in the parking lot outside the Beacon Arms, crouched behind a vehicle and watching for her arrival. She imagined herself getting out of her Outback, and then, before she could take a step—a hand over her mouth, a gun to her back and a whispered threat as she was forced into a waiting car.

She told herself to calm down. She was letting her imagination run away with her. A few deep breaths and she'd be fine—in for the count of ten, out for the count of ten and repeat.

It seemed to work. Enough, at least, to stop her hands from shaking as she pulled into the lot outside the Beacon Arms. She found a parking space and sat in the darkness, sizing up the distance from the car to the front door. Fifty yards, more or less. A quick sprint and she'd be home free.

Her gaze shifted to the rearview mirror and then to the two side mirrors. The coast was clear. No one wanted to kill her, and why would they—she knew nothing and was a threat to no one. Tonight's jitters were an entirely predictable response to the news of Rachel Leventhal's unexpected death. Nothing more and nothing less.

She got out of her Outback, and at the same moment, a car door slammed nearby. It was just as she feared—someone had been waiting for her. She looked up at the lights gleaming from five floors of apartments. The night was chilly, the windows closed. If she screamed, would anyone hear her?

Thirty-six

She flew toward the door and stumbled into the lobby. When she screamed, doors cracked open on both sides of the corridor and startled faces peered out. Further down the hall, a muscular guy with a thick black beard burst out of an apartment, a rifle raised to his shoulder. Brushing Brooke aside, he strode toward the door, his sight fixed on whoever'd followed her.

"Put yer hands up, ya scumbag!" he roared. "Do it now, or I'll blow your head off!"

By now Brooke had stopped screaming, but she was trembling from head to toe and terrified at the thought of being so close to the person who'd murdered Nina and Rachel. But she wasn't the only one who was alarmed. Residents crouched in their doorways, hands covering their ears as they braced themselves for the blast.

But there was no blast. Thanks to the guy with the beard, the rat was cornered and justice was about to be served. But when Brooke turned around, the face she saw took her by surprise.

"Ted!" she gasped. "What are you doing here?"

He didn't answer—he was too busy staring down the barrel of the gun.

"My mistake," she stammered to the gunman. "I thought he was someone else." She glanced sheepishly at her neighbors quivering in their doorways. "Sorry," she called out. "False alarm."

Scowling, the residents of the Beacon Arms slammed their doors and disappeared into their apartments. They'd been primed for a show, and this one had fizzled out.

The gunslinger lowered his rifle and grabbed Ted by the collar. "Watch yer step, ya piece a crap. Understand?" When Ted nodded, the guy with the beard released him with a shove and turned to Brooke. "You okay?" he asked.

She nodded. "Sorry for the misunderstanding. And thanks so much for your help."

His gaze lingered a while longer than seemed necessary. "If you ever need anything..." He smiled—sort of—and gestured down the hall with the barrel of his rifle. "I'm in number 107." With that, he strode to his door and disappeared.

For a moment there was silence.

"That was quite a greeting," Ted said as he straightened his shirt and adjusted the collar.

"I thought you were a murderer."

He nodded sympathetically. "I heard the news and came running. I tried calling and texting, but I guess your phone was off. I had to make sure you were alright."

Brooke was about to tell him she was fine and he could leave now, but the words got stuck in her throat. She didn't want him to leave. She wanted him to stay. Not because he was Ted, but because he wasn't Chris Van Auken or Rodney Cavendish or some unknown killer who'd been waiting to attack.

Ten minutes later they sat at the kitchen table and sipped Earl Grey tea while Brooke filled him in on the things they hadn't had a chance to discuss that night at Don Giovanni's. She spared none of the details. Her visit to Rodney Cavendish's office. The phone call from Mordonna. The vampire ceremony at the farmhouse. Her chat with Steve Haskins. Her encounter with Cavendish at her uncle's apartment and later outside the Hewitt Gallery.

Ted's frown deepened as the story progressed. "Just because the police couldn't pin anything on this Cavendish guy doesn't mean he's not dangerous," he said once she'd finished. "Look at the creepy stuff he's into. Vampires. Drinking human blood. Following you to the art gallery. Things get pretty freakish when people start acting out their delusions."

Brooke took a sip of tea and fell silent. She knew where this was headed. At any second Ted would launch into one of his wild stories. Not about Nazis this time, but about vampires. Maybe it was time to thank him for his concern and send him home.

But he didn't launch into a wild story about vampires. Instead, he got to his feet, walked over to the window and gazed down at the fire escape. Frowning, he looked back at Brooke and then back at the fire escape.

"These stairs go straight down to the alley. Anybody could climb up."

"That's why I keep the windows locked.

"Windows break."

"So I've heard."

He looked back at the fire escape and scratched his head. "That does it," he said after a lengthy pause. "I'm staying here tonight."

Staying here? That was the last thing Brooke expected him to say.

"Two teachers from Sussex Academy are dead," he continued, "and I'm not going to stand by and let you be the third. But hey," he held up both hands and backed off a bit. "You've got nothing to worry about from me. I've got a sleeping bag in my Jeep. I'll sleep on the floor."

She eyed him suspiciously. "A sleeping bag? How convenient."

"I got prepared. I don't want you to be killed."

"I don't want that either."

"That makes two of us. You're not safe with that Cavendish guy on the loose, and the same goes for your Viking buddy and that Nazi kid who plays Count Dracula."

"And if one of them climbs the fire escape and smashes the window in the middle of the night—what then?"

Ted patted his pocket. "I've got a gun—remember?"

She did remember. It had scared the wits out of her a year ago, but it didn't scare her now. In fact, she wished she had one of her own. Her late husband had tried to make a markswoman out of her, but she'd resisted his attempts. Was it too late to learn?

She took another sip of tea and considered her options. She could send Ted home and spend the night waiting for Cavendish, Van Auken, Count Dracula or some other deranged lunatic to crash through her window. Or she could accept Ted's offer of protection. Would that be so bad? In the last several weeks, she'd endured enough angst to last a lifetime. For just one night it would be nice to drift off to sleep with an armed guard nearby.

"I guess that would be alright." she agreed. "And who knows. I might actually get a good night's sleep for a change."

"I'm glad we see eye-to-eye. And here's something else we need to see eye-to-eye on. First thing tomorrow morning, you need to share your vampire story with the detectives."

"Ron Webster spoke to them so I wouldn't have to."

"Maybe so, but the story should come from you. You were there; Ron Webster wasn't."

"It's not that simple. You seem to be forgetting about Detective Burleigh at the Nazi compound."

"I'm not forgetting anything, but Burleigh's not the not the only cop in town. It doesn't matter who you talk to—just make sure the details get from your lips to official ears."

With that settled, Ted went down to his Jeep to get his sleeping bag, and Brooke made up the sofa bed. When he returned, he arranged the sleeping bag on the floor between the sofa and the windows, kicked off his shoes and crawled inside. Brooke tossed him a couple of pillows and nestled beneath the covers while he got settled on the floor.

"I hope you don't snore," she said.

"Did I snore a year ago?"

The question took her back to that night in the cabin in forest in the middle of nowhere. "No, you didn't."

"See. You've got nothing to worry about."

She turned off the light and lay in the darkness, listening to the rhythm of Ted's breathing. It was an unfamiliar sound in this apartment where the rumble of trash trucks in the alley and the clomping of footsteps in the hall were the sounds that typically greeted her ears. It was a gentle sound, and it felt good having someone near.

▾ ▾ ▾

Brooke woke with a start. She'd heard a noise. Was it real or was she dreaming? Footsteps—she was sure of it. Close by— right here in the apartment. She relaxed when she remembered that Ted was with her. At least, that is, until she noticed him tiptoeing across the room, his gun pointed at the door.

"Shh," he whispered. "Don't say a word." The instructions that followed were drowned out by the sound of angry fists pounding on the door.

"Open up!" a voice roared. "I know you're in there."

Ted inched closer. "Keep still," he whispered. "Maybe the

person will give up and disappear."

But the person didn't disappear. Instead, the pounding got louder and so did the voice. "Open up!" it roared. "Now!"

Brooke threw back the covers and scrambled to her feet. "I know that voice. It's Detective Burleigh."

Ted hurriedly tucked his gun away while Brooke undid the locks. When she opened the door, Burleigh burst inside, a warrant held out in front of him. Jason Radley was right behind him, a smirk on his face.

"We're looking for Amy March," Burleigh snarled, his eyes darting around the tiny apartment. "Where are you hiding her?"

Without waiting for an answer, he bolted to the closet, yanked it open and rummaged through the contents. Meanwhile Jason Radley headed for the bathroom, and Brooke could hear him flinging back the shower curtain to see if Amy was hiding there.

Burleigh eventually gave up on the closet, but his face brightened at the sight of Ted's sleeping bag under the window. "Aha! She was here all right."

"No, she wasn't," Brooke argued.

"Of course, she was." He nodded at Radley who'd returned empty handed from the bathroom. "The March kid must have crawled out of the sleeping bag and down the fire escape. Follow her!"

Nodding, Radley threw open the window and clattered down the steps and into the night.

"Excuse me, Detective," Ted interrupted. "Amy wasn't in that sleeping bag when you started pounding on the door. I was."

Burleigh looked at Brooke's sofa bed and at the sleeping bag on the floor and back at the bed. "Hah! How stupid do you think I am? I knock on the door. A few seconds pass. I knock again. A few more seconds pass, I knock again, and a few more seconds pass. That gives the two of you time to throw on your clothes while the March kid runs down the fire escape."

He walked over to the sleeping bag and poked at it with his foot. "I'll have to take this to the station. Who knows what we'll find? Fibers. Hair. Some sort of evidence to prove Amy March was here." He pulled a pair of latex gloves from his pocket. "Now if you two lovebirds will excuse me—" He knelt down and rolled up Ted's sleeping bag.

"Get your jackets," he ordered once he'd finished. "I'm taking both of you with me."

▾ ▾ ▾

The interview lasted until four in the morning. In the course of the interrogation, bits of information emerged to clarify the details of Amy's disappearance. She'd disabled the security system at her house and sneaked out while her dad was working in his study with the door closed. Once March wised up, he called the police and said that Amy must have hightailed it to Brooke's apartment as she'd done once before.

It wasn't easy to convince the detectives that Brooke knew nothing about Amy's disappearance. Eventually, however, they accepted her story, and bit-by-bit Brooke told them the things she'd learned in the last few weeks. She kept silent about the Nazi compound and the pepper spray, but she was completely forthcoming about Dr. Cavendish, Steve Haskins and the midnight ritual at the farmhouse in New Jersey.

The detectives didn't say anything to indicate that either Ron Webster or Rupert March had shared this information at some earlier date. Instead, they let Brooke tell her story as though this was the first time they'd heard it. There was an occasional raised eyebrow followed by requests for further details, but for the most part, they followed their usual protocol with Burleigh asking questions and Radley writing down answers.

Eventually they dismissed Brooke and Ted with a promise of further interviews to follow.

Back inside the apartment Brooke locked the door and sank into a seat at the kitchen table. Amy was out there somewhere, whether with Steve Haskins, Rodney Cavendish, Chris Van Auken or someone else, no one knew. She looked up at Ted. "Where is she?" she asked. "What happened to her?"

Ted sat down and placed his hand over hers. She was about to pull it away, but didn't. The gesture was comforting, and at the moment she needed comfort.

"There's only one thing we can do at this point," he said softly.

She knew Ted well enough to guess his meaning. He was going to pray.

"Care to join me?" he asked.

She didn't see the point, but she was too tired and too worried to object. She listened to the kind words he spoke and felt herself wishing there was someone on the other end, hearing what he said and acting on that request.

When the prayer ended, Ted heaved a sigh and gazed at the spot where his sleeping bag had lain. "I'm really tired, Brooke."

She got that. So was she.

"I'm not accustomed to being dragged to police headquarters in the middle of the night. To be honest, it hasn't happened at all since that night a year ago. You remember, don't you?"

Remember? The memory was permanently etched in every cell in her body.

"What I'm trying to say," he continued, "is that I'm exhausted and way beyond desire." He glanced longingly at the sofa bed. "I promise not to touch you."

"I'm too tired to notice."

She lay down on one side of the bed, and as she closed her

eyes, she felt Ted's weight settle in next to her. That was the last thing she remembered until, like a recurring bad dream, she was jolted awake by the sound of someone pounding on the door.

"Go away," she mumbled, half-awake and half-asleep.

"It's me," Maggie's voice trilled. "Open up!"

Brooke reached for her phone to check the time "Please," she moaned. "It's not even seven. I have dress rehearsal tonight and I…"

"I've got news about Amy March!"

Brooke hit the floor running. She opened the door, and Maggie bounded inside, wearing flannel pajamas and fuzzy slippers, her eyes wild and her hair sticking up in bright yellow clumps. She pointed toward the TV. "It's on every station. They found Amy March but…"

She caught sight of Ted and let out a shriek. "What's he doing here? You told me he was just a friend but…."

"Don't worry about it," Brooke said as Ted stretched and let out a yawn. "I'll explain later."

She turned on the TV and caught the tail end of a mouthwash commercial. When the news came on, she understood why Maggie had tried to break down her door.

"Amy March, daughter of real estate developer and radio host, Rupert March," the anchor began, "was found early this morning in a patch of woods near her house. Sources tell us she'd been strangled and left for dead with the telltale mark of the vampire on her neck. At present, there is no word as to her condition. Stay tuned for further details on this breaking story."

Thirty-seven

Ted staggered out of Brooke's apartment, bleary-eyed, sleep-deprived and worried. The news about Amy March had put the kibosh on further attempts at shut-eye, and while he'd tried to console Brooke, she was distraught and asked to be left alone. He hated to leave her. The danger wasn't over yet—not when the perpetrator of these crimes was near at hand.

An idea came to him as he unlocked the door to his Allentown rowhome. He'd drop in at tonight's dress rehearsal. Afterward, he'd follow Brooke home and stay with her like he'd done last night. He doubted she'd object. Not with the danger moving closer and narrowing the circle in which she stood.

After a shower and a gallon or so of coffee, he turned his attention to a video he needed to edit, but he couldn't focus on the task. Around eleven, he gave up and headed out the door for a final meeting with Reggie Ray. Tomorrow would be her last day as pastor.

He entered the old stone building and found Reggie in the sanctuary seated in the same pew where they'd sat on earlier occasions. She looked back at him with a smile, but there was more sadness in it than joy. And no wonder. Scaffolding stood in front of the plywood paneling covering the opening where the Shepherd window once stood. That could mean only one thing—in just a few days the goddess would preside over this place of worship.

He took a seat next to Reggie, his eyes still fixed on the scaffold.

"The goddess arrives next week. Reggie said. "As much as I hate to admit it, the window will be beautiful once it's finished."

"Beauty's in the eye of the beholder."

Reggie didn't respond. She didn't have to. She and Ted had already spent hours discussing the ordeals she'd faced since her sermon repudiating the goddess.

"Last time we talked," Ted said, "You hadn't decided what you'd do next. Any changes on that front?"

"Nothing concrete. Other than renting a cottage at the shore for a week."

He pretended to shiver. "A bit chilly for that, isn't it, with November right around the corner?"

"I don't mind. I'm looking forward to walks on the beach with the waves crashing on the sand and the air nipping at my face. I expect to get a lot of thinking done that way. Praying too. And I'm looking forward to crab cakes, clam chowder and fried shrimp. But just for a week. I can't stay still for long."

Ted understood the part about not staying still. He was a tad hyperactive himself. And he totally got the part about crab cakes, clam chowder and fried shrimp. He was running on a bellyful of coffee and was starting to feel a bit hollow. But he didn't say as much.

"And then what?"

"I intend to study and catch up on things I've missed over the years. And who knows—I might even head back to seminary to fill in the blanks. But one thing's for certain—my days as a pastor are over."

"Any thoughts on your next venture—beyond studying I mean?"

She nodded. "I think the Lord's calling me to full time ministry with trafficked women and children—without the goddess's help this time. She and I have parted ways, and sad to say, the same goes for most of the women in this church."

Ted could hear the sorrow in Reggie's voice. There'd been a huge backlash after her sermon. The loss of relationships built over twenty years had been particularly painful.

"I've still got a few friends," she said with a smile. "They're holding a luncheon tomorrow in my honor, and…"

The door crashed open behind them. Startled, Ted whipped around, and saw a space alien standing there. He blinked and looked again. No, it wasn't a space alien. It was a guy in a white padded outfit and matching helmet.

Reggie leapt to her feet. "I'm the pastor here. What's this about?

"A bomb threat. We're evacuating the building."

She drew back, clearly startled by the announcement.

The alien pointed to the door. "Out of here—now!"

"But I can't leave. The daycare center's full of children."

"We'll take care of them, ma'am. Just get out."

Ted wasn't about to make an exit, not when others' lives were at stake. Sliding out of the pew, he brushed past the alien and raced down the basement steps with Reggie following close behind.

"The babies," Reggie cried, as they pressed through the crowd of agitated workers, shrieking children and space aliens. "The nursery's up ahead on your right."

Ted darted into a large room lined with cribs and rocking chairs. The caretakers had already sprung to action, but there were too few of them to manage the number of babies. Ted scooped a kid out of a bouncy seat and another from a blanket on the floor while Reggie grabbed two sleeping infants from their cribs. Once outside, the police shunted them down the block to watch from a distance. Instead of waiting on the sidelines, Ted handed the babies to a caretaker and turned back to the building. He stopped in his tracks when an officer with a megaphone announced that the task was complete—the church was empty.

By then Reggie was on the phone, calling parents, grandparents and caregivers to pick up the children. Within minutes, those who worked or lived nearby began arriving at the scene. A youngish mom approached, her eyes scanning the little faces.

"I can't find Jamaal," she cried. "I've looked everywhere, but he's not here."

"He has to be," Reggie told her. "The police got everyone out."

"No. I'm telling you, he's missing."

Reggie grabbed Ted's arm. "Her son's on the autistic spectrum. When things get noisy, he hides under my desk and covers his ears. The police must have missed him."

Reggie called out to a nearby policewoman, but by then, Ted was already racing back to the church, zigzagging past a cop, crawling under a sawhorse barricade and scooting around a space alien who stood in his way. Inside the church, he took the basement steps two at a time, his footsteps echoing in the empty stairwell.

"Jamaal!" he shouted, but there was no answer. He continued to Reggie's office, threw open the door and found a boy who looked to be about four huddled underneath the desk, his eyes closed and his hands over his ears. The kid was clearly terrified, a fact that became evident when Ted tried to pull him out of his hiding place. There was a lot of biting, kicking and screaming, but Ted eventually extricated the child and lugged him up the stairs, out the main door and down the exterior steps. He spotted Jamaal's mom smiling and waving in the crowd. "Your mama's waiting for you," he told Jamaal. "Just a few more seconds and…"

A powerful explosion erupted from the building, filling the air with smoke and scattering debris in all directions. Something heavy struck Ted in the back of the head and knocked him to his knees. He struggled to regain his footing, but instead, he fell forward with Jamaal pressed tightly against his chest. As they hit the ground, Ted's thoughts flew from Jamaal to Brooke. He'd promised himself that he'd see her safely home after tonight's rehearsal. He tried to cling to the thought, but it slipped through his fingers and disappeared.

Thirty-eight

Amy's story dominated the news throughout the day, but as the hours ticked by, not a single new detail emerged. Frustrated with the lack of information, Brooke decided to stop by the hospital before rehearsal. Would she learn anything? Probably not, but it beat sitting in her apartment waiting for time to creep by.

She found a space in the crowded hospital parking lot and made the long trek to the main entrance. The area surrounding the double doors was packed with reporters. No surprise there—she'd watched all afternoon as these same reporters told the audience to stay tuned for further details on the Rachel Leventhal and Amy March stories—details that never materialized

A couple of cops stood by, holding the media at bay so the public could enter the building. Ron Webster was there as well, exuding empathy and saying the words politicians were expected to say at times liked this. He had the bases covered. Grief. Empathy. Thoughts and prayers. When he noticed Brooke, he fought his way through the sea of faces to join her.

"I need to apologize for the way I acted last night," he said, his expression sheepish. "I made things look bad for Amy. I've been beating myself up about it ever since."

"How is she?" Brooke asked. "Have you seen her?"

"No, but that's not why I'm here. I stopped by to visit my sister."

"Excuse me, Mr. Webster," a reporter shouted.

Webster smiled apologetically at Brooke. "Sorry. Gotta' run."

"Wait a minute," she called after him. "Your sister—is she okay?

He gave Brooke a thumbs-up. "The vitrectomy was a success. She's waiting for the doc to sign the discharge papers."

A reporter barged in between them with questions about the release date of Webster's therapeutic computer games. Brooke left them to their discussion and hurried through the double doors to the information desk in the lobby.

"Can you tell me what room Amy March is in?" she asked the white-haired volunteer.

"I'm sorry, ma'am. Ms. March is unable to have visitors."

"I'll only be a minute. Just long enough to look in on her."

"I said 'no visitors,' and that's exactly what I meant." The woman cast a wary glance toward the door and the reporters gathered outside. "They've been pestering me for information all afternoon. For all I know, you could be one of them."

Her message was loud and clear. There was no way she'd let Brooke see Amy—not when every reporter in the region had the same request. "If you can't let me see her," Brooke persisted, "can you at least tell me how she is? Amy's special to me, and I need to know if she'll be okay or if she'll..." She choked back the thought that had haunted her throughout the day—the thought that Amy might die.

Seeing Brooke's distress, the woman's expression softened a bit. "I wish I could help you, dear—I really do—but I'm not privy to that information. And besides," she nodded over her shoulder toward an officer who stood guard nearby. "We've been given strict orders regarding this particular patient."

The cop's stony gaze told Brooke all she needed to know. Amy was a crime victim, and a high-profile one at that. There'd be no news until the authorities said so.

An elevator door slid open nearby and a crowd shuffled into the lobby. Rupert March was among them, his head lowered and his shoulders sagging. When he saw Brooke, he drew himself up sharply and hastened in her direction.

"There's something I think you should see," he said, his tone accusatory. He glanced at the volunteer. "It's all right, ma'am. She's with me." After that, he went over to the cop and exchanged a few words. Once that was done, he took Brooke by the arm and hustled her toward the elevator. They rode together in silence, and when the door opened on the seventh floor, he steered her through a maze of corridors, past a nurses' station and down a long hallway to a door guarded by a man Brooke recognized as one of March's bodyguards. The guard stepped aside and allowed them to enter the room where Amy lay, an IV in her arm and medical equipment beeping all around her.

"Go ahead," March instructed. "Take a look."

Brooke approached the bed and looked down at Amy. Her complexion was a deathly white, her breathing barely discernible, her hair a golden halo against the pillow. Once again Brooke thought of a cemetery angel, carved this time in alabaster instead of granite.

"I tried to warn you, didn't I?" March said, his voice brittle as he joined Brooke at his daughter's bedside. "I told you these were perilous times and the school was out of line for allowing this vampire nonsense to go unchecked. But you thought you knew better and so did Dr. Pierce and the schoolboard. It's healthy fun, everyone said, and now…"

He leaned over the bed and brushed a strand of hair from Amy's face. A glance confirmed what Brooke had heard on the news. Two puncture wounds—the mark of the vampire.

March grasped his daughter's hand and pressed it to his lips. "Who did this to you, Sweetie?" he whispered, his voice quavering. "Wake up—please—and tell me."

He remained like that, fragile and broken as he gazed down at the face on the pillow. The moment was a tender one, so tender that Brooke felt like an intruder—at least until a nurse bustled into the room, all business and efficiency as she hustled from monitor to monitor, checking digital readouts and blinking lights. She made a few notes in a tablet and exited as quietly as she'd entered, leaving behind, not the tender-hearted father of a moment ago, but the bellicose individual Brooke had come to know.

"I warned the administration that Chris Van Auken was up to no good," but Dr. Pierce wouldn't hear of it. 'He's one of our most popular teachers,' he told me. 'The students love him.' Well, this is what comes of ignoring trouble when it's right under your nose."

Brooke's thoughts flew to Dr. Cavendish and his vampire cult. "What about Rodney Cavendish?" she asked. "What are the police saying about his role in all this?"

Before March could answer, a woman's voice rang out from the hall. "Sorry to take so long. There was a line in the cafeteria, and I didn't…" Fern March's jaw dropped when she entered the room and saw Brooke standing beside Amy's bed. There was silence for a moment, and then Fern turned angrily toward her husband. "The police said no one was to enter this room except us," she told him, her voice shrill. "For Amy's safety, Rupert. They made that clear from the start."

"The matter was left to our discretion," March responded defensively. "And as it turns out, Ms. Roberts was just leaving." He turned to Brooke. "Weren't you?"

Brooke nodded—what else could she do? "Before I go," she said, "can you at least tell me how the detectives handled the information about Dr. Cavendish?"

March seemed perplexed by the question. "I have no idea who you're talking about."

"Of course, you do. Ron Webster told you all about him."

"Ron and I haven't spoken in months."

"That's not possible. Dr. Cavendish is a music professor who…"

"Why are you bothering us with this?" Fern interrupted "Can't you see how upset we are?"

"Please Mrs. March," Brooke begged. "You have to listen to me. In my opinion, Dr. Cavendish…"

"My husband and I aren't interested in your opinion. You laughed in our faces when we tried to warn you about Amy's obsessions, and now you have the audacity to barge into her hospital room and expect us to listen to what you have to say?" She pointed at the door. "Leave! And if you tell the reporters about your visit, we'll sue you for everything you're worth. Do you understand?"

March's bodyguard poked his head through the door. "Is there a problem, Boss?"

March shook his head. "My wife is distraught. Would you be so kind as to show Ms. Roberts to the elevator?"

The guard glared at Brooke like she was a bug he'd be happy to crush. "This way," he said.

"That won't be necessary. I can find the elevator myself."

Brooke fought back tears as she made her way past the nurses' station and through the maze of corridors to the elevator. There was no denying it. Webster hadn't told Rupert March about Rodney Cavendish. If he had, Amy might not be lying in that hospital bed. She thought back to the conversation with Detective Burleigh in the early hours of the morning. No wonder he hadn't mentioned having heard the Cavendish story before—Webster hadn't bothered to follow through.

"Are you alright?" the woman at the information desk asked when Brooke walked by. She nodded but said nothing. If she stopped to talk, she'd either scream or break down in tears. Neither response would be helpful. Not when she had a mission to accomplish.

Outside, she scanned the faces gathered around the door. She was determined to find Ron Webster and tell him off, right there in front of the reporters with their cameras and their microphones. She wouldn't be specific—she'd respect the Marches' privacy—but she'd make sure the media knew that Webster was a liar, a fraud and a self-centered, arrogant jerk whose promises meant absolutely nothing.

Two minutes later she still hadn't spotted him.

"He left a short time ago," a reporter told her. "You just missed him."

Fuming, Brooke hurried toward her car, her eyes searching for Webster among those coming and going in the parking lot, but he was nowhere to be seen. Halfway to the school, a billboard appeared on her right—Webster, dressed head-to-toe in black spandex, his hands raised in victory as his bike raced across the finish line. *Elect a Winner!* it instructed. A few miles later another billboard loomed in front of her, this one showing Webster whooping it up in his Native American costume in front of a bunch of wide-eyed Cub Scouts. She didn't bother reading the message. Whatever it said would be a lie.

Her anger was still raging when she arrived at Sussex Academy, but instead of storming into the building, she turned off the engine and sat for a while in silence. Running a dress rehearsal required focus and clear thinking, and at the moment, she was incapable of either. She tried the deep breathing routine—in for ten, out for ten—but it produced only meager results.

Even so, she was pleasantly surprised when she entered

the fine arts lobby and saw what the theater students had been up to all day. Paper bats hung from the ceiling, and an inflatable Dracula stood in one corner, creating the campy, fun feeling that went with this version of the story. A refreshment table decorated to look like a coffin added to the vibe, as did the gothic candelabras at either end. One wall was lined with black and white pictures of the cast, manipulated in Adobe® Photoshop® to include a touch of red, but the main focal point was the poster Nina'd designed: a huge image of Count Dracula in black and white with a drop of red blood on one fang. Underneath were the words, *Black and White, Undead All Over*—Nina's publicity slogan for the play.

Tom-the-Rent-a-Cop stood nearby, studying something mounted on the wall near the auditorium door. Brooke assumed it was related to the play, but when she went over to take a look, it turned out to be a smaller version of Webster's Native American Billboard. The sight threw fuel on her anger, and it was a struggle to maintain her composure.

"That show coming along all right?" Tom asked.

"Fingers crossed. Count Dracula's still a wild card."

Tom chuckled at the remark. "He's a wild card all right. One look at that young fella and I could tell he was up to no good. I should know—I've seen plenty like him in my day."

He noticed her staring at the photo. "That picture caused quite a stir around here a few weeks back, bringing out all those protesters like it did. Think I should take it down before it causes more trouble?"

"Absolutely. This is the fine arts lobby, not Webster's private campaign headquarters."

"Would you like it?"

"Sure. I'll use it as a dart board. Or better yet, I'll rip it to shreds and burn it."

Tom eyed her curiously. "I'd hang onto it, if I were you. Mark my words. Ron Webster's headed for big things. I wouldn't be surprised to see him in the Senate one day. Or even the White House."

"If that happens, I'll pack my bags and leave the country."

Tom ignored her cynicism. "Ya know," he said as he removed the image from the wall, "Ron let me in on a little secret about this photo. Looks like it was shot at night, doesn't it? Well, guess what? It was shot late in the afternoon and edited in Photoshop® to make it seem like night. Look at that starlit sky and the firelight gleaming on the Cub Scouts' faces. Hard to believe it's not real."

"Hah—it's a fake—just like Ron Webster."

She left Tom contemplating the photo and went into the auditorium to greet the students as they arrived. Before long, the place was buzzing with the nervous excitement that precedes the final rehearsal.

"You guys decent?" she called through the door of the boys' dressing room. Hearing a chorus of yeses, she went inside for an inspection. Whiskers in place. Costumes buttoned and zipped. Makeup applied. There was only one problem. Dracula was nowhere in sight. Was Erik pushing her buttons by refusing to arrive on time? Or worse—did he intend to sabotage the play by ditching dress rehearsal? The former she could deal with; the latter spelled disaster.

As it turned out, neither was true. She found him center stage beneath the lights while the makeup person, a ditzy sophomore named Isabel, covered his short, sandy hair with black spray. That done, Isabel started in on the white face makeup and ended up smearing it in his hair. She dabbed at the blotch and inadvertently wiped off the black spray, revealing the lighter hair beneath. "I'm making a mess of this," she moaned.

"Do it this way," Brooke instructed. "Spray his hair and cover it with a shower cap before you apply the makeup. That way the colors won't get smeared. There should be a couple of shower caps in the make-up kit."

Isabel shook her head. "There aren't, but now that you mention it, I noticed one in Mr. Webster's office when I spoke to him the other day. He was here a few minutes ago—maybe he'll let us borrow it."

Brooke resisted the impulse to tell Isabel what she thought of Ron Webster. "Why would he have a shower cap in his office?" she asked instead.

"Beats me. It was more of a black bathing cap sort of thing." She paused to wave at someone. "Oh, hi. We were just talking about you."

Brooke turned and saw Webster strolling down the center aisle.

"Talking about me, Isabel?" he said with a smile. "I hope you were saying something nice."

"We need a shower cap. I knew you had one in your desk."

He looked perplexed. "In my desk?"

"That's right. I was talking to you last week—remember? You opened a drawer and I saw a black shower cap."

"You must be mistaken."

"It doesn't matter," Brooke said impatiently. "I'll stop at a drugstore on the way home and pick up a few for tomorrow night."

By now the cast and crew were gathering on the stage for a final assessment under the lights. Webster took advantage of the moment to make a flowery speech about the kids persevering through tough times, and once that was over, he told them to break a leg and promised that he and his wife would be in the audience on opening night. He excused himself to dash off to what he termed "a super important campaign engagement," but stopped halfway to the door and looked back at Isabel.

"That was a skull cap, not a shower cap. It lessens wind resistance in a bike race—like the one I was in last weekend. That explains the confusion."

Isabel nodded. "I guess so."

"And by the way, I won the race. Are you going to congratulate me?"

"Sure. Congratulations."

Brooke watched in disgust as Webster continued on his way. He had time to run a political campaign, create computer games and win bike races, but he didn't have time to follow up on a commitment that could have kept a young girl from harm. He was a phony, just like the phony billboard picture that magically turned day into night.

A tech kid barged into her thoughts. "We're ready to start when you are."

She smiled at the boy's bright expression. "Okay—let's do it." She took a seat in a middle row, and on cue, the house lights went down, the creepy Dracula music boomed from the speakers, the curtains opened, and the stage lights came up. It was showtime!

"Sorry to interrupt," Dr Pierce shouted from the back of the auditorium.

Once again she fought back the urge to scream. Didn't this man understand what these kids had been through? Didn't he realize how important it was for dress rehearsal to go off without a hitch?

"A word with you in private," Pierce said. "Out in the lobby, if you don't mind."

Sighing, Brooke rose to her feet and followed him out of the auditorium and into the lobby with its Dracula decorations.

"I'll make this brief," the headmaster began, "The school board just met in an emergency session. After everything's that happened, they've decided that it doesn't make sense to go forward with our bicentennial activities. That means the play and everything else will be postponed until a later date."

Brooke threw her hands in the air. "So, after all we've been through, Dracula's cancelled the night before we open?"

"Not cancelled. Postponed."

"Until when?"

He shrugged. "Our calendar's full for the remainder of the year. It will be tough to move things around."

"Oh, really? So, you're planning to rent storage and pay someone to haul the sets and the costumes there?"

Dr. Pierce stared down at the floor—he obviously hadn't thought this through. "We'll come up with something," he assured her. "You agree, don't you, that the decision's appropriate?"

"Of course, I agree that it's appropriate. I thought we should have cancelled the night Nina was murdered. Instead, we slogged through weeks of rehearsals only to have you pull the plug at the last minute. What am I supposed to tell the kids?"

"I'll break the news." Pierce said somberly.

The students seemed to accept the board's decision. There were no arguments, just a quiet sadness as they shuffled into the dressing rooms and got out of their costumes and makeup. The whole process took about half-an-hour, and as they left the building, Brooke gave each student a hug—even Erik—not knowing if she'd ever see any of them again.

Once they were gone, she climbed the steps and went backstage. The boys' dressing room was a mess, and she took a few minutes to put away tubes of makeup, cans of hairspray and the costume pieces that lay scattered about. She made a similar visit to the girls' dressing room which was in only marginally better shape. Afterward, she closed the heavy velvet curtains and turned off the lights, leaving only the dull orange glow of an emergency light shining on the Act I set.

She glanced at the Victorian wallpaper, the velvet settee and the marble-topped tables. A lot of work had gone into this project, and her disappointment at cancelling it was profound— but not nearly as profound as her anger at Ron Webster. He'd been at the hospital today, not to apologize to the Marches for his negligence, but to pay a visit to his sister and to turn Amy's suffering into a photo op. Brooke recalled the term he'd used to describe his sister's medical procedure. For some reason, the word was stuck in her head, but she had no idea what it meant. It would take only a few seconds to look it up.

Thirty-nine

Reggie turned her gaze back to what was left of the place that had been her spiritual home for the last twenty years. The front of the church lay in ruins while the left side slumped listlessly toward the center. In the morning FBI agents would arrive to sort through the debris, and then cranes and bulldozers would arrive to complete what the bombers had begun. In the meanwhile, police tape lent an eerily festive note to the scene, like yellow crepe paper at a child's birthday party. Spotlights lit the sky, and a jovial mood hung over those who'd gathered in the chilly darkness to sip coffee and gawk at the spectacle. Reporters were there as well, their presence adding to the carnival atmosphere as they made their way through the throng in search of details to spice up the eleven o'clock news.

"We've posted a couple of officers to keep watch overnight," a tired policewoman told her. "Other than that, there's not much more we can do."

"Any recent updates?"

The cop shook her head. "Not a word since the most recent press conference"

Stories related to the bombing had filtered down to Reggie throughout the afternoon. Initial reports called it a hate crime perpetrated by white supremacists, notably a band of neo-Nazis rumored to be headquartered in the area. The FBI and Department of Homeland Security had initially supported these claims, but in the last hour, another story had begun to take shape. It seemed that a left-leaning anarchist group had carried out the bombing with the intent of laying the blame on their political opponents. A false flag in other words, orchestrated to slant the media narrative now that election day was drawing near. Three people had been arrested—two men and a woman—but a search was on for those who'd organized and funded the attack.

Reggie sighed at the thought of people doing such a thing to further a political agenda. Was the country really that divided? She laughed inwardly at the question. Of course, it was.

The bright spot in the midst of all this dismal news was that none of the children and none of the daycare staff had been injured in the explosion. Even Jamaal had only a few minor bumps and bruises thanks to Ted Roslyn's protective care. Ted's condition remained uncertain—he was apparently still unconscious, but there'd been no word as to the extent of his injuries. Reggie closed her eyes offered a silent prayer for his recovery—the hundredth time she'd offered this prayer since the bomb blast shattered the silence of this late October afternoon.

A wave of fatigue told her it was time to go home and rest up for the difficult day that awaited her. A handful of women from the church—those who were still speaking to her—had arranged a farewell luncheon in her honor. But now, instead of spending her final hours with those she loved, she'd spend it with trustees and insurance agents, answering questions and slogging through mountains of paperwork.

She pulled her coat collar tighter around her neck and brushed something from her shoulder. The night had grown chilly, and the wind was sending bits of ash billowing through the air. She heard someone approach from the rear, and feeling a hand on her arm, she steeled herself for yet another encounter with the press. Instead, she was greeted by gallery owner, Madeleine Hewitt.

"I wish I could do something," Madeleine said softly. "Light a candle. Lay a wreath. Something. I feel so helpless."

"Being here is enough."

The two women stood together in the crowd as ashes floated in the breeze. They'd shared much in the last few weeks—Madeleine about her failing marriage; Reggie about her faltering ministry. In spite of their many differences, they had a lot in common. Both lives were in chaos. Both futures uncertain. Were they ships, shining a light to help the other navigate dark and treacherous waters? Or were they friends, traveling the sea together? Reggie hoped it was the latter.

▼ ▼ ▼

Brooke fished her phone out of her pocket and sat down on the Victorian settee in the Act I set. "*Vitrectomy,*" the online dictionary said. "*A surgical procedure to correct a condition known as diabetic retinopathy.*" She had to read the definition twice. Webster's sister was diabetic? Really? Did that mean he had access to insulin? And if so…

She thought back to that night when Detective Radley came to her apartment. He'd mumbled something about the storage closet being too clean, referring, of course, to a lack of fibers, hair, fingerprints and other tangible evidence to tie a suspect to Nina's murder. And then he'd added, "*It was like the perp was some kind of reptile.*" Brooke pictured the billboard of Webster in his racing gear. Spandex didn't shed fibers like other fabrics, leather gloves didn't leave prints and skull caps prevented loose hair from drifting to the floor.

The thought was ludicrous. She was getting carried away again, just like she'd done last night when she thought a killer was stalking her in the parking lot outside the Beacon Arms. And yet...

Her mind drifted from Detective Radley's comments to something Webster had said when he stopped by her apartment to discuss the plans for Nina's memorial service. *"I'm sure everyone at Sussex Academy will remember where they were at the time of Nina's murder. I was at home hosting a Cub Scout event with my wife. There I was, dressed as a Native American and whooping it up around a bonfire in our back yard while..."*

But that was a lie. The Cub Scout event had taken place hours earlier and the photos had been altered to make it look like night. Could Webster have exchanged his Native American buckskins for spandex and hurried off to the school to confront Nina? And what about his wife—did she go along with his story, and if so, was she an accomplice to murder?

The idea was laughable. The Webster's were an upstanding couple, and besides, the computer evidence linked Van Auken to the crime. Or did it? Webster had the programming skills to create computer games. Could he have hacked into the school's network and planted the evidence that incriminated Van Auken?

You're a bit of a sleuth yourself, Webster'd told Brooke that day outside the Hewitt Gallery. At the time, it seemed like a compliment, but what if the comment had a different meaning? What if Webster was afraid she'd find him out?

Calm down, she told herself. There was nothing to fear. Not tonight anyway. Not when Webster was at a campaign event with election day right around the corner.

Unless he'd lied. Unless there wasn't a campaign event. Unless he knew the play was cancelled and he was waiting for her outside the building.

She glanced toward the parking lot. She couldn't go out

there alone.

Hands trembling, she called Tom-the-Rent-a-Cop, but instead of his cheery voice, a tape instructed her to leave a message at the sound of the beep.

"This is Brooke," she began, and then stopped.

She'd heard something. A sound—muffled and barely audible. She listened, and heard it again. Footsteps. Catlike. Stealthy. Nothing like Tom's self-assured tread.

"Tom?" she whispered, but there was no response.

"Tom," she tried again, her voice catching in her throat. "Is that you?"

No answer.

The velvet curtain rippled slightly, causing the shadows to shift.

"Tom!" she shrieked, and this time her voice exploded from her throat. "Answer me, Tom. Is that you?"

The curtain parted and her screams died on her lips.

Forty

Webster eased through the opening in the closed curtain. Spandex. Leather gloves. Skull cap.

"Sorry to disappoint you, Brooke," he said. "Tom left with Dr. Pierce a few minutes ago. There was a phone call about an accident involving some of your theater students. A false alarm, but they don't know that yet. Since it's Mischief Night, the police will assume a couple of kids called in a bogus report. That means you and I have the building to ourselves."

Brooke backed slowly toward stage right. Could she dash down the steps and out the emergency exit without Webster stopping her? No. He was an athlete. She didn't stand a chance.

"I tried to warn you about Amy, didn't I?" he continued. "I told you to set boundaries. To keep your distance, but you didn't listen, did you? And you didn't listen when I slashed your tires and sent a warning. No—you had to keep snooping and prying. Believe me, I'm not the first therapist who's found himself in a compromising situation with an underaged client. It happens more frequently than you might imagine—an occupational hazard, so to speak. Amy was a frequent visitor to my office, and knowing how she thinks, it didn't come as a surprise when she described a love potion she'd purchased. I can still remember the look on her face when she offered it to me. Tempting. Daring. And above all—willing.

"Steve Haskins acted as a go-between, and for a while, things went smoothly. But when Rachel and Nina started asking questions, I knew I had to act. I couldn't stand by and let a couple of meddling women spoil everything I've worked so hard to accomplish. I have a destiny to fulfill. Not just for our county, but in years to come, for our great nation. Believe me, Brooke, I didn't want Nina to die. Or Rachel. And I didn't want to silence Amy. But they chose their fate—just like you've chosen yours."

He opened his hand and revealed a shiny object resting against the palm of his black leather glove. "A stiletto," he told her. "Forged in Tuscany by a master craftsman." Holding it up, he pressed a button and a blade sprang out. And then, ever the showman, he paused his recitation and carved a figure-eight in the air.

That moment of showmanship gave Brooke gave an opportunity. She lunged at Webster, intent on knocking the knife from his hand, but he jerked it away, laughing as she raced toward the curtain and groped for the opening. In an instant he was behind her, the knife poised above her head.

She heard it whiz past her ear, just missing her by an inch and getting tangled in the thick, velvet curtain. She pivoted away, ran back into the Act I set and took refuge behind a Victorian settee. When Webster came after her, she shoved the settee in his direction, hoping to knock him off his feet. He surprised her by leaping over it, and in a couple of strides, had her pinned against the Act I backdrop with the stiletto at her throat.

"If you'd heeded my warning, we wouldn't be here tonight,

would we?" he hissed through clenched teeth. "But you persisted, and now…" He pulled back the knife, but before he
could plunge it into her, she sprang forward and shoved her
hands against his chest, causing him to miss his mark and carve
a long, gaping incision in the canvas backdrop.

There was nowhere for Brooke to go but backward through
the torn canvas and into Dracula's crypt. She was trapped now
by cave walls on either side, an open coffin to her rear and Webster in front, blocking the only means of exit.

"When we're finished here," he said, his voice soothing,
like a priest performing last rites, "I'll lay you to rest in the spot
intended for Count Dracula. Days will pass before anyone
thinks to look for you backstage, and when they do, it will be
the stench of rotting flesh that gets their attention." He laughed
at the thought. "Perhaps I'll place something in the coffin with
you. Something to send the police scurrying in all the wrong
directions. The mark of the vampire on your neck or a swastika
on your face—painted with your own blood. That should keep
the heat turned up on Chris Van Auken, don't you think?"

Brooke said nothing—in part because terror had left her
speechless and in part because she knew something about
stagecraft Ron Webster didn't know. Her fingers found the edge
of the coffin. It was here somewhere—she just had to find it.
Yes—there it was.

With a push of a button, the plastic Dracula bat dropped
from the fly space and collided with Webster's hand. The im-
pact sent the stiletto flying through space, at the same time
throwing Webster off balance. When he reached out to steady
himself against the coffin, Brook brought the lid crashing down
on his wrist. A sickening crunch followed by profanities and
howls of pain echoed in her ears as she darted out of the crypt,
down the stage steps and into the parking lot.

But she wasn't safe yet. In a matter of seconds, Webster
was out of the building, racing toward her with a stake in his

good hand. The stake was supposed to end Count Dracula's life, but Webster's intention, Brooke knew, was to end hers.

She rounded her car, dove inside and started the engine. She backed out and the vehicle trembled—not from flat tires this time, but because Webster rammed the stake into the passenger side door. That first attempt was nonproductive, but on the second try, the window shattered, sending shards of glass flying over the upholstery. Brooke shifted into drive, but before she could get away, Webster took a flying leap and landed on the hood. She sped forward and slammed on the brakes, hoping to dislodge him, but, he held on, his face distorted with pain and rage. Their eyes met through the windshield, and it seemed to her that the man was no longer human. He'd become a monster, a crazed spandex serpent writhing closer and closer.

Another inch and he thrust the stake into the windshield. The first attempt accomplished nothing and neither did the second. The third, however, sent a spider web of tiny cracks rippling across the glass, reducing visibility to zero. Brooke rolled down the window and leaned out to gauge her direction, but ducked back inside as the stake came at her.

There was nothing else to do but speed forward, steering wildly—blindly—toward what she hoped was the exit. This time when she slammed on the brakes, Webster lost his grip, flew off the hood and landed in a heap on the asphalt.

She continued in the direction she'd been going, her eyes glued to the speedometer. Five—ten—twenty—twenty-five miles per hour—and then…

Blam!

The air bag deployed and shards of glass ripped into her hands as she held them to her face. She parted her fingers enough to peer through what used to be the windshield. She thought she'd slammed into the building, but to her surprise, Detectives Burleigh and Radley looked back at her from inside their vehicle.

"Brooke Roberts," Burleigh said as he got out of his car and eyed the damage. "I might have known." He mumbled something about a bogus accident report tipping him off that there might be trouble at the school, but Brooke didn't wait for him to finish. Instead, she pointed a bloody finger at the crumpled form moaning on the macadam.

"Ron Webster," she gasped, barely able to find the words. "He killed Nina Powell and Rachel Leventhal. He intended to kill Amy March, and he just tried to kill me. Arrest him now, and I'll explain later.

Forty-one

The next day was Halloween, and the hospital halls were filled with nurses dressed up in wigs and crazy makeup. Brooke sat by an empty bed and waited for Ted to reappear. He didn't seem too concerned about the bruises and lacerations he'd suffered in the explosion but he was definitely bent out of shape about the concussion that left him with a raging headache, ringing ears and nausea. The nausea explained the sounds coming out of the bathroom—he was puking up his lunch. The good news was that there were no broken bones, no internal injuries, and no serious blood loss. In fact, he'd be going home as soon as the doctor signed the papers.

While she waited, Brooke watched videos of Reggie Ray hailing Ted as a hero. The claim was supported by the mother of a young child Ted rescued, but when he emerged from the bathroom, he didn't seem interested in listening to these words of praise. Instead, he found footage of EMTs lifting a stretcher from the back of an ambulance and carting a bruised and battered Ron Webster into the emergency room. The piece was followed by clips of county residents expressing horror at the charges that had derailed the frontrunner's political career just days before an anticipated landslide.

Once the story played out, Ted raised his foam coffee cup in a toast. "I have to hand it to you, Brooke. You're a dangerous woman."

▾ ▾ ▾

And just like that, November rolled in, bringing with it dark, dreary days balanced by shining hours of harvest and plenty.

When he realized he'd been framed, Chris Van Auken panicked and went into hiding. Once the veil of suspicion lifted, he decided to bag Sussex Academy and head off to Sweden to study the Vikings up close and personal. After that, he had his eyes set on grad school for a PhD in Nordic studies.

As it turned out, Detective Burleigh wasn't the nasty Nazi Brooke had feared. He'd been at the compound that night to find out if any cops were tangled up in that sordid business. His motives were of the highest order—he wanted to clean things up and restore the integrity of the force. And the neo-Nazis at the compound? They'd disbanded but as was often the case, they were expected to reassemble once the heat was off.

To Brooke's surprise, the police determined that Rodney Cavendish, while totally creepy, had done nothing illegal. He remained free to lead vampire tours to Whitby England and to preside over his secret circle of vampire wannabes. It was a free country, after all.

Amy March emerged from her coma after ten days, and while the doctors expected her to make a full recovery, emotional healing promised to be a bigger challenge—not just for Amy, but for her parents as well.

And finally, the Sussex Academy School Board voted unanimously to strike the set and move on as though Dracula had never darkened their doors. Even so, memories of those dark, dreary days lingered inside the ivy-covered walls and in the hearts and minds of those who walked its corridors.

Memories, after all, are a lot like Dracula.

They walk among us. Black and white. Undead all over.

Acknowledgements

Thanks so much to Sandra Carey Cody, Linda King, Andrea Mihaly, Wendy Kemmerer, David Kempf, Carol Billman, Marielena Zuniga and Mike Gerow for reading and commenting on different iterations of *Undead All Over*. Your insights at various stages of the journey have been amazing. Kudos to Jon Labs for creating and maintaining my website—your skills are greatly appreciated. And finally, a special thanks to my multi-talented husband, Wayne Labs, for sharing his expertise in all facets of editing and publishing.

About the Author

Author and artist Nancy Labs lives with her husband, tech editor and fine arts photographer Wayne Labs, in Bucks County, Pennsylvania. In addition to undergrad and graduate studies in English, History, Theater and Shakespeare, she's studied creative writing, screenwriting and painting in workshops and private studios. Her career has included forays into selling antiques and collectibles, teaching English and theater, writing features for local publications, editing for trade journals and book-length projects and coaching aspiring authors in the areas of screenwriting and fiction. She and her husband have collaborated on theater productions, publishing projects and art/photography exhibitions.

The Brooke Robers Mystery/Suspense Series springs from a lifetime fascination with historical puzzles, contemporary enigmas, theological conundrums and things that go bump in the night. *Undead All Over* is the second novel in the series.

You can visit her website: www.NancyLabs.com or contact her by email at BOOKS@Nancylabs.com.

Also Available

Wishing You Harm

Artist Karl Erikson hasn't been himself in the days before his death. He's been anxious. Fearful. Obsessively religious. Odd for someone who's been a lifelong atheist. His house is broken into six weeks after the funeral. The investigator asks his widow: Is there anyone who wishes you harm? Brooke can't think of a soul who wishes her harm, but how else to explain the break-in? Drawers emptied onto the floor. Upholstery slashed. Valuables left untouched. Did Karl hide a treasure somewhere in the house? Did the intruder find it, or will he be back to search again?

Brooke's search for answers leads her into a dark world of secret societies, coded symbols, ancient prophecies and spiritual warfare. She soon realizes that high-tech security cameras, motion detectors and alarms can't protect her from those who are out there in the night, watching, waiting, and wishing her harm.

Coming Soon

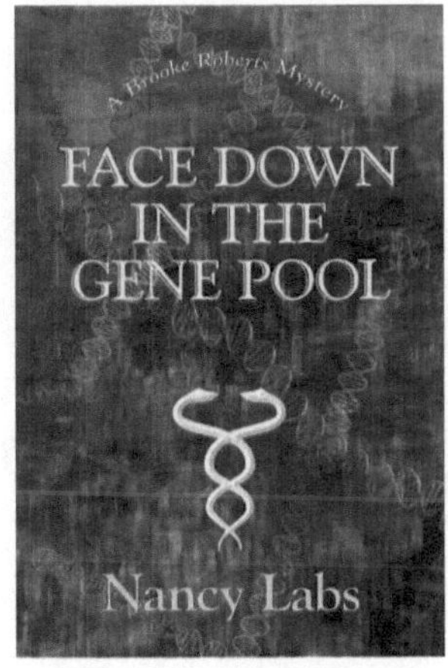

Face Down in the Gene Pool

Brooke can think of lots of things she'd like to do on the first day of spring. Shopping. A walk in the park. Lunch with a friend.

Finding a body at a genealogy conference? That wasn't on her list.

She's grieving her husband's death, and with the pain still tugging at her heart, she needs to put this more recent horror behind her. But friends with ties to the victim and others with ties to the suspects draw her into an investigation she didn't exactly go looking for. The evidence she uncovers has more twists and turns than a strand of DNA, and before long, she's treading water in a gene pool that's a lot deeper—and a whole lot murkier—than it appears on the surface.